*continued . . .*

# IT'S NOT A PRETTY SIGHT

## GAR ANTHONY HAYWOOD

BERKLEY PRIME CRIME, NEW YORK

IT'S NOT A PRETTY SIGHT

A Berkley Prime Crime Book / published by arrangement with
The Putnam Berkley Group

PRINTING HISTORY
G. P. Putnam's Sons hardcover edition / 1996
Berkley Prime Crime mass-market edition / January 1998

The Putnam Berkley World Wide Web site address is
http://www.berkley.com

ISBN: 0-425-16196-X

Berkley Prime Crime Books are published
by The Berkley Publishing Group, a member of Penguin Putnam Inc.,
200 Madison Avenue, New York, NY 10016.
The name BERKLEY PRIME CRIME and the BERKLEY PRIME CRIME
design are trademarks belonging to Berkley Publishing Corporation.

PRINTED IN THE UNITED STATES OF AMERICA

10  9  8  7  6  5  4  3  2  1

# ACKNOWLEDGMENTS

The author wishes to thank yet another member of the on-line services universe, Prodigy subscriber

Lorraine Thompson,

for sharing her medical expertise with me.

If I sound like I know what I'm writing about this time, it's at least partly her fault.

For Connie and Cheryl
The Roads Not Taken

# IT'S NOT A PRETTY SIGHT

# summer
## 1 9 7 8

"HE'S GOING TO KILL ME," JOLLY'S WIFE SAID.

And if it wasn't true, you wouldn't know it from looking at her. Her lower lip was busted and there was a bruise just below her right eye that seemed to be turning colors as she spoke. She was a pretty lady, Jolly's wife, caramel-skinned and nicely built, but she didn't look pretty today. No one who got into it with William "Jolly" Mokes ever did.

"That's crazy," Gunner said.

Because he didn't think Jolly would go that far, number one, and because Jolly was his friend, number two. Or had been, once, back in the living nightmare that had been the Vietnam War. Long Binh, 1971. A thousand lifetimes ago.

"I'm tellin' you, he *is*!" Jolly's wife insisted. Gunner remembered now that her name was Grace.

They had only met once before, out at Jolly's apartment down in San Pedro. He hadn't even known Jolly was married. The two men hadn't seen or spoken to each other since they'd both come home, which was just fine with Gunner, but then Jolly called him at the house one day, out of the blue, and kept right on calling after that. Not from his hometown of Oklahoma City, but from San Pedro, of all places. Two, three times a month the phone would ring, and there on the line would be Jolly, primed with liquor and bursting with melancholy, having nothing to say and taking all day to say it. He must have given Gunner his address a hundred times before Gunner finally agreed to come see him, thinking he was lying through his teeth, until he found himself in the car on the southbound side of the Harbor Freeway, pushing into the stench of freighters flooding the docks just outside Jolly's front door.

He'd had no idea what he was doing or why he was doing it, but Gunner had gone all the same, to see a man he no longer wanted to know, to reminisce about a time he was desperate to forget. And to meet the wife. Grace. Gunner thought they made a nice couple. Jolly, big, dark, childishly plodding, and Grace, short, big-boned, soft-spoken. The field hand and the chambermaid. A natural combination.

That had been three weeks ago.

Discovering now that all was not well between them— that Jolly had the bad habit of slapping his wife around whenever the spirit moved him—was disconcerting, perhaps, but by no means surprising. Gunner had seen the way Jolly treated women before. Whereas most of the less scrupled grunts Gunner knew could be satisfied just having their way with the occasional Vietnamese village girl or two, Jolly always had to throw his weight around, too. It was just his way. Giving him hell about it had been useless, and his COs always looked the other way, consoled by the fact he never seemed to hurt anyone seriously. There were, after all, more pressing matters for them to attend to.

Now, the battle scars on his wife's face clearly proved that Jolly had brought this predilection for violence against women home with him, where it had probably originated in the first place. Some men needed a war to bring out the devil in them, and some men didn't. Apparently, Jolly was one of those who could raise hell just fine without.

Not that it was any of Gunner's business.

Jolly's wife had a fat lip, and a mouse under one eye, but she wasn't dead. She was perfectly capable of saving herself from the monster she was married to, if survival was really that important to her. She didn't need a private investigator like Gunner to run interference for her. All she needed was a bus ticket.

"I can't do that," she said, shaking her head at the suggestion. "He'd find me."

"Not if you did it right," Gunner said.

"Please. Just talk to him for me. If you tell him to leave me alone, he will. He respects you."

"Why should he respect *me*?"

"I don't know. But he does. I can tell by the way he speaks your name."

Gunner dropped his head and sighed. She wasn't asking for much, she was just asking the wrong man. He'd had to see Jolly again to remember how little he cared for the man. Jolly had been an oafish, brutal jackass as a GI and he was still one today. What real friends Gunner had made in Vietnam were all dead now, and pretending Jolly had ever been one of them had been a mistake. A mistake Gunner would hardly rectify now by sticking his nose into Jolly's affairs here at home.

So he told the wife he was sorry, but there was nothing he could do. Get a good lawyer, throw some things in a suitcase, and go see the folks back east, he said. Three times. When the recommendation finally stuck, the lady stood up, tucked her purse under one arm, and walked briskly out of his office.

He never saw Grace Mokes again.

Although he did catch a brief glimpse of her on TV two days later. Just a body under a sheet on a late-night local newscast. A couple of kids had found her under a freeway overpass in Long Beach early that morning and the coroner's boys were just now carting her away. Jolly was already in custody, the voice-over said, having offered the police more confessions to the crime than the DA's office would ever need to convict him.

To say that Gunner felt responsible for Grace Mokes's fate would be an overstatement of the facts. He hadn't told her to take the vows with Jolly any more than he'd told her to take the big man's abuse for the two years that followed. She'd been standing in front of that runaway train for a long time, and it wasn't Gunner's fault that she'd waited until the last minute to try and get out of its way.

Hell, no.

Showing somebody the palms of your hands when they were looking for a way out of an open grave wasn't murder. It just felt that way.

As it probably would, Gunner knew, for the rest of his miserable life.

# one

THE FIRST MISTAKE BEST WAY ELECTRONICS MADE WAS giving Russell Dartmouth credit. The second was losing sight of him after he'd used it.

In two visits to the store, a converted retail shoe outlet on Central Avenue and 135th Street in North Compton, Dartmouth bought a nineteen-inch color TV, two VCRs, one bookshelf stereo system, and a pair of microwave ovens. Over $2,000 in merchandise, and all Best Way had to show for it was $47.18, the first and only payment Dartmouth ever made on the debt.

The three Best Way bills which followed went ignored, as did numerous phone calls to Dartmouth's residence. Only once did someone at the store actually manage to speak with Dartmouth over the phone. Dartmouth made a host of assurances that some form of payment was forthcoming, then proceeded to completely disregard them. Best Way was never able to contact him again. First his phone was disconnected, then his mailing address went away. Best Way tried tracing him through his employer, B & L Tool and Die in Southgate, only to discover the firm had laid him off six days after he'd made his last Best Way purchase.

That's when Roman Goody called Aaron Gunner.

Goody was the owner of Best Way, and the loss on Russell Dartmouth's account was his alone to bear. As was the embarrassment of having ever allowed the machinist to leave the Best Way premises with so much as a pocket calculator in his possession. Goody had built Best Way's reputation in the community on an all but foolhardy willingness to grant people credit when no one else would, so he was accustomed to getting burned now and then, but people like Dartmouth tried his patience. He could let folks miss a few payments on a four-hundred-dollar washing machine, he said, but there was no way he could allow a customer to take him for two thousand in electronics without completely losing face. Not to mention the two thousand dollars.

"It's a helluva way to make a livin'," the stumpy, fiftyish black man said, "but it works. I can't offer people all the things the major chains can—price, service, selection—but I can sure as hell make it easier for 'em to buy. They appreciate that." He clasped his hands over his belt buckle and threw himself farther back in his chair, making the giant coiled spring beneath its seat groan in distress. "Of course, every now and then, I get taken advantage of."

Goody frowned and shrugged like this last didn't really matter. He didn't have the look of a particularly easy mark, Gunner decided, but he did look like someone you could try to screw over without fear of getting your teeth kicked in. He had the soft, unassuming body of a frog, round and fleshy everywhere, and his hair was an ongoing argument; it was dry and brittle and, against his better efforts, stood up on his head like a flag blowing against a stiff tailwind.

"I would like to believe Mr. Dartmouth made his purchases here in good faith, and merely fell on hard times," Goody continued, "but I'm afraid that's not the case. I think Mr. Dartmouth is a thief, and I want you to find him for me. Before people get the idea our generous credit policy here at Best Way can be similarly abused for fun and profit."

"I understand," Gunner said simply. The disheartening austerity of Goody's office was beginning to get to him a little.

"So. How long do you think it will take?" Goody asked.

The investigator considered the question briefly, and then shrugged. "That's hard to say. How long did you say he's been missing?"

"About ninety days. Maybe a little longer than that. Last

bill we sent out to him that didn't get returned went out back in November sometime.'' He consulted a document on his desk. "November twenty-fourth, to be exact.''

Gunner nodded and thought a moment. "It's just a guess, but I'd think I could draw a bead on him in a week or two. Three at the most. Unless, of course—''

"A week or two? Are you joking?''

If it *was* a joke, Goody wasn't laughing.

"Joking? No, I'm not joking.'' Gunner could see what was coming with both eyes closed, and it wasn't much fun to look at. "You had some other time frame in mind?''

"You damn sure better believe I did. I was thinkin' more along the lines of three *days,* not three *weeks.* Who the hell can afford to pay you for three weeks?''

Gunner started to laugh. Slowly at first, then in earnest. Goody just watched him in silence, until the younger black man finally shook his head, rose up from his chair, and headed for the door.

"Hey! What the hell's so funny?'' Goody demanded, calling out after him.

Gunner stopped and turned around, holding Goody's office door open in his left hand. He wasn't laughing anymore, but he still found the round little man's naiveté worth a smile. "Mr. Goody, I couldn't find a lost *dog* in three days. And a lost dog *wants* to be found.''

Goody just stared at him.

"I tell you what. Keep your money. Maybe Dartmouth will turn up on his own, you never know.'' He started to walk out again.

"Waitaminute, waitaminute. Hold on a minute! You're gonna need more than three days, is that what you're tryin' to tell me?''

Once more, Gunner postponed his departure to turn and regard Goody directly. "I'm trying to tell you there's no way to predict how much time I'm going to need. Depending on how well Dartmouth's made himself disappear, I could find him next week, or never at all.''

"*Never at all?*''

"That's right. There is always that possibility. Of course, that's not very—"

Goody grunted derisively and, waving his right hand to shoo his guest out the door, said, "In that case, Mr. Gunner, don't let me keep you, please. You obviously need to find yourself a richer client, and I need to find myself a more confident private investigator. No hard feelings."

Gunner raised an eyebrow. "What?"

"You heard me. I am not a fool. I will not pay you to do nothing. My pockets are not that deep."

"I see. I'm trying to scam you, is that what you think?"

"That is my impression, yes. You walk in here and talk about nothing but all the things you *can't* do for me, instead of all the things you *can*. And I'm supposed to hire you anyway. Why? If you can't promise me results, why in God's name shouldn't I just go out and look for Dartmouth myself?"

"Because you're not a skip tracer, Mr. Goody. You're a camcorder salesman," Gunner said.

"But if you can't find him any better than *I* can—"

"I never said that. What I said was that I can't guarantee you anything. There's a difference. Perhaps I should have explained to you what that difference is."

This last comment was designed to make Goody feel stupid, and it achieved the desired effect. The store owner was shamed into silence.

"But look, I'm easy," Gunner went on. "You're right— I'm the detective and you're the prospective client, whatever you want you should get. You tell me what you want to hear, and I'll say it. You want guarantees, I'll give you guarantees. Never mind that I won't be able to make good on any of them. If it's your preference to be disappointed later, rather than now, that's *your* business, right?"

"It's my preference not to be disappointed at all," Goody said.

"Yes, well, disappointment sometimes comes with the territory, Mr. Goody. Skip tracing is not an exact science, it often takes a great deal of luck to locate a subject. And time. Generally, however, it takes neither. Generally, the man or woman you're looking for turns up rather easily. I'd say the average time invested is about three weeks. Maybe Mr. Dartmouth would turn up sooner than that, who knows? But I'm not going to tell you now that he *will,* and then have you bitching and moaning to me later when he doesn't. I don't do business that way. I promise what I know I can deliver, and nothing more.

"So here's the deal: I charge you a fair fee for my time, and then I charge you again for the results of that time, if and when there are any. If you still think that sounds like some kind of a rip-off . . ." He shrugged. "Then I guess you were right the first time. You need to find yourself another private investigator, and I need to find myself another client."

Gunner struck a confident pose and waited for Goody to make up his mind.

Which apparently required the store owner to do little but return the investigator's stare and twiddle his fingers, both in complete and unnerving silence. Gunner watched the fingers work to keep from going insane, meaty little stubs of flesh rolling about one another in a furious ballet of concentration. It was almost fascinating. But not quite.

"I'll pay you for ten days," Goody said at last, his voice weighed down by the humiliation of concession. "And if you haven't found Dartmouth by then . . ." He didn't bother to complete the sentence, knowing he didn't have to. His meaning was clear.

"Fair enough," Gunner said.

He closed Goody's office door and sat back down.

There was a pay phone just around the corner from Best Way, outside a liquor store on Manchester Boulevard. In fact, there were two, but only one was working; the handset on the other was hanging from its shredded cord like the victim of a lynching, which, in a way, it was. Stripped of both its receiver and transmitter, it was only a plastic shell now, just one more slice of inoperative blight for the people of South-Central to get used to. The working phone, meanwhile, was in use, providing the means for a dark-skinned, fat woman with a thousand pink curlers in her hair to relate the story of her life to a girlfriend who, as near as Gunner could tell, never had a word to say of her own.

Fortunately, Gunner had no interest in the phones themselves, but in the directories that dangled beneath them. All but the lower third of the cover on the White Pages was missing, but what remained was enough to identify the volume as a relatively new one. Gunner opened the book and started flipping through it, hoping the page he needed would not be among those previous users had ripped out and walked away with like so many coupons in a neighborhood flier.

It wasn't.

Three Dartmouths were listed in the book: *Dartmouth, L.*; *Dartmouth, William B.*; and *Dartmouth, R. R.*, as in Robert, or Richard, or . . .

Russell?

Life was not supposed to be this good to anyone, but every now and then it honored Gunner with a gift, all wrapped up in fancy paper and tied with a bow. Go figure.

He snatched the page out of the book and rushed back to his car before the Fates could change their minds.

"You gonna tell him?" Howard Gaines asked, several hours later.

"Who? My client?"

Gaines nodded and grinned. Gunner knew damn well who he was talking about.

"Tell him what? That I've found an 'R. Dartmouth' in the phone book?" Gunner shook his head. "I don't think so. I've gotta check it out first, make sure the 'R' doesn't stand for Rodney, or Rachel. Something like that."

Gaines laughed, risking the loss of what few healthy teeth remained anchored in his mouth. "Shit. You know what it stands for. You just tryin' to keep the man on the clock a few more days, that's all." He gulped down the last of his beer—by Gunner's count, his sixth of the night—and slid the empty bottle across the bar, toward the huge black woman in the dirty apron standing behind it. "Ain't that right, Lilly?"

Lilly Tennell grunted, offering her usual response to most things said about Gunner. She and the investigator were friends of many years, but this was obvious to no one, least of all the two of them. The Acey Deuce was the lone point of commonality between them. Gunner liked to drink here, and Lilly liked having him do so. Not because she needed his business, exactly, but because her customers seemed to find him entertaining. Hell if she could figure out why.

Gunner, meanwhile, liked to think of Lilly as an overweight, overbearing, humorless example of Afro-American sisterhood wearing too much red lipstick. Other than that, she was great.

As was the Deuce itself—for a dump. The South-Central bar was ice cold in the winter and a steambath in the summer, as inviting to strangers as a lumpy mattress in a cheap motel room. Its mirrors were cracked and its chairs all listed to one side or another, and there wasn't a red vinyl booth in the entire house that wasn't coughing up balls of foam padding somewhere. But it felt like home. Everything about the Deuce was as dirt poor and bone tired as the people it shared the neighborhood with, so walking through its doors into the stifling despondency of its ambiance had a certain comfort to it.

In short, it was a hot spot, if any place so far south of Wilshire and east of La Cienega could be called such a thing. It had personality, it had a loyal following, and some nights, like this one, it even had a crowd. Despite all of Lilly's smart-ass, sarcastic grunting.

"What's that supposed to mean?" Gunner asked her.

"It means Mr. Goody better sell himself a mess of TVs this week, he wants to pay the bill you're gonna send 'im," she said. She glanced at Gaines and winked.

"Who's 'Mr. Goody'?" Gunner asked, trying to sound as if the name were new to him. He hadn't mentioned who his client was, just that he was a local businessman looking for a credit holder named Russell Dartmouth.

"Brother, you must forget what I do for a livin'," Lilly said. "I knew it was Goody you was talkin' 'bout the minute you opened your mouth."

Gunner thought about asking her how, but decided he might be better off not knowing. Lilly was scary enough as it was.

"You workin' for Mr. Goody?" Gaines asked. "Over at Best Way?"

"That's confidential," Gunner said, discreet to the bitter end.

"Man, don't play Mr. Goody like that. He's all right. I buy stuff over at Best Way all the time."

"Don't play him like what? I'm not 'playing' anybody."

"But you found the man he told you to find, an' you ain't gonna tell 'im."

"I found a name in the phone book, Howard. That's all."

"You found *his* name in the phone book."

"I found a name *similar* to his in the phone book. You don't listen."

"But—"

"Look. I'll make a deal with you. I won't tell you how to sweep floors, if you won't tell me how to run a skip trace. All right?"

"How to sweep floors?"

"That's right. You think it's funny, accusing me of trying to cheat somebody, but if the wrong people ever heard you—"

"What wrong people?"

"—I could lose my goddamn license. Then you and I would have to go somewhere to do something about your mouth. You understand what I'm saying?"

"Hell no, he don't understand," Lilly said, breaking in before Gaines could say another word. "And neither do I. Why the hell you goin' off on him like that? He didn't do nothin' to you!"

"The hell he didn't. He said—"

"Look here, Gunner. Enough is enough. Every time you come in here lately, you lookin' for a fight with somebody, an' I ain't gonna have it no more. You hear what I'm sayin'?"

"What?"

"You heard me. Every man in this place got some kinda

woman trouble, but you the only one waits till he comes
through my door to decide he wants to get pissed off about
it. You need to grow the hell up!''

Gunner had no immediate retort for that. What she was
saying was basically true: He *was* looking for a fight. And
Claudia Lovejoy was the reason.

Gunner's on-again, off-again relationship with Lovejoy
had finally come to an end, less than a week ago, and the
investigator was not dealing with it well. Twenty-one months
of trying, and the pair still couldn't synchronize their levels
of commitment. For the most part, Gunner had been the one
ready to go forward, Claudia the one holding back. Being
careful for them both, she called it. Like the two of them
together were a bomb that needed defusing, or something.
Gunner had hung in as long as he could, hoping she'd lose
her reluctance to trust him with time, but she never did, and
worse, gave him no reason to believe she ever would.

So he finally pulled the plug.

It would have been a painful thing to do in any case, but
the way Lovejoy reacted to it only added insult to injury. No
tears, no heavy sighs, no words of regret; just relief masked
over by a thin layer of melancholy.

Still, after all this, Gunner had thought he was doing a
pretty good job of being cool about it, keeping his confusion
and resentment to himself. He didn't think anyone would be
able to read what really lay below the surface. He didn't
think anyone knew him that well.

Leave it to Lilly to prove him wrong.

"Come on, Lilly, damn," Gaines said, throwing an arm
around Gunner's shoulders. "Leave the man alone. He didn't
mean nothin'."

"I don't care if he meant somethin' or not. You ain't his
whippin' boy, an' neither is anybody else in here. You hear
what I'm sayin', Gunner? Or you gonna find yourself another
place to hang?"

"Aw, Lilly—" Gaines started to say.

"She's right, Howard," Gunner said, cutting him off.
Looking at Gaines and not at her, because he couldn't meet

her gaze. "I was out of line, and I'm sorry." He offered Gaines his hand, and Gaines took it.

"That's better," Lilly said.

Somebody had been shouting at her for the last five minutes, trying to get her attention, but she'd been resolutely ignoring the distraction. Now that she'd put Gunner's head back on straight, she didn't have to pretend anymore that she couldn't hear the fool, wearing her damn name out from clear across the room.

"Who the hell is that callin' me?" she asked, peering out over the crowd.

"Me!" the irate customer said, standing up and waving. "We want some service over here!"

It was Beetle Edmunds, the carpet cleaner, sitting in a corner booth with two overdressed women Gunner had never seen before. He was shorter than an upright ironing board, had a head the size of a cantaloupe and a backside the shape of a giant steel kettle, but Beetle's own self-image was that of a Zulu warrior. Not even the nickname people had given him years ago could convince him that he looked just like a bug.

"Beetle, you better sit down and shut up," Lilly said, her use of his name getting a laugh the way it usually did. "I'll get there when I get there."

"Woman, I been callin' you for a half hour! You gonna come over here right *now*!" Beetle said, sounding to Gunner as if he was only half joking.

"Or else what? What you gonna do?"

"Or else I got somethin' for you, that's what." He didn't want to, but he had to smile when he said it, betraying his lack of any genuine intent.

"Is that right? You got somethin' for me? Well, honey, guess what—I got somethin' for you, too." With that, Lilly reached down, felt around under the bar for a moment, then finally withdrew a giant can of insect spray, careful to hold it label out so that everyone could see it. "And you gonna get some of it, right now!"

As the house erupted in laughter, Beetle included, the big bartender scurried around the bar and ran toward his table, the spray can held aloft as if she was going to give him a shot on the top of his head as soon as she could reach him.

Chuckling, Gunner turned around to watch the two of them go at it, and caught a glimpse of Gaines's face as he did so. Not only was the janitor the only man at the Deuce not laughing, but he looked like he was going to be sick. In fact, it appeared to Gunner that he'd actually broken out in a cold sweat.

"You all right?" Gunner asked him.

Embarrassed, Gaines shrugged, trying to play his condition off. "Yeah, sure. I'm cool." He turned to take another hit of his beer, forgetting that he'd emptied the bottle several minutes ago. "I just . . ."

Gunner waited for him to go on, but Gaines didn't say anything. "What?"

Gaines tried a brave smile. "I just sort of freaked out when Lilly reached up under the bar like that. You know? I thought she was gonna . . . I thought what she was reachin' for was . . ." He couldn't get the rest of the sentence out.

"J.T.'s gun?"

Gaines nodded. "I know she wouldn't do that, bring it out just to be funny an' all, but still . . . I don't know. It spooked me, that's all." He shrugged again.

Gunner didn't ask for any further explanations because he didn't need any. He understood what the man was talking about completely. The last time Gaines had seen the shotgun Lilly kept fastened to the underside of the Deuce's bar, in the middle by the beer taps where she could get to it easily if she had to, Lilly's late husband, J.T., had been wielding it, just before a crazy white man using an old army Colt had splattered him all over the mirrored wall Gunner and Gaines were facing right now. It had happened a long time ago, but some nights, Gaines often admitted, he could walk into the Deuce and still hear Mean Sheila screaming, and see the corpse of Buddy Dorris—the killer's second victim that night—crumple to the floor like a headless rag doll.

It was something Gunner and Lilly would forever be envious of, Gaines's sensitivity to any reminder of J.T.'s death. Lilly had been asleep in the bar's back storeroom that fateful night, and Gunner had been drinking at home, having run up a bar tab at the Deuce his old friend J.T. had finally grown tired of begging him to pay. How things might have been different had either of them been around to witness, let alone prevent, J.T.'s murder no one could say, but Gunner and Lilly liked to punish themselves for being absent that night all the same. They felt like they owed J.T. that much, at the very least.

Gaines slid off his stool and shoved a hand in his pocket, rummaging for whatever meager cash might be found there.

"You taking off?" Gunner asked him.

"Yeah. I gotta get home." He shrugged one last time.

When he tried to toss a couple of balled-up bills on the counter, Gunner pushed them back into his hand and told him to forget it, the beer was on him tonight.

"You don't have to do that," Gaines said.

"Nobody said I did. But I want to. For jumping all over you like I did a minute ago. It's what Lilly would want me to do, I'm sure."

Gaines didn't buy that explanation, of course—he knew Gunner was just feeling sorry for him—but he seemed to lack the energy to press the matter any further. "Okay," he said, shoving his two pitiful little bills back into his pocket. "Thanks, man."

Then he was gone.

Afterward, with Lilly still busy elsewhere, Gunner got up and went around to the other side of the bar to refill his own glass, something Lilly always gave him hell for doing, but that he occasionally did nonetheless. He was putting the bottle of Wild Turkey back on the shelf when somebody he hadn't heard coming said, "Hey, Gunner. I been lookin' all over for you, man."

Gunner spun around to see Too Sweet Penny, acting like he'd been planted on a stool at the bar all night. It wasn't an unusual place for a lush to be, a barstool, but this lush of late was the homeless kind, the kind who generally did all his drinking from a brown paper bag while perched on a bus bench or a stoop. Too Sweet used to be a regular at the Deuce, when he had both a job and a wife with one of her own, but now that he had neither, he almost never entered the place. Lilly gave him too much grief for begging her customers for the cost of a drink from time to time.

Still, rare as this visit to the Deuce was, Gunner wasn't nearly as surprised by Too Sweet's presence in the bar as he was by the expression on the old man's face. He'd either been crying, or was giving a lot of thought to doing so. The Lord knew Too Sweet had enough reasons to cry if he wanted to, hard as three years on the street could be on a man his age, but the fact of the matter was, crying wasn't Too Sweet's style.

So why, Gunner had to wonder now, was he sitting here tonight with the unmistakable shadow of mourning draped across his face?

"What's going on, Too Sweet?" the investigator asked, making out like he couldn't tell something was wrong.

Too Sweet swallowed once, hard, and said, "I come lookin' for you 'cause I thought you'd wanna know. 'Fore it's all on the TV, an' shit."

"What?"

"I remembered you an' the girl used to be tight, almost got married once, even. I said, man, that used to be Gunner's girl . . ."

"Who?"

"Nina Hillman," Too Sweet said. "You knew her, right? Wasn't she the one you almost married?"

"Nina Hillman?"

"That ain't her name no more, Hillman. She goes by 'Pearson' now, her married name. But I know it's the same girl, I used to see her around all the time."

Gunner's throat was suddenly dry. "Something happened to Nina?"

Too Sweet nodded. "I just come from over by her house. Cops and people all in the street over there, sayin' she's dead."

"Dead?" Gunner stiffened.

"They say the husband did it. Took a shotgun an' blew that poor child's head off, they said. They lookin' for him now." He shook his head at the pointlessness of it all, and just kept right on shaking it, as if that might somehow change something.

"Too Sweet. Are you sure about this? You have to be sure, man. If you're not—"

"Man, I'm sure. I'm as sure 'bout this as anything I ever said in my life." He bit down on his lower lip as tears began to glisten in his red-rimmed eyes. "I wouldn't lie 'bout somethin' like this, man. Beautiful girl like that . . ."

Gunner believed him. It was the last thing he wanted to do, but he believed him.

Nina Hillman was dead.

Gunner came around the bar to where Too Sweet sat and put five dollars on the counter in front of him. "Thanks," he said, gently patting the old man's shoulder. "Lilly gives you any trouble, just tell her why you came. She'll understand." He started for the door.

"What you gonna do?" Too Sweet called after him, wiping his eyes with the back of one wrist.

But Gunner never stopped to turn around. Not because he didn't hear, but because he had no answer for the question.

# two

HE HAD SEEN THE HOUSE ONLY ONCE.

Ten years ago, the day of Nina's wedding, he'd driven past it twice, unable to make himself do anything more with his invitation than sample the festive sounds of her reception from a moving car. The little two-bedroom on Ninety-fifth Street between Main and San Pedro had been clean but unremarkable, a single-story California cottage done up in white and charcoal gray. "Nice" and "pleasant" were both the best and worst things one could possibly say about it.

As they were today, Gunner discovered. Though the gray trim had given way at some point to a pale, lifeless blue, the house remained as ineffectual as ever. Only now, its dull veneer was beginning to show some age, even in the poor light of dusk. Its red shingled roof was dry and discolored, the screen door out front had a hole in it the size of a medicine ball, and the address marker on one of the two pillars standing on the porch was missing a digit, the last one of three. It was still a better-looking house than most on the block, but it offered the eye nothing to latch on to, save for one conspicuous detail: the yellow strands of crowd control tape the LAPD had looped around its perimeter.

It was the tape that finally brought Gunner to the end of his waning optimism. The crowd of people and law enforcement officers Too Sweet had described were nowhere in evidence, save for one lonely black-and-white parked at the curb, but the tape was proof enough that the old man's story had been accurate, at least in part. Because the tape was the Man's way of saying "Keep off the grass" at a crime scene, and while the crime wasn't always a homicide, it was more often than not, especially here in the 'hood. The wide yellow bands and the coroner's wagon just seemed to go hand in hand.

Gunner forced himself out of the car and approached the house.

Two uniforms were pushing through the front door when he reached the porch. The cleanup crew left behind to put the site to bed. One looked like a high-school weight lifter, the other the little brother who looked up to him. Both were Caucasian males in their mid-twenties, and both eyed Gunner like a nail they wanted to drive into the nearest wall.

"I'm sorry, sir, but you have to get back behind that tape," the smaller man said brusquely. "You can't be up here."

"This is a crime scene," the other added, sounding even more annoyed than his partner. "Just like the tape says. You should have bothered to read it before you stepped through it—"

Gunner reached for his wallet and produced his ID, being careful to be quick so that neither man would have time to misinterpret the motion. "I just want to ask a few questions," he said.

"If it's about what happened here—" the smaller man started to say. The name on the tag pinned to his breast was "Tripplehorn."

"The lady of the house was a friend of mine. I just want to know if she's okay," Gunner said.

"I'm sorry, sir, but we can't answer any questions," the big cop said. His name was Finch. "If you're not a member of the direct family—"

"Was this a homicide?"

"Sir, I believe we asked you to get back behind that tape."

"Was this a homicide?" Gunner asked again.

After a while, Finch said, "Possibly."

"Was the deceased a female? Black, late thirties, five

nine, five ten, about a hundred and thirty pounds?''

Finch and Tripplehorn eyed each other; then the latter said, ''That's right.'' Not even trying to hide his burgeoning suspicions.

Gunner looked away for a moment, feeling himself starting to lose it. ''Has the body been identified yet?''

''I'm afraid that's all we can tell you right now, sir. But maybe you'd like to come down to the station and talk to the detectives in charge of the case. I'm sure they'd be happy to answer any questions you might have about your friend.''

Clever man, Gunner thought. Get the potential suspect to turn himself in by offering him a hot cup of cocoa and a shoulder to cry on down at the friendly neighborhood police station.

''Who should I ask for?''

''Lieutenant Matt Poole and Detective John Gruber,'' Finch said, anxious now to get in on the glory he could see his buddy Tripplehorn setting himself up for.

''Matt Poole? This is his case?''

''That's right. You know him?''

Gunner nodded, somewhat relieved. ''Yeah.''

''Well, you wanna talk to him, like Mike here suggested, we're going in right now, soon as we lock up. You want, you can follow us.''

Another clever young man.

Gunner just nodded and told him he had a deal.

''So what's your interest?'' Matt Poole asked. Looking as always like a fully dressed mannequin that had fallen off the back of a truck and onto the Santa Monica Freeway. During rush hour.

''I think the lady was a friend of mine,'' Gunner said.

Poole put his coffee cup down slowly and eyed the black man in earnest, his eyes filling up with something that strongly resembled sympathy. ''I'm sorry to hear that,'' he said.

He was sitting and Gunner was standing in the former's new cubicle at the LAPD's Southwest station, where Poole stood out like a Packard in a Ferrari showroom. His old digs at the department's now defunct Seventy-seventh Street station had suited him better than these, Gunner thought; old paint and scarred linoleum made the detective look almost human. But against a backdrop of walls without plaster patches and bright, almost cheery overhead lighting, well . . . he looked *sick*.

"Her name's Hillman," Gunner said. "Nina Hillman."

"Hillman?"

"Sorry. Pearson. Nina Pearson. I keep forgetting, Hillman was her maiden name."

Poole hesitated again, delicacy requiring the effort that it did with him. "We don't have a positive ID yet, but that's who we believe the deceased is, yeah. Mrs. Nina Pearson."

Gunner's jaw tightened up for a moment, then relaxed. He was only vaguely aware that his right hand had curled up into a fist as hard as a mallet's head. "What happened?"

"Domestic homicide. At least, that's the way it looks right now. The ex-husband's been abusing her for years, apparently we've been out there to pull him off her three times in the last ten months alone. And he's turned up missing. What's that add up to to you?"

"How did he do it?" Gunner asked.

"He did it. What's the difference how?"

"Come on, Poole. Don't play with me, man."

Again Poole hesitated, trying to decide how much Gunner did and did not need to know. He glanced around the squad room briefly, then said, "It was a shotgun. There were casings all over the kitchen where the body was found."

"Jesus," Gunner said. He was fighting back tears.

"Like I said, I'm sorry."

Gunner nodded to say thanks.

"I take it she wasn't just any friend."

The black man lowered himself into the chair in front of the policeman's desk and shook his head. "No."

Poole just stood there and waited, letting him elaborate when it suited him.

"We were engaged once. Eleven years ago," Gunner finally said.

"I see."

But of course he didn't. Poole and Gunner didn't go that far back.

So Gunner told him the story, hard as it was to tell.

He had met her on a bus.

The 204 line, southbound on Vermont between South-Central and Hollywood. He was on his way to a football game, USC versus Arizona State, and she was on her way to work. An angel-faced sister in her late twenties or early thirties, sitting in the back reading a book. He had to pass fifteen empty seats to take the one next to her.

"That's a classic," he said.

She looked at him, curiosity and annoyance in perfect balance. Giving him the benefit of the doubt before telling him to get lost.

"What?"

"*Childhood's End*. Some people think it's one of the greatest science fiction novels ever written."

She was the only black woman he'd ever seen reading Arthur C. Clarke.

"Really." She smiled. Not because his line deserved it, but because she wanted to.

Jumping into the breach before his luck could change, he introduced himself hurriedly, and things progressed nicely from there. He stayed on the bus until she got off at Olympic, a dozen stops past the Los Angeles Memorial Coliseum and his football game, but by that time he knew where she worked and what she did—she was a clerical assistant in the admissions department at Orthopedic Hospital—and her phone number was on an old transfer slip in his pocket.

He thought he had made an easy catch.

Six weeks and eight phone calls later, however, he was still waiting for her to agree to see him again. Because once the introductions were over, Nina made things easy for no man. She was a woman who put a price on everything she had to give, and you either gave her the respect she demanded or you took your act down the street. Putting Gunner off as long as she did had simply been her way of preparing him for this reality, so that when they actually did start dating, he was ready for the hard work to come.

Not that work was what he was looking for. He was just looking for a few good times. He hadn't counted on one good time with Nina leading to another, and another after that, until she was the only woman he could make any time for. It just worked out that way. Nina was beautiful and smart, smarter than anyone he had ever been with, and she loved him with an open, unapologetic zeal that he could not help but find addicting. She was ambitious and independent, two things he rarely found in the same woman, and her laugh could bring a smile to his face no matter how dark his mood. In short, life with Nina was good, and eventually it became so good that he actually found himself wondering if life with her as his wife wouldn't be even better.

So he proposed.

How the wheels of their relationship came off after that was not easily explained, save to say that Gunner called their wedding off with three months to spare. Cold feet, people called it, and Gunner could only agree, not knowing what else to say. That he loved Nina was never in doubt; he was more certain of that than he was of her feelings for him. But he was afraid. Afraid and finally, after eighteen months of unprecedented monogamy, just a little bit bored. Nina was too much of a good thing, if that was possible, and too much of anything could only hold Gunner's interest for so long. He was thirty-one years old, closer to a young man than an old one, and he thought he'd be losing more than he would gain if he conceded to the permanence of matrimony now, no matter who he chose to share his vows with.

He was wrong.

What he gained by setting Nina adrift was very little, and what he lost turned out to be much of what made life worth living. Love; friendship; family. Eleven years of transient, unfulfilling relationships later, he was still waiting for these things to come his way again, secretly convinced that they never would.

Nina, meanwhile, had declined to wait. Less than eleven months after Gunner left her, she became another man's wife. Her mother told Gunner she'd met Michael Pearson at the hospital one day and was dating him the next. He was a dispatcher for one of those package delivery services, Mimi Hillman said, she couldn't remember which one.

And he was bad news.

Maybe he was, and maybe he wasn't; Gunner didn't know the man, and had no desire to. To start worrying about Nina now would have been the height of hypocrisy, he decided, so he left the question of her husband's moral character—and Nina herself—alone. That day in the car, driving past her raucous new home with his invitation to her wedding going to waste on the seat beside him, was the last time he gave any thought to seeing her again. He'd written himself out of Nina's life, and she deserved to have him stay out of it, for better or for worse.

So he did.

He started treating Nina like a memory, and hoped that she would treat him similarly. He never heard the stories about Pearson's dark side, and she never tried to tell him any. In his mind, Nina was happy, and would be happy all the rest of her days, and he didn't want to know anything that might threaten that idea.

His ignorance was bliss. At least, until now.

"She have any kids?" Gunner asked Poole, when he was done poring over his regrettable past.

"Kids? No, no kids. None that we're aware of, anyway." Poole was still eyeing the other detectives in the squad room, watching to see how much attention he and Gunner were getting. He was no collaborator, Poole, and he wanted no misunderstanding about that.

"Does her mother know?"

"Her mother?"

"Nina's mother. Mimi Hillman. Come on, Poole, get with the program. Has anybody told her mother yet?"

Poole nodded. "We sent a car out to her house about an hour ago. They're taking her downtown now."

"Downtown? For what?"

"I told you. We still need an ID on the body. Look, Gunner, it's been fun, but—"

"I'll ID the body. No point in putting her through that shit."

"You? You haven't seen the woman in twelve years, how the hell are you gonna ID her?"

"I can ID her. Believe me."

"I don't think you understand. There isn't—" He stopped himself, reconsidering his choice of words. "She doesn't look anything like she used to, all right? I think her mother's gonna have a hard enough time recognizing her as it is."

"All the more reason to spare her the grief."

"Goddamnit, Gunner, I'm trying to tell you she's a mess! She took a head shot from a sawed-off twelve-gauge at point-blank range, how the hell are you gonna know if it's her or not?"

"We shared the same bed for a year and a half, Poole. I could ID her body in the dark."

"After twelve years?"

"Twelve, fifteen, twenty-five—makes no difference. If it's her, I'll know it."

"Yeah, well, I think I'm gonna decline the offer all the same. Thanks anyway."

"What?"

"I said you're not IDing the body, and that's final."

"Poole—"

"Look. It's like this. I let you down there and you go ape on me, I'm gonna be kicking myself in the ass for a month. Because any fool can see what's on your mind. Even a fool as big as me."

"Yeah? And what's that?"

"Shit. You want the husband. What man wouldn't, under the circumstances?"

Gunner didn't say a word.

"But it's not gonna happen, partner. Not on my watch. So you can forget about it right now. The mother's gonna view the body, as planned."

"All right, all right." The black man threw up his hands, begging the cop off. "So maybe I *was* thinking about going after the husband. I confess, the thought did enter my mind. But no more. You want me out of the picture, I'm out of the picture. Just don't ask Mimi to do the ID, Poole. As a personal favor to me, let me do it instead. Please.''

"Gunner . . .''

"You want to lock me up afterward, that'll make you feel better, do it. I don't give a damn. Just don't let that woman find out Nina's dead like that. I'm begging you.''

He could see Mimi now, bravely following Poole down to the morgue, mouthing a mantra of prayers with every faltering step until a coroner's assistant pulls the sheet off a headless corpse she cannot help but place immediately . . .

Poole let out a heavy sigh. "Jesus Christ. You're a pain in the ass, you know that?''

Gunner nodded, in no position to argue. "I know.''

"You're gonna ID the body, then you're gonna get the hell out of my face.''

"Right.''

"And you're gonna keep your fucking nose out of this investigation after that. You get in the way on this one, Gunner, and I'll have your license revoked before the sun goes down. You hear what I'm sayin'?''

"I hear you.'' Gunner nodded again and waited.

"You know, the mother's gonna see that body anyway, sooner or later,'' Poole said. "You really don't have to do this.''

"I'm a big boy, Lieutenant. I think I can handle it.''

Poole shrugged. "Okay. Just thought I'd give you one more chance to back out. Before . . .''

He gave the investigator one more hard look, trying to say with his eyes what he obviously couldn't—or wouldn't—articulate verbally, then finally got out of his chair.

It took them twenty-five minutes to drive down to the county coroner's office.

Gunner could have sworn it was twenty-five years.

# three

MIMI HILLMAN WAS A ROCK. ALWAYS HAD BEEN, ALWAYS would be.

The devil took his chisel to her more than he did to most, targeting her health here, her family there, and all she ever did to retaliate was survive. Shed a tear and push on, suffering no loss of momentum by looking back to bemoan her fate or wonder what might have been. Her faith in God and all the Catholic saints was a fuel she fed on perpetually, and it never left her feeling down or dejected about anything much longer than a day.

The lady was impenetrable.

So it was hard for Gunner to see this squat, wide-bodied giant of a woman hurting so profoundly, crying now instead of weeping, railing rather than suffering in dignified silence. Reaching with both arms for the comfort of an embrace she had never before required no matter how dire her circumstances. Gunner had known Nina's death would cut her to the quick, but he had not expected this. The mountain no earthly object could move, collapsing in shards like a shattered crystal vase.

Nina had been her last living child, and now she was gone. Mimi had seen the proof with her own two eyes. Poole had told Gunner his word would not be good enough for her, and he was right. Mimi had insisted upon viewing the body for herself, buying in the process one final memory of Nina she would never be able to forget. Just as Gunner never would.

She offered no resistance when he offered to drive her home. She just nodded her head and let him lead her away, not speaking again until they had entered the house and he had locked the door behind them.

For Gunner, it was like passing through a portal in time. The house was exactly as he remembered it. Overstuffed Victorian-style furniture dressed in burgundy velour, red wooden legs and arms buffed and polished to an almost obscene perfection. Throw rugs in huge ovals arranged over a glistening bare wood floor. The smell of fresh flowers everywhere. Photographs of Mimi's three children crowding each other out up on the mantel above her fireplace: Teresa, her oldest, who had died at the age of eighteen after a long battle with leukemia; Charles, Mimi's only son, who was killed in a car accident during Gunner and Nina's courtship; and Nina herself, the baby. Even the arrangement of all the gold and silver frames seemed unchanged.

Mimi asked Gunner if he wanted coffee, actually intending to play the polite hostess, but he cut her off before she could reach the kitchen and steered her into a living room chair, ordering her to remain there while he put the coffee on himself. He didn't have to tell her twice.

Later, when there were no more amenities to use as a means of avoidance, they sat in Mimi's living room and talked, unable to sustain the silence to which they'd both been clinging another moment longer.

"You have somebody you can call who can stay with you tonight?" Gunner asked gently. "Or would you like me to?"

Mimi shook her head. "I don't need anybody to stay with me. I'm fine."

"You really shouldn't be alone tonight, Momma." At some point during his time with Nina, he had started calling Mimi "Momma Hillman," and he'd been doing it ever since.

"Why not? I killed that girl. I deserve to be alone."

"Momma, don't," Gunner said, reaching out to pat her hand.

"It's true. I killed her. It's nobody's fault she's dead but mine."

"That's ridiculous."

"It's not ridiculous! I should have gotten that child some help! I should have bought myself a gun and killed that man a long time ago!"

Without knowing it, she'd all but answered the question Gunner had been working his way up to asking. "You mean Michael?"

"He's sick. There's something . . . *wrong* with that man. I thought . . ." She shook her head and turned away. "I thought he could change. I thought if we both prayed for him, if we just kept *praying* for him . . ."

Her voice trailed off, her eyes fixed on the floor.

Gunner waited a moment, then said, "You're convinced he's the one who killed her?"

She looked up to face him again slowly, clearly dumbfounded by the absurdity of the question.

"Momma. Listen. I know you don't want to talk about this right now, but . . . I have to know for sure. It's *important.* If there's any chance it was somebody else, any chance at all—"

"It was *him,*" Mimi said, making sure he understood her this time. "It was *Michael.* He told her he was going to kill her, and he did. He was the only one could've done that—" She stopped abruptly, suddenly remembering the butchery she was referring to, and had to pause a moment to gather herself before going on. "He was the only one could've hated my baby that much."

Gunner nodded, anxious to get her mind—and his—off the subject of Nina's remains. "In that case," he said, "I only have one more question to ask. I need to know where can I find him. If you have any ideas—"

"Find him?" The big woman glared at him. "What do *you* want to find him for?"

Gunner didn't say anything.

"Aaron, no. Don't even think about it, you hear? Nina is dead. The time to help her is past. There is nothing you or

I can do for her now except pray for her soul in heaven. Do you understand what I'm telling you?''

"I'm not going to hurt him, Momma. I just want to help the police bring him in.''

"The police don't need your help. And neither does Nina. What are you doing here, anyway? Who told you Nina was dead?''

Gunner shrugged. "A friend. Someone who happened by the house while all the police were there and heard what happened.''

"And you just all of a sudden came running to help. Is that it?''

"I don't—''

"None of this is any of your business, Aaron. It's not your problem. Ten, eleven years ago, it might have been, but not now. Not anymore.''

"Momma, that's not true.''

"It *is* true! You didn't care about that girl! You haven't given her a single thought since the day you let her go! But *now* you want to be outraged because somebody killed her. Now that she's not here to see it, you want to come runnin' to her rescue, like she was *your* wife, and not *his*!''

She stood up, before Gunner could offer any kind of rebuttal, and said, "Go home. Go home and mind your own business, like you've been doing for the last ten years. There's nothing you can do for Nina, or me, now. Except maybe make things worse.''

Her insistent stare would not relent until he had risen to his feet, yet he made no immediate move for the door. "Maybe I deserve that, I don't know. I'd have come around once or twice, like you say, just to make sure she was doing okay . . . maybe none of this would have happened. It's for sure if I'd known Michael was abusing her . . .'' He had to bite down on the thought, his eyes narrowing with anger. Thinking as much of Grace Mokes as he was of Nina.

"Anyway, none of that does anything to change the fact I'm hurting right now, same as you,'' he went on. "Whether you think I'm entitled or not. And I'm going to keep right on hurting until the man who killed your daughter is off the street. Either in a cell, or in a box, one or the other.''

"That's not what Nina would want," Mimi said.

It was so true he almost nodded his head. "Nina wanted a lot of things she didn't get," he said instead.

Before his voice could crack again, he kissed his Momma Hillman on the cheek and went home.

"Well? Anything to report?"

Nine o'clock in the morning, and Goody was on the phone looking for results.

Gunner had no time for him today. "You'll be the first to know when I do, Mr. Goody."

"You're not just getting started, I hope."

"No. I've been up since three. Surely I'd be cheating you otherwise."

"Excuse me?"

"I'll give you a call later this afternoon, Mr. Goody. Say around four." He hung up, not caring if the big man was offended or not.

Then he rolled out of bed.

In the end, he did Goody's bidding anyway. He didn't have any choice. Finding Michael Pearson was foremost in his mind, but there was the little problem of Poole to deal with. All the promises the cop had made to Gunner the day before, he had sincerely meant to keep, so he was almost certainly out there somewhere, in one form or another, watching and waiting. Looking for Gunner to drop Pearson's name, just drop his name, so he would have an excuse to take him downtown and get him started in a new line of work.

It wasn't worth the risk.

Besides, it wasn't going to take long to get Goody's business out of the way. Despite all his protestations to the contrary, Gunner felt confident that the address he'd found in the phone directory yesterday would indeed lead him to Russell Dartmouth. It had been a while since he'd had this kind of break, and he was due.

The "R. Dartmouth" he had found in the phone directory lived in Venice, down in the Oakwood section where blacks

and Latinos had been waging war with each other for years.
Three minutes from the beach, less than two miles north of
Marina del Rey's billowing white sails and luxury oceanfront
condominiums, Oakwood was a pocket of blight equal to
anything Watts or Compton had to offer. Here, poverty had
wielded its broad brush like a scythe, littering the sidewalks
with black men and women, teenagers and little children, all
dressed down and properly sedated for the business of being
poor. They lived in tiny little houses with boarded-up windows and apartments filled with smoke. They trod upon grass
that had never known a lawn mower, and kicked around
empty beer cans just to hear the clatter.

And they eyed the passing of a stranger's car like it was
a messenger from Death, coming to claim them all.

It was nothing Gunner had never seen before, but the
scene shook him up all the same. Because there was nothing
a man or woman could do to deserve so cruel an existence.
Nothing. Simply being born into a legacy of such squalor
was not crime enough. And yet, here they were. The com-
placently condemned, crowding onto the trapdoor of the gal-
lows for the hangman yet to come.

Gunner found the building he was looking for and parked
the red Cobra right out in front of it, no longer as concerned
with discretion as he was with expediency. He knew the car
would attract the attention of all the wrong people sooner or
later, but he wasn't planning on being away from it for more
than five or ten minutes. He was going to run up to Dartmouth's apartment, establish that he'd found the right man,
then leave. Throw Goody his bone to make him go away
and then get back to the only work that really mattered to
him right now: finding Michael Pearson. Poole or no Poole.

Gunner didn't know what Russell Dartmouth's last place
of residence looked like, though Goody had supplied him
with the address, but he felt safe in assuming the man's move
to Oakwood hadn't done much to improve his living conditions. The apartment building in which Dartmouth now
lived—if Gunner was indeed as lucky as he felt—was a
two-story stack of cracked and crumbling stucco on Brooks
Court between Sixth and Seventh Avenue that seemed to

promise nothing but grief for visitors and inhabitants alike. Fronted by dead landscaping and covered in diverse, over-lapping layers of unsettling brown paint, it appeared about as steady on its foundation as a drunk was on his feet; like something that had been destroyed by the Northridge earth-quake of '94 but had forgotten to fall down.

Gunner went inside, past a set of double glass doors ren-dered opaque by grime, and followed a mailbox labeled DARTMOUTH up to the second-floor balcony and room 21, the blare of dueling televisions and radios flooding the open courtyard behind him. He knocked on the door and waited. There was a window to his left, but a closed set of dirty blinds blocked his view of the apartment beyond, though it appeared to be completely dark. He knocked again.

Down below, a little boy was suddenly running rings around a dead palm tree, giggling like he'd never had so much fun in his life. Gunner turned to watch him, amused, and didn't see the huge blur coming up on his right until it was too late to do anything but flinch.

A fist the size and approximate weight of a truck battery hit him just above the right ear and put him flat on his back on the balcony floor, blinking into a wash of white light he thought would never fade. The need to drift off into uncon-sciousness was strong and immediate, but he fought it with all he had, convinced he was a dead man if he didn't.

"Why the hell you keep messin' with me, man? Why you keep *messin'* with me?" he heard the voice of a madman demand.

The guy had surprised him by coming at him from out on the balcony, rather than from the inside of the apartment. He was little more than an outline to Gunner, but an outline was enough to make one thing, at least, perfectly clear: He was *big*. Not heavy or muscular, particularly, but tall; some-where in the neighborhood of six seven or six eight. A giant. And Goody had placed Dartmouth's height at around six one or six two.

The fool needed glasses.

"Waitaminute . . ." Gunner murmured, trying to get to his feet. But none of his limbs would work as intended and the leviathan standing over him wasn't interested in talk.

"Wait a minute, my ass! Fuck wait a minute!" the big man howled, using his right foot to kick Gunner twice in the ribs. Gunner rolled over and curled up like a pill bug, fighting to breathe and hold on to his breakfast at the same time.

*Who in the hell does this maniac think I am?* Gunner wondered.

"I'm sick of this shit, man! I'm sick of you people fuckin' with me! You motherfuckers gonna learn to leave me alone! You gonna *learn*!"

He was lifting Gunner up by the shoulders, preparing to throw him over the railing.

While his vision was improving, all of Gunner's other faculties were shot; he couldn't breathe, his ribs were killing him, and his head felt like the core of a detonating grenade. A gun would have come in handy, but he wasn't carrying one today; he'd left his Ruger P85 at home, as he did most days. Smart.

The big man had him up in the air now, about waist-high.

There was no time to throw a punch, and not much reason to; with what he had to put behind one at the moment, a punch might not even get his friend's attention. And he definitely needed more than the man's attention. With what he figured to be five, maybe ten seconds left to live, he decided to try the one thing—the *only* thing—he felt relatively sure he could pull off with any real hope of success.

He grabbed hold of the big man's balls.

First with one hand, then with both. Squeezing with all the power he could generate, not caring a bit if he tore something loose. But the giant cared. He abruptly went rigid and lowered Gunner to the floor, his grip on the investigator's shoulders rapidly relaxing. He didn't even feel like screaming, anymore.

Carefully maintaining his hold on his victim's genitals, Gunner rose slowly to his feet and looked the big man over, able to see him clearly for the first time. He was a pale-skinned black man in his early thirties, with an oval bald patch on the top of his head and a long, narrow face; he had a thin man's potbelly and a rat's-nest beard, and eyes set so close together they nearly climbed up the sides of his nose.

Russell Dartmouth. Goody had gotten the height all wrong, but he'd been right about everything else.

"Say good night, Russell," Gunner said, feeling revitalized.

He threw a quick right hand at the underside of Dartmouth's left jaw and leaned into it, hoping to do with mass alone what he ordinarily accomplished with mass and velocity combined. Maybe it helped that Dartmouth had been caught unawares, and maybe Gunner had merely found his second wind, but either way the big man's head snapped back nearly ninety degrees and he went down, falling all at once like he'd been lopped off at the knees. It was probably unnecessary, but Gunner went over afterward and kicked him in the side of the head, just to make sure his lights were out for good.

Not that any of Dartmouth's neighbors gave a damn. Gunner was still waiting to see or hear so much as one, the kid who'd been playing down in the courtyard earlier notwithstanding. And even he was gone now, making the building's odd desolation complete. Either the people who lived here were deaf, or they'd raised the act of minding one's own business to the level of art.

Crazy.

Gunner had lost his wallet in the scuffle. He spotted it and some loose change scattered about nearby. He gathered it all up hastily, his ribs giving him hell for the effort, then went through Dartmouth's pockets, looking for a set of keys. When he found it, he unlocked the door to the big man's apartment and swung it open gingerly, waiting for another surprise. But he never got one. The apartment was empty, save for all the TVs and stereos, clock radios and assorted VCRs that stood in the middle of the front room, arranged neatly in little warehouselike stacks.

Goody would have been moved to tears.

# f o u r

GUNNER SPENT THE BETTER PART OF THE NEXT TWO DAYS in bed. He had a mild concussion, his doctor said, and bed was the only place for him, he didn't want to be throwing up every three hours, or blacking out at the wheel of a car doing sixty-five in the middle lane of the Harbor Freeway. It was the kind of exaggerated physician-speak he generally liked to ignore, especially when there were things on his "To do" list that wouldn't wait, but this time he had to believe there might be something to the prognosis. He had already blacked out once, getting in his car right after his final visit to Best Way Electronics had made an ex-client out of Roman Goody, and his head had been pounding like a swordsmith's anvil ever since Russell Dartmouth's right hand had tried to lobotomize him. He waited twenty-one hours for the pain and nausea to subside, then sought a physician's counsel, convinced at last that he was suffering from something significantly more serious than a Goody-induced migraine.

Not that Goody wasn't capable of giving someone a major-league headache. The big man had been a pain in the ass from the start of Gunner's dealings with him, and he'd been one right up to the end. Even as the investigator was handing Dartmouth over to him on a silver platter, Goody was whining and complaining, defending himself against the constant and wholly imaginary threat of being taken advantage of.

"How do I know this is really him?" he had asked, after

he had read and reread the written report Gunner had furnished him with.

"What do you mean?" Gunner asked. Wondering how much worse his headache would get if he got up from his chair to give Goody the backhand he so richly deserved.

"I mean, you found him awfully fast. How do I know this address here is for real, and not just somethin' you made up?"

Gunner took a deep breath, held it. "That's what the VCR's for," he said. Goody glanced over at the tape machine Gunner had set on his desk along with the report, acting as if he hadn't noticed the thing until this minute. "You check the model and serial number, I think you'll see it's on the list of items Dartmouth purchased from you."

Taking the unit out of the unconscious Dartmouth's apartment hadn't exactly been ethical, but Gunner had suspected he might need something more than his word to convince Goody that he'd found the right man. And short of dragging Dartmouth himself into Goody's office . . .

"Okay. Fair enough," Goody said. Suddenly and unexpectedly appeased, he was writing out a check before Gunner could even ask for one.

"So what happens now?" Gunner asked him.

"Now? Now I serve him with papers. What do you think?" Goody looked up from his checkbook, said, "In fact . . ."

"Forget about it. That's not why I asked."

Goody waited for an explanation.

"I was going to suggest you make the next man or woman you send after him a little more aware of Dartmouth's size and temperament than you did me. Otherwise, you're going to get somebody killed."

"I don't understand."

"I think you do. You see what he did to me, don't you? The man is certifiable. And he's big enough to cast a shadow over half a city block. Or didn't you notice that about him?"

"I believe I mentioned that he was tall."

" 'Tall'? He's a fucking *giant*. And he's crazy. I'd been a little less lucky today, he would have killed me, without even bothering to ask who I was or what I wanted with him.''

"So he's crazy. So what?''

"So you're playing with fire with this guy, that's what. As would anybody else you hired to approach him again. Surely you understand that.''

"I understand that he's a thief who owes me money. That's what I understand. Him bein' big and crazy don't change that.''

"No, it doesn't. But it does make him somebody you don't want to fuck with and then turn your back on.''

"Nonsense,'' Goody said.

And that was how Gunner left him, comfortably cocooned in a blanket of tightly woven ignorance. It was how Gunner imagined he spent most of his time, in denial of one reality or another that failed to suit his purposes. Goody didn't know it, but he was getting off lucky; another day as Gunner's employer and he would have found himself lying flat on his back in a dark alley somewhere, getting his attitude adjusted. Now, no such unpleasantness would be necessary. Gunner's business with Goody was over, and he was free once more to concentrate on the task his work for the owner of Best Way Electronics had so rudely interrupted—locating Michael Pearson.

Unfortunately, being free to find Pearson and being in shape to find him were two different things. Having to waste all day Thursday on Goody's boondoggle had left Gunner feeling more anxious to get his hands on Nina's ex-husband than ever, but it had also left him in no condition to do anything about it. Bedridden with a concussion, all he could do to track Pearson down was count on others to do the job for him. All day Friday, he used the phone like a gregarious bookie, spreading the word to every friend and family member he had on the street that he needed Pearson found. He called in favors and offered up rewards; he coerced and cajoled, charmed and terrorized. He took every tack he could think of to reel Pearson in remotely.

And then he waited for his own phone to ring.

It was a long wait. He tried to watch television, but that was impossible; the talk shows were brainless and the soaps hedonistic, the latter to the point of vulgarity. Five minutes into any one of them, and you felt like a total failure, the only human being in the world who wasn't rich, beautiful, and sexually ecstatic.

Gunner turned to books and jazz instead.

Grover Washington, Jr., and John Coltrane; Miles Davis and Dexter Gordon; Thelonious Monk and Sonny Rollins. He reread Harlan Ellison's *Paingod* and wore the grooves off *Killer Joe,* the classic Quincy Jones LP.

And he dreamed of Nina.

Sleep was what he needed most, but sleep was where her memory found him most vulnerable. She came to him in dreams of every variety, from the fantastically illogical to the painfully realistic. He heard her laugh a thousand times, and felt her body rocking beneath him over and over again. All he had to do was close his eyes, and she was there.

But she wasn't real.

She was dead, and there was nothing he could do about it. That was the fact he was left to consider, and reconsider, every time a dream did a slow dissolve to startle him awake: Nina was gone. Forever.

Maybe he was crazy, thinking he was to blame, and maybe he wasn't. The only thing he knew for sure was that the guilt building up inside him was real, and it had to be dealt with. Soon.

Before it made him feel more like the world's greatest fool than he already did.

Nina's funeral was held at two o'clock Saturday afternoon. It should have been a gray day, an ugly day, but it wasn't; the skies were clear and blue, and temperatures were in the low seventies. Great conditions for a picnic, lousy conditions for mourning. Nina had deserved something far less picturesque.

There was a short service at Mother of Sorrows Catholic Church, followed by the interment of the body at Holy Cross Cemetery. Gunner attended both, his landlord, Mickey, serving as both his driver and his nursemaid, but he passed on the gathering at Mimi's home that was scheduled to come

later. He had a hard time dealing with the anguish grieving
black people liked to lavish on their dead under the best of
circumstances; today, looking and feeling very much like a
corpse himself, he had even less stomach for it than usual.

"Take me home, Mickey," he'd said, after offering Mimi
his apologies and saying good-bye at the grave site. She had
taken one look at him and sent him on his way, making him
promise to call her later so that she'd know he was doing
okay. Not fifteen minutes removed from burying the last of
her three children, and *she* was worrying about *him*.

But that was Momma Hillman for you.

By nine o'clock that evening, the pain that had been pounding out a steady cadence on the inner walls of Gunner's skull
mercifully began to subside.

He wasn't recovered by any means, but he was able to
eat, drink, and walk to and from the toilet without getting
sick or falling on his face, and that was something. He was
still a little unsteady on his feet, and his stomach threatened
trouble if he remained upright for too long, but beyond that,
he was progressing nicely. Nicely enough that he felt confident he could go back to work the next morning.

Then Weldon Foley called.

Foley was a fixture at the barbershop Gunner used for an
office, Mickey Moore's Trueblood Barbershop on Wilming-
ton and Century. The old man never needed a haircut, he
just liked hanging around. Gunner couldn't remember the last
time he'd been at the shop that Foley and his landlord
weren't arguing about something, trading insults and insipid
theories in some comical excuse for a debate, Mickey trying
to concentrate on the head he was butchering at the moment,
and Foley just sitting there, watching and instigating. The
two men were inseparable.

But Foley wasn't just a fly on the wall; he also worked
for Mickey. He hardly needed the additional incentive to be
there, but Mickey also paid him a few dollars to clean up
the place. Foley ran a broom across the floor at regular in-
tervals during the day, then came in every other night after
closing time to do the rest. Sometimes at six, sometimes at

nine, sometimes as late as midnight; Mickey allowed him to set his own schedule.

"I found your boy," he said, the instant Gunner answered the phone.

It took Gunner a moment to place the voice. Phone calls from Foley were not a common occurrence. "Foley?"

"I found 'im, man. The boy you lookin' for."

"Pearson?"

"Yeah. The one . . . the one you been askin' about."

Foley sounded odd.

"Where is he?"

After a long pause, Foley said, "You gotta meet me here at Mickey's. I'll show you."

"Mickey's?"

"Yeah. I'm here right now, finishin' up. Come on down an' I'll show you where the boy's at."

"Come on down? What do I want to come down there for? Just tell me where he is now and I'll go find him myself."

"No! You . . . It ain't gonna work that way, man. I gotta take you to 'im."

"I don't understand," Gunner said.

"Look. It's like, where the boy's at, you'd never find it on your own. I gotta *take* you there. Otherwise . . ." He let his voice trail off.

"Yeah?"

"Otherwise, you ain't gonna get there in time. 'Cause he ain't likely to be there long. Fact, he *might* be gone already, I don't know."

He wasn't making a great deal of sense, but Gunner had the feeling he could talk to him all night and he still wouldn't. Foley could be like that, especially with a drink or two in him.

"I'll be right down," Gunner said, only halfway sure he was strong enough to make it as far as his front door.

The first thing he saw when he came in was the man in the barber chair.

The third and last chair in the shop, furthest from the door.

Mickey's chair. The lights weren't working and the room was black as coal, and the chair had been turned around to show its back to him, but Gunner could see the man—if it was a man—sitting there just the same, reflected many times over in the shop's mirrored walls. A silent and motionless ghoul, wearing one of Mickey's striped barber aprons over his head like a shroud.

He was about Foley's height.

Gunner called Foley's name once, twice, but the body in the chair didn't move. He tried the light switch again, and again received the same result: nothing. His head began to swim. He'd come halfway prepared for something like this, but now that he'd found it, he wanted no part of it. He never did.

He lifted the nine-millimeter Ruger automatic from the waistband of his pants and started forward.

"Foley! Is that you?"

The head under the apron shifted, then grew still again. Foley coming around, or Michael Pearson playing possum; it was impossible to tell which.

He hoped to God it was Foley.

The chair wasn't more than fifteen feet away, yet it felt like a distance he would never live to cross. The silence in the room was paralyzing. Just beyond the chair, past a beaded curtain hanging in an open doorway, more darkness loomed: the office in the back. A black pit offering him nothing but one more thing to fear.

He made it to the chair.

The clothes and shoes beneath the barber's apron looked like Foley's, but he couldn't be sure. It was still too dark to be sure about anything. He held the Ruger out with his right hand, aimed directly at the hooded man's skull, and spun the chair around with his left, yanking the apron away as he did so.

Gagged and unconscious, Foley fell forward toward him just as the beaded curtain nearby exploded, thrown aside by someone entering the room like a projectile fired from a cannon.

Gunner tried to swing the gun around, but too late: He

was knocked off his feet before he could complete the motion, ducking a right hand thrown at his head that only partially missed. The two men hit the floor hard, Gunner leading with his back, his right cheek burning strangely.

He figured he was good for ten, maybe fifteen seconds of serious horseplay; any more than that and he was dead. And maybe he was dead anyway, because he knew now that his cheek wasn't burning, it was *bleeding;* cut open with the pair of Mickey's scissors he could see in his foe's right hand. He tried to get up, but couldn't; the black man above him was kneeling on his chest, hard, pinning him down. Rolling to one side or the other proved equally impossible. He had no strength to fight. There was nothing to do but watch the scissors ascend, high overhead, and then—

He pulled the Ruger's trigger.

The shop flashed white with the weapon's report and his would-be killer froze, Mickey's scissors suspended in time above his right ear. The bullet had hit him only inches above and to the left of his groin, leaving behind an entry wound slowly staining his pants red. His face was a mask of utter disbelief. Gunner bucked to throw the man off him and scrambled to his feet. He heard the scissors hit the floor and skitter off to distant parts unknown.

When he thought he could afford the luxury, he located the nearest wastebasket and threw up in it, feeling only slightly better than he had immediately after his dance with Russell Dartmouth. Two days of lying on his back down the fucking drain.

The bleeding man on the floor stirred, moaning, but was clearly capable of little else, so Gunner turned his attention to Foley. He found him with his eyes open, staring sideways at Gunner's shoes. He was struggling to free the hands taped behind his back, and was shouting against the hand towel that had been stuffed into his mouth. Blood was leaking from his nose, and his left eye was nearly swollen shut, but otherwise he appeared to be okay.

"How you doing, Foley?" Gunner asked him, when he'd removed the gag from his mouth. "You all right?"

"He made me call you, man," Foley said, sounding sad

enough to cry. "I swear I didn't want to, but he *made* me! Motherfucker said—"

"Forget it. No harm done. Come on, get up off the floor, I'll call you a doctor."

He lifted the older man onto his feet and guided him back into the barber chair he'd fallen out of. He could hear their friend on the floor grunting and groaning as he worked to unbind Foley's hands, but he didn't bother to turn around until he was done, satisfied that the man was no longer a threat to anyone. And he was right. The man he saw when he finally looked for him again was far closer to the dead than the living. He'd forced himself up to a sitting position, back braced against the nearest wall, and grown still, eyes open but unseeing, both hands clasped over his ruptured middle. Only the faint movement of his lips lent any credence to the idea that he was not already dead.

Gunner had only seen Michael Pearson two or three times in his life, but he felt relatively certain this was he.

"Is he . . ." Foley started to ask.

"No," Gunner said. "Not yet. But he will be soon, I don't get an ambulance out here for him fast." He went to the phone on the counter nearby and called 911.

"An ambulance? What you wanna call an ambulance for *him* for? Sonofabitch almost killed us both, he wants a doctor, let him go get one for hisself!"

"I wish I could, Foley, but—" He had to cut the sentence off and gesture for Foley's silence when his 911 call abruptly went through. He made it brief, reporting a shooting and requesting an ambulance without preamble. Then he hung up, in the face of a determined dispatcher gamely trying to press him for more details.

Afterward, he went to check on Pearson.

"I didn't kill the bitch," the wounded man said when Gunner knelt down beside him, blood bubbling up at both corners of his mouth. A thirty-something pretty boy, light-skinned, square-jawed, thinly mustachioed. His voice had been almost too soft to hear, but his tone was unmistakably upbeat. He thought what he'd said was funny.

"Shut up and save your strength," Gunner said.

"I *wanted* to kill her sorry ass, but somebody else did it for me. Ask Goldy, she'll tell you." He coughed spasmodically and spit up some more blood.

"Who is Goldy?"

"The bitch . . ." He fell silent, as if his train of thought had deserted him. He turned his head to one side and kept it there, for no apparent reason. Gunner was beginning to think he'd passed on when he suddenly spoke again, picking up right where he'd left off. "The bitch I was with that night. Who the fuck you think?"

Incredibly, he actually managed to laugh, making a sound deep down in his throat like a handful of rusty screws being rattled about at the bottom of a tin can. Gunner couldn't help but wince. "She thought if she lef' me, I wouldn't have nobody. Like I was gonna be lonely, or somethin'. Sheeit . . . Dumb-ass bitch, I was gettin' busy with a diff'rent ho every goddamn night!"

The supreme irony he found in this last compelled him to laugh again, and again he paid for the privilege with a bloody cough, long and loud and coarse as sandpaper.

"I told you to shut up," Gunner said once more, and this time it was no mere suggestion. He'd heard Nina referred to as a *bitch* twice now, and he wasn't going to hear her dishonored like that again. He didn't have that kind of patience.

When he stood up and walked back to the telephone, Foley said, "Man wants to talk, let 'im talk. An' if he wants to die, let 'im die. What the hell should we care, he wants to laugh hisself to death?"

"You want to know why we should care?" Gunner asked, flipping through the pages of a pocket telephone book for Matthew Poole's number at home. "I'll tell you why: Because I just shot a man who murdered an ex-girlfriend of mine. With my own gun, at my place of business. After calling all over town for two days, trying to run him down. Are you getting the picture yet, Foley, or do I have to go on?"

"They gonna think you set this up."

"You'd better believe they are."

"An' if the boy dies . . ."

"I'm going to be in the deepest of deep shit. Yeah."

"Jesus," Foley said.

"Go keep an eye on him, will you? I've got one more call to make."

It was like asking Foley to keep an eye on the back row of teeth in a live alligator's mouth, but he did as he was told, limping slowly away like an old arthritic turtle.

When Poole answered the phone, picking up after only three rings, Gunner said, "You want Michael Pearson, come get him."

"Who the hell is this?"

"Get your fat ass out of the bed and think about it. It'll come to you."

"Gunner?"

"Hurry up, Poole. We're here at Mickey's, waiting. How much longer Pearson'll be around, though, I can't say."

Rather than ask what that was supposed to mean, the cop said, "You were told to leave Pearson to me." Understanding that what Gunner was leaving unsaid was not good, and already pissed off about it.

"Do me a favor, Lieutenant. Get down here first, and give me my thirty whacks later. Okay?"

He hung up the phone.

Somewhere off in the distance, many worlds away, the baleful song of a siren began to grow from a whisper to a scream.

Gunner prayed to God it was singing for him.

# f i v e

"YOU'VE JUST MADE A CAREER CHANGE," POOLE SAID. "Your cousin the plumber's gonna have himself a partner again."

"Del's an electrician," Gunner said. "How many times do I have to tell you that?"

"Plumber, electrician. Same difference. Either way, you're gonna be doin' somethin' else with your time besides makin' my life miserable. Unless you wanna play private dick in some other state of the Union. You could always try that, I suppose."

"If any other state'd have you," Detective John Gruber said. Poole's partner on the Nina Pearson murder case, Gruber was a short, disagreeable white man with a gap-toothed grin and flat head; a cop who never opened his mouth unless he had something nasty or vulgar to say. Most of the time, Gunner noticed, it was a little of both.

"Goddamnit, Gunner, I'm not fuckin' around this time!" Poole roared, knocking a half-empty coffee cup off the table and across the room, spraying cold coffee everywhere. "I told you to leave Pearson the hell alone, and you went after him anyway! If he doesn't make it—"

"Listen to me, Poole. Read my lips this time, will you, please? *I didn't go after anybody*! I've been in the goddamn bed for the last two days, *he* came after *me*!"

"Bull*shit*! He had no reason to go after you! He was too busy runnin' from us to be thinkin' about you!"

"Yeah, well, he thought about me anyway, and that's a fact. He shanghaied Foley, lured me over to Mickey's, and tried to ambush me. So I shot his ass, hell yes. He didn't give me any other choice."

He'd been telling the same story now for over two hours, as he suspected poor Foley had been doing in another room elsewhere, until even he was tired of the sound of it. Trouble was, it was the truth, and the truth was all he had to offer these two, give or take a few minor details. Like the manhunt he had started for Pearson with a few dozen phone calls, which may have explained to Poole's and Gruber's satisfaction the fugitive's view of Gunner as somebody who needed killing, if Pearson ever hoped to show his face in daylight again.

"I think you had a choice," Gruber said, "and you made it. Leave Pearson to the law, or take care of him yourself. You chose to do the latter."

"So I could have you two come down on my ass like a ton of bricks, is that it?" He turned to the other cop in the room, said, "Christ, Poole, listen to what you're saying. I'm not that stupid, and you know it."

"Nobody's accusin' you of being stupid, Gunner. Just crazy."

"Let me tell you what's crazy. What's crazy is you bozos leaning on me like this when you know damn well I'm telling you the truth. That's what's crazy. Or are you gonna stand there and tell me Foley hasn't been backing my story up one hundred and ten percent?"

Poole had nothing to say to that, but Gruber said, "Foley's been tellin' us what you told him to say, wiseass. That's all."

"And Pearson? What about him?"

"You know the answer to that. He's in no condition to talk. He hasn't said a word to anyone since they took him to County Hospital."

Which was probably just as well, Gunner knew; if Pearson *had* talked to the police, he would have been unlikely to say anything even remotely similar to Gunner's account of his shooting.

"Okay," Gunner said. "So forget Pearson and Foley. What about the physical evidence at the scene? You guys have heard about physical evidence, haven't you?"

"The physical evidence at the scene proves nothin'," Gruber said, "except maybe how good you are at makin' attempted murder look like self-defense. At least, that's all it proves to *me*."

"Aw, hell . . ." Gunner dropped his chin to his chest and shook his head, genuinely exhausted. He had already been physically sick once since they'd brought him in here, and he was beginning to feel sick again.

After a short silence, Poole turned to his partner and said, "Johnny, go have another talk with Mr. Foley, will you?"

"Excuse me?"

"I'd like a minute or two with this clown alone. You don't mind, do you?" Poole glared at him, waiting.

Clearly, Gruber minded a great deal, but there wasn't much he could do about it; Poole had him outranked.

"Sure. Why not?" He shrugged, staring daggers at both men alternately, and walked out. Gunner couldn't help but feel sorry for Foley, if that was indeed where Gruber was headed.

When the door had closed behind him, Poole said, "Looks like you've made another friend at the department."

Gunner smiled, not wanting to seem impolite. "Yeah. Man in my line of work can never have too many, can he?"

Poole thought about taking offense at that, but chose to let it pass. "I don't have to tell you you really stepped in it this time. Do I?"

"After what you and laughing boy have just put me through? No, Lieutenant, you don't. I'm knee-deep in the brown stuff, I understand that."

"Then why—"

"I've already told you why. Why, what, when, where, and how. As God is my witness, Poole, the man tried to do me before I did him. It's that simple. I mean, hell—what kind of moron would I have to be to shoot him without provocation, and then call you to come get him before he was dead? You ever ask yourself that?"

"Sure I have. And the answer I come up with is that you got cold feet. Chickened out at the last minute and tried to cut your losses."

Gunner shook his head again. "No. *No!* You know me better than that, Poole. I *know* you do!"

"All right. All right! So it all happened just the way you say. Why the hell didn't you call me *before* you went out to Mickey's? If you knew Pearson was there waiting for you—"

"I never said I knew he was there. I said I suspected he might be. There's a difference."

"Yeah, but—"

"Besides. I wake your ass up in the middle of the night to tell you where I think Pearson *might* be, only thing you're going to do about it is rip the phone cord out of the wall and go back to sleep. You know it, and I know it."

Again, he had rendered Poole speechless. A state of being cops looked upon with the same fear and dread as paraplegia.

"Listen, Lieutenant," Gunner said, trying his best to sound conciliatory, "I can't do this anymore. I'm tired, and I'm not well. You've seen that for yourself. Another ten minutes of this shit and I'm going to have a stroke, I swear to God."

"My heart bleeds," Poole said.

"Okay. Your heart bleeds. So read me my rights and stop fucking around. Right now, let's go." When Poole failed to respond to that, he said, "Shit. You're not going to charge me, and we both know it. Gruber might be too thick to know the truth when he hears it, but not you. You've been around too long. Pearson got shot tonight exactly the way I've been saying he did, and you've known that from the start."

Poole still refused to speak.

"You told me what would happen if I went after Pearson on my own, and you meant it," Gunner said. "So since you've made no effort yet to put your foot in my ass—"

"All right, smart guy. So maybe I do think you're telling the truth. Today, right now. Pearson's shooting isn't a homicide, yet—I can afford to be charitable. But tomorrow, or the next day, or the day after that . . . when and if the man *dies . . .''* The cop shook his head. "It's not gonna be so easy to believe you. Not for me—and not for the DA. You remember the DA, don't you?"

Gunner had never actually met the woman, but he knew more than a few of her assistants. None of them cared for him very much.

"Go on home, Gunner. I'm tired of this shit too. We wanna see you again, we'll know where to find you."

Gunner didn't move. He thought Poole was putting him on.

"I said, get the hell out of here! What do I have to do, put it in writing?"

The black man got up from the table and said, "What about your pal Gruber? This going to be okay with him?"

"You let me worry about Gruber, Gunner. You wanna worry about somebody, worry about Pearson. Maybe even say a prayer for him while you're at it. I know I would, I was you."

There was nothing Gunner could say to that but amen, and he knew it. "Thanks, Poole. You're a stand-up guy."

On his way to the door, he blew a kiss at his reflection in the one-way glass of the room's observation window, just on the outside chance John Gruber was standing on the other side.

Ira "Ziggy" Zeigler was eating grapes today.

He was always eating some kind of fruit, Ziggy. Apples, oranges, peaches, pears—Gunner had seen the seventy-something lawyer eat them all. The stuff was like candy to him.

Today, Monday, he was eating grapes.

Gunner only knew this because that was the first thing he'd asked when Ziggy answered the phone, what kind of fruit was it today?

"You know, you could do worse than try to eat a little fruit yourself, sometimes," the old man said, after he'd answered Gunner's opening question. "Or maybe you don't want to live to be my age. Maybe forty-five, fifty years of living is enough for you."

It was the last lighthearted thing he had to say. Once Gunner told him how he'd spent the better part of his Saturday night and Sunday morning, Ziggy had no interest in anything but ripping his client's lungs out.

And Gunner had thought it would help, waiting until Monday morning to break the news to him.

"Kid, you're killing me," he said, his voice rising. "I tell you every time I talk to you, so help me God. *Call me first*, I say. Before you do anything else, before you say a single word to anybody. *Call me first!*"

"Ziggy—"

"I don't want to hear any excuses! We've gone over this a million times, you and me, I shouldn't have to be telling you this anymore. You pay me good money to watch out for you, Aaron, why the hell won't you let me earn it every once in a while?"

"Ziggy, they couldn't hold me. Okay? I *knew* they couldn't hold me. I had a *witness*."

"It doesn't matter that you had a witness. I don't care if you had a *thousand* witnesses, you talk to *me* before you talk to the *cops*! Always! What kind of licensed professional are you, you don't understand that yet?"

As many times as they'd had the same argument, Gunner had never won it. He fell silent.

"So what's his present condition? This guy you shot?" Ziggy asked, finally ready to change the subject.

"I've got no idea."

"You didn't check on his condition yesterday?"

"I was back in the bed all day yesterday. Recovering. I told you that."

"What's his name again? Peterson?"

"Pearson. Michael Pearson."

"P-E-A-R-S-O-N?"

"Yeah."

"And you say he's at County?"

"That's what they said, yeah. You going to send him a card?"

"A card wouldn't be a bad idea, I'll tell you that. Especially if it'll pull him through. But what I had in mind was calling down there to see how he's doing. Find out if the worst is over, or just beginning.''

"He's in the jail ward, Ziggy. They're not going to tell you anything down there.''

"Not officially, no. But off the record, as a favor to a friend . . . I might know somebody works there who'd answer a question or two, I asked politely.''

That Ziggy knew at least a *dozen* people fitting that description, Gunner had no doubt. He was the most well-connected man the investigator had ever met.

"And I better talk to your friend Foley, too. Just to hear his side of things. Think you could have him call me this afternoon?''

"Sure. Just do me a favor and go easy on the poor guy, huh? Pearson roughed him up pretty good Saturday night, like I said, and he might not be feeling so hot himself.''

Ziggy said he'd treat him like a newborn baby.

"And you get any more requests to do a Q and A downtown, I'm going to be the first to know about it. Correct?''

"Correct,'' Gunner said. "You have my word on it.''

"Your word. Terrific. I've got the price of a cup of coffee, my life is complete.''

Fresh fruit and one-liners. That was Ziggy.


Mickey said, "Next time you two wanna fight a war with somebody, fight it somewhere else, all right? This is a barbershop, man, not Madison Square Garden.''

"Madison Square Garden? You mean Caesar's Palace. They ain't had a big fight in Madison Square Garden in thirty years,'' Winnie Phifer said, cutting Alonzo Moe's hair at the next chair over. She'd just started working for Mickey three weeks ago, but she had never been the least bit uncomfortable about correcting him in front of his friends.

"He thinks it's our fault,'' Foley said to Gunner, still looking as hurt and tired as he had the last time the investigator had seen him, stepping into the backseat of the taxi Gunner had called for him outside the LAPD's Southwest station more than thirty-two hours earlier. "Like it was *us* tried to jack *the boy* up in here, 'stead of the other way around. Ain't that a bitch?''

"You didn't have to let 'im in," Mickey said. "What the hell you let 'im in for?"

"'Cause he looked like he needed *help*! I *told* you that! Man come knockin' on the door, holdin' his arm all funny an' shit, an' said he just been jacked up, could he please use the phone. What was I s'posed to do, say no?''

"Yes. Yes! Just say, 'I'm sorry, brother, but the boss ain't here, I can't let you in. You're gonna have to use the pay phone down the street.' ''

"Man, that's cold," Morris Bingham said.

"Sure is," Winnie agreed.

"Cold? I'll tell you two what's cold," Mickey said, stopping his work on Bingham's almond-shaped head to more directly confront his detractors. "Cold is comin' in here this mornin' and findin' blood all on the floor, that's what's cold. On the floor, on the walls, in my chairs—"

"All right, Mickey, we get the point," Gunner said, finally entering the conversation outright. "We fucked up the place. We're sorry." He was sitting in a chair against the wall, four chairs removed from Foley and everyone else, acting like the magazine he had open in front of his face was actually holding his interest. No one was fooled. Both his silence and the distance he had placed between himself and the others had been a clear indication to everyone that his mind was elsewhere, and he wanted it to stay that way.

But Mickey wouldn't allow it.

"'Sorry'? You can be sorry if you want to," Foley said, "but not me. I almost got killed Saturday night, I'm just happy to be alive."

"Amen to that, brother," Alonzo said.

"Besides—who the hell you think cleaned the place up this mornin', 'fore all the rest of you got here? *Him*?" Foley pointed at Mickey. "Hell, no! It was *me,* that's who. He didn't even have to say a word, I just come in here an' did it. Didn't I? Didn't I?"

He was talking to Mickey, but Mickey wasn't listening. He was studying Gunner instead. He turned his clippers off, dropped them to his side, and said, "Hey, Gunner, man, don't be like that. I'm just messin' with you guys, that's all. You know that."

"Forget it," Gunner said. He still had the magazine open in his hands.

"It's just, I walk in here this mornin' and see blood all over the place, man, I didn't know what to think. 'Cause you guys didn't call me to tell me what happened, so I thought—"

"Anybody know a girl named Goldy?" Gunner asked, tossing the magazine back onto its pile on the table beside him.

Everybody stopped what they were doing to look at him, surprised by the question.

"Goldy?" Bingham asked.

"Like Goldie Hawn, the actress?" Winnie asked.

"I guess so. I'm not sure," Gunner said.

"Who the hell is Goldy?" Mickey asked.

Gunner shook his head. "Probably nobody. Pearson said he'd been with a girl named Goldy at the time of Nina's murder. I'm sure it was just bullshit, but . . ." He shrugged. "You never know."

"Yes you do. That nigger's full of shit," Winnie said. "He killed that girl, an' he knows it. Only girl named Goldy he knows is the one in that fairy tale, 'Goldilocks an' the Three Damn Bears.' "

"I heard that," Alonzo said.

Gunner nodded his head, agreeing. "That's what I think too. It just bothers me a little, I guess. Him picking a name like that out of the hat, I mean. 'Goldy.' "

"What's wrong with 'Goldy'?" Bingham asked.

"Nothing. Except that a man usually isn't that creative when he's telling a lie he hasn't had time to think through, that's all."

"I don't follow you," Mickey said.

"What I'm saying is, it's not the kind of name you'd expect him to come up with on the spur of the moment. Is it? Betty or Debra, maybe, but Goldy? Why would he say Goldy?"

"You're thinkin' he was tellin' the truth. Is that it?" Alonzo asked.

"No, but—"

"That nigger wasn't with nobody named Goldy," Winnie insisted, starting back to work on Alonzo's hair. "I already told you."

"Okay. So he was lying. That's what I think too, like I said. But—"

"But what?"

"But answer the question anyway. Just to humor me. Anybody here know somebody named Goldy?"

The room fell silent as everyone gave the matter some thought.

"I knew a *brother* whose name was Goldy, once," Alonzo said. "That was ten, fifteen years ago, back when I was workin' for GM, out in Van Nuys. He worked in the tool shop. They called him Goldy 'cause he had a gold front tooth, you could see it every time he opened his mouth. I never understood that, why somebody would want to put a gold tooth in their mouth like that, right up front where you can't miss it, but—"

"Alonzo, we supposed to be talkin' 'bout a *girl* named Goldy," Winnie said. "Remember?"

"Oh, yeah. That's right," Alonzo said, embarrassed.

"*I* know a girl named Goldy," Foley said, "but I don't think it's the one you got in mind. This is a white girl."

Everyone waited for him to explain.

"She works in the car wash over on Manchester and Vermont. She's the cashier there, been there forever."

"I know her," Bingham said, nodding. "He's right, her name *is* Goldy, now that I think about it. It's on her name tag, 'Goldy.' But—"

"She's an older girl," Foley said.

"Yeah. That's what I was about to say."

"How old is that?" Gunner asked. "Approximately?"

Foley and Bingham looked at each other, neither wanting to be the first one to take a guess. Shrugging, Bingham said, "I don't know. Forty-five or fifty, maybe."

"Yeah. That sounds right," Foley said, nodding.

"Forty-five or fifty?" Gunner asked.

"That don't sound like nobody that boy would've been with to me," Mickey said.

"Sure don't," Winnie said, laughing.

" 'Less he was fucked up even *before* he got shot," Mickey added, laughing too. Alonzo and Bingham cracked up next, followed by Foley, leaving Gunner the only one in the shop not getting—or appreciating—the joke.

Being the first to notice this, Mickey wiped a tear from his eye and said, "Come on, Gunner, man, you're worryin' about nothin'! Like Winnie said, that boy's full of shit, there ain't no Goldy. So he came up with an original name, so what? That's what *good* liars do, tell lies don't *sound* like lies. He's a good liar, that's all."

"Exactly," Winnie said.

Bingham and Alonzo both uttered various forms of concurrence, equally eager to set Gunner's mind at ease on the subject.

After a while, the investigator nodded and stood up, ready to go. "Yeah. I'm sure you're right," he said. His friends would have liked to see him smile, but they weren't so rewarded; he looked a little less distracted than before, but that was all.

When he started out the front door, Mickey said, "Where you gonna be, you get an important call? Or you just want me to hold your messages?"

"Hold 'em," Gunner said.

"You better tell 'im to write 'em down," Bingham said, trying to make a joke.

But Gunner was already out on the sidewalk.

# six

HE HAD BILLS TO PAY, SO HE WENT OUT AND PAID THEM. HE
had the money, for a change, so he figured what the hell. His
cable service had been lousy lately, so he paid the cable
company last, hoping the wait would bring them to the brink
of bankruptcy and change the way they handled customer
service forever.

That killed about two hours.

When his last check had been written, he found a pay
phone and called his cousin Del. Poole had suggested he
might have to go back to work for the electrician soon, if
Pearson didn't make it and Gunner's PI license got yanked
out from under him, and maybe the cop had something there.
Gunner had worked for Del before, and almost learned to
like it, so his doing so again was not completely out of the
question.

Of course, there was no guarantee that Del wanted to be
bothered with him again. In fact, it was sometimes all his
cousin could do just to talk to him over the phone.

"What do you want?" Del asked him today, the minute
he realized who was calling. Not to be rude, but merely time-
efficient. Gunner had a reason for calling, he always did, so
there wasn't any point in either of them pretending otherwise.

"I need to talk to you, Del. Five, ten minutes, that's all
I need."

"When? Now?"

"Right now, yeah. Can you meet me somewhere?"

"No. I'm busy."

"Del—"

"I'm goin' over to Mother's in about a half hour, you want to meet me over there. What's this all about?"

"Mother's? *Big* Mother's? When the hell did you start going to Mother's?"

Del had tripped on a treadmill the first time he'd visited the popular South-Central gym as Gunner's guest, nearly two years ago, and the humiliation of the experience had been so severe he'd sworn never to return again.

"I've been a member for almost a year," Del said. "What's the big deal?"

"Nothing. I just thought you said—"

"Look, you wanna meet me there or not? I've got work to do here, I've gotta get going."

"Sure, sure. I'll see you in a half hour."

"And you're gonna have my money, right?"

"Your money?"

"Don't bother comin' without my money, Aaron. Save yourself a trip."

He was talking about the seventy-five dollars Gunner had borrowed from him eight weeks before. Somehow, Del never asked for a loan to be repaid until Gunner actually had the money. Which, of course, he did in this case, thanks to Roman Goody. It was as if the man had a direct line to Gunner's bank account.

"That was fifty bucks, right?" Gunner asked.

Talking to no one but a dial tone.

The answer to the question everyone always asked was yes, there really *was* a Big Mother.

His name was Ozzie Bledsoe, and he was as big as a weight lifter could get without bursting out of his skin like an overcooked hot dog. Gunner didn't know his exact age, but he figured the former Mr. California to be somewhere in his late forties to early fifties, though he looked much younger than that. There were lines beneath his eyes and his hair was turning gray almost as fast as it was falling out, but other than that, the goateed black man seemed completely unaffected by age.

According to Ozzie himself, he had picked up the Big Mother name in the county joint, back in the mid-seventies when he was still more interested in pulling armed robberies than pumping iron. Some kid in the next cell over had just started in calling him "Big Mother," yelling it out at the top of his lungs every time he addressed him, and pretty soon, everyone was doing it. Even the guards. What else could you call a black man who was six four, 265 pounds, with a back as wide as a four-lane highway and biceps as big as beer kegs?

In any case, the name came in handy when, in the fall of '91, he decided to open a gym of his own. He'd been a retired felony offender for over ten years at that point, and had made a few dollars doing bodyguard work for various people in the entertainment industry. He bought an old gas station with a large service bay to start, stayed there for a couple of years, then found a warehouse building near the Compton airport and converted that. Big Mother's Gym had been there ever since.

He saw Gunner walk in the door and immediately started shaking his head. The teacher confronted by his most unproductive student.

"Uh-uh-uh," he said. "Look at you. Just *look* at you!"

"Come on, Mother. I'm a sick man, have a heart."

"I'll say you're sick. Look at what you've done to yourself! Man, Gunner, was a time you were in here every other day. Had arms as big as me an' a stomach you could iron clothes on. And look at you now. Just look!" He appraised Gunner's waistline critically. "All that muscle gone to waste . . ."

"It's called getting old, brother. Some people do that, you know."

"Yeah, well, that don't mean you have to get fat an' ugly, too. You'd bring your behind in here more often than two, three times a year—"

Gunner waved him off and said, "Never mind all that. My cousin make it in here yet?"

"You mean the one—"

"Yeah, him. Del."

Mother jabbed a thumb at the room behind him, chuckling, and said, "You can usually find 'im over at the abdominal station, harassin' the females. I haven't seen 'im today, but if he's here, that's probably where he's at."

"You haven't been giving him a hard time, I hope."

"Who? Me?"

"About his accident, I mean."

"Oh. That." Mother started chuckling again. "Last time we talked about it was the day he came in here to sign up. I told him we were happy to have 'im, under one condition: He wants to use the treadmills, he's gotta wear a *helmet*."

Mother fell out, laughing like Gunner had just told *him* a joke, and not the other way around. Heads turned throughout the gym, reacting to the sudden blast of sound. When Mother laughed, he laughed for the world to hear; it was a deep, booming laugh that shattered silences and made a shambles of conversations taking place zip codes away. Only an air raid siren could be more conspicuous.

Gunner shook the big man's hand and went to find Del.

It was a brief search. He wasn't in the first place Gunner looked for him, at the gym's abdominal station as Mother had suggested, but he did turn up in the second: the free-weight area, where he was actually engaged in doing incline bench presses. He was huffing and puffing, pushing a relatively light amount of weight, but other than that, he appeared to be as comfortable doing physical exercise as anyone else on the premises. Gunner was amazed.

"I can't believe what I'm seeing," he said.

Del glanced up at him, surprised. "Ha-ha," he said, in midrep. "So what's so important?"

"I'm fine, cuz. Thanks for asking. And you?"

"I thought you were in a hurry. But if you wanna make small talk—"

"You're right. I *am* in a hurry."

"So what's goin' on?"

Gunner told him. He talked and Del listened, both men moving from weight station to weight station as Del doggedly continued his workout, until Gunner finally fell silent and waited, looking to his cousin for some kind of reaction.

"So? What's the question?" Del asked. He was seated at a preacher bench now, both arms busy doing barbell curls.

"Question is, are you going to be where I can find you if the shit hits the fan? Or should I make other plans?"

"Say that again? I don't understand."

"Look. This isn't just the usual bailout I'm talking about here, Del. The kind of trouble I'm in this time can't be fixed with just a few dollars for meal money and a place to crash for the night. I'm going to need more help than that."

"You talking about a job?"

Gunner shrugged. "Only if I can't find something else. And only if you can really use me."

"Use you? Man, I can *always* use you," Del said. "You know that. I just wish—"

"Yeah, I know. You wish I'd make it permanent this time."

This was an old refrain of Del's, and Gunner had known he'd have to hear it sooner or later, the topic of discussion being what it was.

"Listen. I'm tired of bein' just any port in a storm for you, Aaron, okay? You've gotta grow up, man, and growin' up starts with havin' a job. A *real* job."

"I've *got* a real job."

"No, what you've got is *trouble*. That's what you've got. That's all you're ever gonna have, line of work you're in. When are you gonna figure that out?"

"Del—"

"Okay, okay. Forget I said anything. We've been through this enough times, I oughta know by now how pointless it is."

Angry now, both men spent the next several minutes not speaking to each other, acting as if the silence didn't bother them in the least. Gunner could feel another headache coming on, resulting from the clang of iron weights being dropped throughout the gym.

Finally, Del said, "Maybe he won't die. This guy you shot."

Gunner shrugged. "Maybe he won't. I've been lucky be-fore."

"But even if he does, you're covered, right? Because Fo-ley was there—"

"Yeah, he was there."

"And he told them what happened."

"Yeah, he told them."

"Then what's the problem?"

"The problem is Poole, and how badly he wants to burn me this time. He told me to stay away from Pearson, and in his mind, I ignored him. Cops take that kind of shit person-ally, Del. If Pearson lives, Poole might get over it, but if he doesn't . . . I'm in for a career change, like he said, whether I want one or not."

Del nodded, resting between sets. "So when are you sup-posed to hear from Ziggy?"

Gunner shook his head. "He didn't say. But I'm going to call him soon as I get out of here, see if he's found out anything yet."

"And then?"

"Then I'm going to ask around some more, find out if anybody's ever heard of this Goldy person Pearson talked about. The girl he said he was with the night Nina was killed."

Del nodded again, rather than give voice to his true opin-ion: that he wouldn't waste a minute of *his* time looking for some nonexistent Goldy woman, if he were in Gunner's shoes.

Instead, he asked about Claudia.

"There is no Claudia anymore," Gunner said.

"Oh."

"Don't look so broken up. It's for the best."

"Yeah. I'm sure."

"Anyway, no one can pin this one on me. I was ready to go the distance, she wasn't. It happens."

Del shrugged. "Yeah. It does."

Gunner stood up and reached into his pocket, suddenly in a hurry to leave. "Before I forget, here's your money."

Two months Del had been waiting to get his seventy-five dollars back, and now he felt like a heel for taking it.

Nobody at the Deuce had heard of Goldy either.

Gunner had made two complete passes through the bar in three hours, hitting every table, booth, and stool, and now he was tired of asking. Watching people shake their heads and say no, the name wasn't familiar, sorry. Everybody polite, trying to be helpful, but no one having anything to offer him but apologies.

He gave up about twenty minutes after nine.

By that time, the Deuce was in full swing, women laughing and men shouting, Boyz II Men on the stereo, tables and chairs scraping across the floor to suit some new arrangement, ice cubes and drink glasses and bottles of booze clinking, clanking, *crashing* together . . .

A typical Monday night at Lilly's.

Except that Gunner had traded his customary seat at the bar for one at a table, trying to put some distance between himself and Lilly's liquor. This was one of those rare occasions when his problems were too monumental to be dulled by good bourbon, even when consumed in massive doses.

He still had no idea how Michael Pearson was doing. He hadn't been able to catch up with Ziggy until almost six o'clock, and his lawyer had had nothing to report at that time.

"Guy I'm talking to, he was supposed to get back to me, but he never called," Ziggy had said. "So I've got to call him at home, try to reach him there. Where can I find you later, I finally hear from him?"

Gunner told him he'd be at the Deuce anytime after seven, and Ziggy recited the number, having used it enough times in the past to commit it to memory.

And so Gunner was here, hours later, waiting for Ziggy's call. Sharing a table with Jetta Brown, who was talking up a storm, not at all minding that Gunner's thoughts were elsewhere. Jetta never needed you to actually *listen* to what she was saying, she just wanted you around to bounce her voice off of, so that she herself might hear it better. She had a cute face and a body built for action, but her runaway mouth kept most men out of range like an electrified fence.

Of course, her husband, Ollie, did too, when he was around, but that was a different story.

"I asked you a question," Jetta said.

She had been silent for several seconds, having finally gotten around to involving him in the conversation, and Gunner had failed to notice.

"What?"

"I asked you a question. You didn't hear me?"

"I heard you. I just . . ." He tried to think. *What the hell has she been talking about?* "You were saying something about Ollie going back home. To Tennessee."

"For?"

"For a funeral. His brother's, or his stepbrother's."

"His stepbrother's. Lincoln. Go on."

"And he'll be gone for a week. So you were wondering . . ." He stopped, enlightened; not really *remembering* what she had asked, just figuring it out, knowing her as well as he did. ". . . if we were going to get together sometime."

"That's right." Jetta smiled. She never used to have time for Gunner, but lately she'd been flirting with him with serious intent.

"I don't think that would be such a good idea," Gunner said.

"Why not?"

"Because Ollie would object, he ever knew. And make dog food out of us both."

"Shoot," Jetta said, swatting the very thought out of the air with an open palm, "Ollie ain't even *thinkin'* about you."

"Exactly what I like about him best. He never thinks about me."

Ollie was big, fat, and consistently ill-tempered, and what he couldn't pulverize with his bare fists, he could mangle beyond recognition. Gunner had seen him do it.

"You're scared of *Ollie*?"

"I tell you what. If you can find a man in this room who *isn't* scared of him, I'll pick up your tab tonight. And call that man a doctor."

Jetta laughed. Cheating on Ollie was a nonstop party for

her because men took all the risks; her husband didn't have it in him to harm a hair on her head, and she had always known it. How could a woman resist having a little fun at such a man's expense when hurting his feelings was the only consequence of getting caught?

"He loves you, Jetta," Gunner said. "Why don't you give the man a break?"

"A *break*? Honey, every time I let that fat fool get in the same bed as me, I'm givin' him a break!" She laughed again. The tight blue dress she was wearing was only barely able to hold her little breasts in check, it was cut so low in front.

Gunner just shook his head, disgusted with her. He'd been amused by her promiscuity only seconds ago, and now he couldn't think of a thing in the world more loathsome.

"What's the matter with *you*?" Jetta asked.

"Nothing's the matter with me. I just don't like being asked to help you fuck over a friend, that's all."

"A *friend*? Ollie ain't your friend!"

"He sure as hell is more mine than yours."

"Say what?"

"You heard me. You—"

"Gunner, baby, I gotta talk to you," Mean Sheila cut in, having suddenly appeared at their table. The Deuce's resident prostitute was in her usual drunken state, too impaired by liquor to realize she was interrupting a full-scale argument in the making.

"Not now," Gunner said, waving her off brusquely.

"Nigger, you're *crazy*," Jetta said to Gunner, doing the investigator one better by ignoring Sheila altogether.

"I'm not crazy. I'm just honest. Your act isn't funny anymore, Jetta. It's old and it's tired, and it's cheap."

"*Cheap*?"

"Gunner—" Sheila said, gamely trying to interject again.

"Who the hell you callin' *cheap*?"

"You," Gunner said flatly. "You see anyone else around here with their legs open?"

Jetta's hand flashed out to throw her drink in his face, but he caught her wrist before she could raise the glass off the table. Furious, she leapt to her feet to attack him properly, as Mean Sheila finally got the hint and backed off, heading for cover. She didn't get far. Within seconds, a sea of bodies swallowed her up on its way to Gunner and Jetta's table, everybody screaming at once, everybody smelling blood.

Eventually, four Good Samaritans managed to pry Gunner and Jetta apart; one for him and three for her. Gunner gave up peaceably, but Jetta did anything but, kicking, scratching, and cursing like a woman possessed.

And then Lilly pushed her way to the center of the crowd.

Jetta stopped struggling and shut up, *boom,* just like that, and everyone else did likewise. Playtime was over.

"All right, what the fuck is goin' on here?" Lilly asked, sounding not unlike a woman about to kick some very serious ass. She was looking straight at Gunner.

"This nigger here—" Jetta started to say.

"Shut up, Jetta. I'm talkin' to *him,"* Lilly said.

Jetta shut up.

Not waiting for Gunner to speak up, Lilly said, "I told you 'bout bringin' your problems in here and startin' shit with my customers, didn't I? Did I tell you I wasn't gonna have it, or not?"

Gunner wanted to answer, to explain that everything he had said to Jetta to incite this mini-riot had been meant not for her but for Claudia Lovejoy—he could see that now with surprising, if belated, clarity—but he couldn't bring himself to do so. He felt foolish enough as it was; confessing to everyone here that his rejection of Claudia was killing *him* more than it ever would *Claudia* would surely just make matters worse.

So he said nothing, which of course made the house grow quieter still. Because of all the things one could do to get on Lilly's nerves when she was trying to chew you out, nothing worked quite as well as refusing to defend yourself.

Nothing.

"Go get the phone," Lilly said.

No one could believe they had heard her correctly.

"What?" Gunner asked.

"I said go get the phone. You weren't so busy tearin' my place up, you'd've heard me the first time." She gestured toward the bar and the telephone nearby. "You got a phone call."

"Who is it?"

"How the hell should *I* know? Do I look like your god-damn secretary?"

Before he could ask any more stupid questions, Gunner went to the phone.

It was Ziggy.

"We got problems, kid," he said.

Gunner threw his head back and closed his eyes. "Pearson's dead."

"No. Not dead. But he's on a respirator, in a coma. His doctors don't expect him to ever come out of it." He paused to see if Gunner would respond to that, then said, "He lost a lot of blood, and there was some kind of internal infection, my man wasn't too clear on the specifics. In any case, he's in pretty bad shape."

Gunner still didn't say anything.

"You there?"

"Yeah. I'm listening."

"Look, try not to worry about it. He might pull out of it, you never know. And as long as his condition is up in the air, the cops will probably sit tight and leave you alone. They wanted to take you in on an assault charge, they could have done that Saturday night. The fact that you're still walking around suggests they're not interested in charging you with anything short of manslaughter. And they may never get that opportunity, if we're lucky."

"I don't feel lucky," Gunner said.

"Relax, kid. It's gonna be okay. Just try to lay low for a while and stay near the phone. All right?"

"Sure, Ziggy. Thanks."

Gunner could feel Lilly's breath on the back of his neck even as he hung up the phone.

"You finished?" she asked. Stunning him yet again with her uncanny ability to cross her arms across the endless expanse of her chest.

"Yeah. Thanks." He tried to slink away.

"Oh, no. I'm not finished with you yet." She stepped to one side, barring his way.

"Lilly, please. Not tonight . . ."

"Oh, yes, tonight. You did it again. Started some shit in here after I told you I wasn't havin' any. Didn't you?"

"Yes. I did."

"Jetta says you called her a ho. That true?"

"A 'ho'?" Gunner looked around, reminded of the woman he'd been brawling with only moments earlier, and found Jetta back at her table, entertaining what stragglers remained from the crowd that had gathered there to watch them go at each other. She appeared to have completely forgotten about him. "No. I did not call her a ho. I just told her I was getting a little weary of watching her come in here all the time, trying to catch flies between her thighs. That's all."

He hadn't really meant it as a joke, but Lilly took it that way all the same. She cracked up.

"Get the hell out of here," she said, using both hands to push him around to the other side of the bar where he belonged. "Go on, get!"

It was a piece of advice he fully intended to take, until he heard a familiar voice call out after him just as he was walking out the door.

Mean Sheila again.

"Sheila, baby, I've got to go," Gunner said, trying to be patient with her. "Lilly says—"

"This is only gonna take a minute," Sheila said.

"Come see me at Mickey's tomorrow."

"But Elvin said—"

"Elvin said *what*?"

Elvin was Elvin Hodge, the young taxi driver sitting in a booth over by the window. Gunner hardly knew him.

"He said you said it was important. That you needed to know right away," Sheila said.

"Needed to know *what* right away? I don't—"

"He said you lookin' for a girl name' Goldy. You wouldn't be talkin' 'bout Goldy Cruz, would you?"

He had almost been out the door. Too concerned with the

life expectancy of Michael Pearson to remember what had
brought him here in the first place: the nagging fear that
Pearson's friend Goldy was real, and not imaginary. If he
had only started for the Deuce's door five minutes earlier . . .

He would not be so afraid now.

The first thing Gunner learned was that her name had nothing
to do with gold teeth.

Nor the color of her hair, nor the kind of jewelry she liked
to wear. It wasn't a play on her last name, nor was it reflec-
tive of any resemblance she might have borne to Goldilocks,
friend to the Three Bears.

It was all about shoes.

They called Carol Cruz ''Goldy'' because every pair of
shoes the hooker owned was gold. Forty-three pair in all, she
said, either bought gold or dyed gold later. It was just a habit
she'd gotten into as a kid.

''I like the way gold looks on my feet,'' she told the
investigator, dazzling him with her mental dexterity by
shrugging, smoking, and chewing gum all at the same time.
The pink wad in the black woman's mouth had to be as big
as a golf ball.

Sheila had said they could find her working the Inglewood
district, standing on the corner of Prairie and 112th Street
like somebody waiting for a bus where no bus stop was apparent, and she'd been right on. There Goldy stood, just another working girl like Sheila, only younger and remotely
more attractive; about thirty, wearing a tight white sweater
that buttoned down the front, and a pair of tattered denim
cutoffs with tassel-like threads ringing the hem of each leg.
A braided mass of phony blond cornrows had been woven
into her hair, clashing violently with her dark brown skin.

When Gunner finally got around to asking her the only
question that really mattered, it took her forever to tell him
the truth.

And even then, it came too soon.

# seven

"YOU'RE PUSHING ME, GUNNER. I SWEAR TO GOD," POOLE said the next morning.

"She was telling the truth, Poole. I'd bet my life on it."

"Your life is already spoken for. If Pearson dies, it belongs to me. I told you that Sunday."

"But if he didn't kill Nina—"

"For Chrissake, we're talking about a hooker here! Somebody he used to throw a little change at every time he needed a hand job!"

"I realize that. But—"

"Hookers do what they're paid to do, Gunner. That's the nature of their profession. If a john tells 'em to jump, they jump. And if he tells them to bark like a dog, or moo like a cow, or tell anybody who asks that he was with them on Christmas morning, between the hours of six and ten-fifteen . . ."

"It wasn't like that, Poole. She didn't *want* to talk to me. I had to *make* her talk."

It was only a slight exaggeration. He hadn't had to tie her to the rack, exactly, but he had been forced to bide his time with her before she stopped playing stupid.

"You know a man named Michael Pearson?" Gunner had asked her, after all of Mean Sheila's introductions were out of the way.

"Michael who?"

"Pearson. Michael Pearson."

The hooker thought about it. Too long.

"Uh-uh. Don't know nobody by that name," she said, trying to mask the lie behind a nonchalant exhalation of cigarette smoke.

"Are you sure?"

"Yeah, I'm sure. Don't know the man."

"Because he said he was a john of yours. Last Tuesday night."

"He wasn't no john of mine."

"Black man in his mid-thirties, light-skinned, handsome, with a square jaw and a thin mustache. Hair all greased back on the sides. You don't remember being with anybody like that?"

"No."

"You're full of shit."

"What?"

Taken aback, Sheila said, "Gunner, baby, what—"

"I said you're full of shit," Gunner said to Goldy, while motioning for Sheila to hold her tongue. "I just described probably half the men you've ever been with, how the hell are you going to tell me you don't remember being with a john like that?"

"I said—"

"I know what you said. And I know it's bullshit. What I don't know is why you're lying. Are you trying to cover his ass, or yours? Or both?"

He let his eyes lean on her for a while, then said, "Maybe you'd remember him better if I told you he was dying. He's at County-USC right now. In a coma."

Her face changed, but not the way he thought it would: She *smiled*.

"That's too bad," she said, taking another long drag from her cigarette. Southbound traffic on Prairie was blasting the trio with cold air regularly, but she seemed to be the only one not to notice. Or care.

"Then you *do* know him."

"I didn't say that. I just said it was too bad what happened to him, that's all."

"Look. Maybe you don't understand. I don't give a damn

for Pearson. If you don't want to do him any favors, that makes two of us. But I'm the one who put him in the hospital, and I need to know how bad I should feel about that if and when he dies. Do you understand? If he was lying about being with you last Tuesday, I've got no reason to lose any sleep over him. But if he was telling me the *truth*—''

"It don't matter *where* he was last Tuesday. Puttin' that motherfucker in the hospital ain't nothin' for nobody to feel sorry about. Believe me.''

"That doesn't answer my question, Goldy,'' Gunner said firmly. He wanted to get off the street before a patrol car inevitably cruised by and ended their little party.

"He likes to *hurt* people. Bad.''

"I know that.''

"He's a sick motherfucker. He treats you good, an' then . . . then he . . .'' She was rubbing her left arm now, trying to erase the memory of an injury that was no longer there—but perhaps had been, only six days before.

"He *was* with you, wasn't he?'' Gunner asked her.

After a long pause, she shrugged. Confessing.

Gunner had known right then he'd have to see Poole in the morning. First thing.

Sadly, he had also known how reluctant the policeman would be to hear anything he had to say. Just getting him to agree to this meeting at Leimert Park had been as arduous a task as falling up a hill.

"So how come you didn't bring her in?'' he asked Gunner now, swallowing the last of three fast-food breakfast sandwiches Gunner had bought for him. "She's such a reliable witness, why didn't you bring her here so *I* could talk to her?''

"You know the answer to that. She doesn't want to talk to you. She's afraid you'll run her in.''

"Run her in? For what?''

"For practicing prostitution at the Nite Owl Motel with a john named Michael Pearson last Tuesday night, that's what. Exactly what she'd be confessing to if she made Pearson's alibi official.''

Poole shook his head, said, "Baloney. Any pro knows

we'll waive a chickenshit charge like that, they can help us work a felony case. She was feedin' you a line.''

''No.''

''She was afraid of gettin' busted, all right, but not for prostitution. She was afraid we'd throw her ass in jail for tryin' to feed *us* the same bullshit she was feedin' *you*.''

''No!''

''If Pearson was her boyfriend, she'd be here. No matter what. Far as I'm concerned, Gunner, that's the bottom line.''

He stood up from the table they were sharing, wiped his mouth with a paper napkin, and dusted the crumbs off the front of his trousers. Preparing for the long drive back to the station.

''So you're not going to look into it. Is that what you're telling me?'' Gunner asked him, not bothering to rise himself.

''In a word? No. Not at this time.''

''Because you still think Pearson's your man.''

''At this very moment, yeah. I do.''

''I guess that means you found the murder weapon. That's why you're moving so slow on this thing, isn't it? You've got a murder weapon.''

''We don't have a weapon yet, Gunner, but we will. Soon. And as for your insulting insinuation that I'm draggin' my ass on this one—not that it's any of your fucking business—I got a dance card full of other cases in much greater need of my attention. So—''

''So you're a busy man who could use my help. I volunteered it to you.''

''Forget about it, all right? I'm not givin' you permission to involve yourself in an ongoing homicide investigation. You're in enough trouble as it is.''

''But—''

''No more buts, cowboy. You wanna keep dicking around in this Nina Pearson case, you're gonna have to do it behind my back, same way you do everything else.''

''What?''

''You heard me. You don't give a damn for my authority, you're gonna do what you wanna do no matter what I say, so why pretend otherwise? What's the point?''

"Nobody's asking for your *blessings,* Poole. I'm just asking for a little breathing room. A little stress-free space to operate in for a while, that's all."

The police detective shook his head again, said, "That ain't mine to give, Gunner. Least, not officially."

"Tell me what you can do for me *un*officially, then."

"Unofficially, best I can do for you is offer you some advice: Stay out of my field of vision. Make it as easy for me to ignore you as you possibly can. That clear enough for you, or do I have to draw you a picture?"

He'd keep his back turned as long as Gunner gave him no reason to turn around. That was basically what the cop was saying.

"It's clear," Gunner said.

"Good. Next time I hear from you, you'd better have something more to offer me than suspicions and theories. And soggy breakfast sandwiches with two ounces of fuckin' meat in 'em."

Poole tossed his balled-up napkin at Gunner's chest and walked away.

The Nite Owl Motel was a run-down eyesore on Inglewood and Magnolia Avenues that served more prostitutes nightly than all the hamburger joints in the city of Inglewood combined. The trio of tiny little bungalows was dirty and graffiti-infested, and there was only one thing worse than spending an evening there: trying to hold a decent conversation with the desk clerk.

He was a gaunt, middle-aged black man with a full head of unruly hair. Gunner found the clerk fighting a nap upon his arrival, and he was as full of information as a duck hunter's decoy.

"You know a working girl named Goldy?"

"No."

"Last name Cruz. Goldy Cruz."

"Nope."

"A dark-skinned sister in her early thirties, average height, average weight, wears her hair in braids. Long, blond braids."

"Uh-uh."

"Always wearing gold shoes on her feet. That's where the name comes from, Goldy."

"I don't never look at nobody's feet."

"But you look at their faces. Don't you?"

"Sometimes."

"Were you looking at faces last Tuesday night?"

"Maybe. Some, I guess."

"You *were* working last Tuesday night, right? Isn't that what you said, that you were the one here on the desk last Tuesday?"

"Yeah. I was here."

"But you don't remember seeing a girl like the one I just described to you?"

"No."

"She would've been with a man."

"Man, they *all* with a man."

"This one would've been a good-looking, light-skinned brother. An inch or two shorter than me, a few pounds lighter. Wears a mustache."

Gunner waited for a response.

"You didn't see *him*?"

"No. I don't think so."

"Mind if I see the motel register?"

"The motel register?"

"The book your guests sign when they rent a room. This." Gunner tapped on the large ledger book sitting on the counter between them, then opened it without waiting for permission to do so.

"You can look at it if you want," the desk clerk said, "but don't none of the girls work here use it. Their friends neither."

It was true; the book was almost empty. Gunner closed it back up and said, "You *do* understand that I'm not a cop, right? I'm a private investigator, working on an insurance fraud case."

"Yeah, you said that."

"So you have no reason to be afraid to tell me the truth. I'm not Vice, or anything."

"I *am* tellin' you the truth."

"Sure you are. But—"

"Maybe you got the wrong motel. Why you so sure they was here, these people you lookin' for?"

"Because Goldy said they were here. The Nite Owl Motel in Inglewood, she said."

The desk clerk paused a moment, thinking. "Maybe she was confused," he said.

"Or maybe she's a friend of yours, and you think you're helping her out, acting like you don't know the lady. Maybe that's it."

The desk clerk just stared at him.

The time had come in this interrogation for Gunner to start thinking about offering the man a few dollars for his candor, but he didn't know what the money would buy. He still couldn't tell if the guy was a hard-nosed Goldy loyalist, or simply somebody who neither knew nor cared who Gunner had been talking about for the last twenty minutes.

It took him about thirty seconds to decide what to do.

Confident he'd be able to spend his money more wisely somewhere else, he handed the man one of his business cards and said good-bye.

His next move was to buy a cup of coffee.

It was a large cup of a West African blend called Safari Black at HiNotes, a neighborhood coffeehouse he liked to frequent on Central Avenue and 107th Street. He had to adulterate it with six packets of sugar to smooth out its rough edges, but it was good. Strong as aged oxen blood, but good.

While Duke Ellington's "Mood Indigo" escaped from the speakers above his head, and sports pages and assorted business journals were being studied by black men and women all around him, he reviewed what he had learned about Nina Pearson's murder so far and came to a very disagreeable conclusion: He still didn't believe her husband had killed her.

Which was odd, considering his little Q and A with the dimwit desk clerk at the Nite Owl Motel seemed to only bolster Poole's contention that Pearson's alibi was bogus.

The guy couldn't remember Pearson *or* Goldy Cruz being there the night of Nina's murder.

Still, the investigator's instincts told him Pearson was an innocent man. And that left him nothing else to believe but that Nina's real killer was still out there somewhere, enjoying the freedom Gunner had inadvertently secured for him or her by providing the police with the perfect fall guy for Nina's murder: a mute. A motionless lump in a hospital bed who could neither deflect nor deny the charges being made against him.

Had he only been able to move Poole to see things his way this morning, and agree to start looking for other suspects in the case, Gunner would not be here at HiNotes struggling to accept the obvious fate that awaited him. But that was life. Always throwing work in your path that would neither pay you a dime nor make you feel any better about yourself afterward.

He put a lid on his half-full cup of Safari Black and got on with it, this business of doing yet one more dirty job nobody else could see their way around to taking off his hands.

"I don't believe it," Mimi Hillman said.

She was sitting in her living room again, Gunner sitting opposite her. She sounded just like Poole.

He had known it would be a hard sell, getting her to believe that someone other than Nina's husband might have killed her, but he had nowhere else to go with his suspicions. He certainly couldn't go back to Poole. Not yet, anyway.

"Who else would want to kill my baby?" Mimi asked him. *"Who?"*

She had spent all of ten seconds reflecting on the news of Pearson's grave physical condition. Heartbroken she obviously wasn't.

"If I knew that, Momma Hillman, I wouldn't be here," Gunner said.

"Then what makes you think it wasn't Michael? If nobody else could have done it—"

"That wasn't what I said. What I said was I don't know

of anyone else who could have. But *you*—you're a different story. You knew Nina's friends, her enemies . . .''

Nina's mother shook her head. "That child didn't *have* any enemies. Only enemy she ever had in this world was Michael. Nobody else ever even looked at Nina sideways. Nobody.''

"You're sure about that.''

"Of course I'm sure. You just don't know Michael, that's all. You don't know how he beat on Nina, and cheated on her, and lied to her . . .''

"I don't think he was lying about this.''

"Why? Why don't you think he was lying?''

"Because it didn't *sound* like a lie to me when he said it. That's why. I know that sounds silly to you, but . . .'' He shrugged. "I can't explain it any other way. I've been in this business almost twenty years, and I still don't always know a lie when I hear one. But the *truth*—sometimes the truth makes a sound all its own.''

"And you think he was telling you the truth. About his being with this other woman when Nina was killed.''

"Yes. I do. Just like I believe the woman was telling me the truth when she told me where and when they'd spent the night together. My instincts aren't much, Momma Hillman, I'd be the first to admit that. But they're all I've got. And what they're telling me now is that Michael's not the man the police really want. Someone else is.''

"Someone like *who*? Everybody else loved Nina!''

"I'm sure it appeared that way to you. Nina was an easy person to love, after all. But people don't always show you their true feelings. Sometimes all the hugs and kisses and kind words are just for show.''

Mimi shook her head again, said, "I don't believe that. Nina's friends are good people.''

"I'm not saying they aren't. I'm just saying I'd like to talk to a few of them to find out for myself what kind of people they are. That's all.''

"But why? Why? If the police are satisfied that Michael killed Nina—''

"We're not talking about the police. We're talking about

*me*. And I don't want to wake up some morning five, ten, fifteen years down the road to learn that somebody other than Michael killed Nina and *walked*. Do you understand? The time to see that justice is done for Nina is *now*, Momma Hillman. Not later. Later might be too late.''

''Seeing that justice is done for Nina is not your job, Aaron. It's God's job. Let God and the police handle justice.''

''I *am* letting them handle it. I'm just giving them a little help, that's all.''

''Aaron—''

''Look. I don't want to argue with you. That's not what I came here for. If you're satisfied that Michael killed Nina, fine. I envy you that. The information I'd hoped to get from you today I can get somewhere else, no problem. But I'm going to do this. One way or another. Whether you think I have the right to get so personally involved or not.''

He moved to kiss her good-bye.

''Aaron, don't. Don't leave,'' Mimi pleaded with him.

''I have to. I'm sorry. I'll call you tomorrow.'' He started for the door.

''Sisterhood House,'' Mimi said, all but blurting the words out.

He looked back at her. ''What?''

''She was staying at Sisterhood House. It's a home for battered women. That's where her friends were. At least, all the ones I knew.''

He walked back into the living room but didn't sit down. ''Where would I find this Sisterhood House?''

''It's up on Sugar Hill. Or what people used to call Sugar Hill. On Adams Boulevard between Crenshaw and Normandie. It's one of those old, mansionlike homes up on the hill there.''

''When was Nina there?''

''She was there just last month. She'd been there since September sometime. The child had only been home three weeks.''

''Did Michael know she was staying there?''

Mimi shook her head. ''Not at first. But he found out

eventually. Nina called him right after serving him with the
divorce papers, and I think she told him then. I told her not
to, but she did.''

"When was this?''

"I don't know. Maybe five or six weeks ago. I'm not
sure.''

"She told him where she was?''

"Yes. The security at the House made her feel very safe,
she had no fear of him getting to her there.''

"By 'security,' you're talking about what, exactly?''

"I mean there's a gate out front. An electronic gate. And
if you don't have a pass, they don't let you through. They
won't buzz you in. That's why she was there, instead of here
with me. The security. Michael might have reached her here,
but he couldn't reach her there.''

"She was there for what? About five months, you said?''

"Yes.''

"Why so long?''

Mimi just looked at him, not following the question.

"I mean, isn't the normal stay in a home of that kind
usually a month or two? How is it she was allowed to stay
there for almost half a year?''

"Oh. Well, I don't know anything about the normal
length of stay. But Nina was there that long because she was
working there too. She wasn't just a resident.''

"Working there? In what capacity?''

"I couldn't really tell you. Nina was never very clear
about that. She was an aide to the director, is all I know.''

Gunner finally produced a notebook and a pen, asked,
"Would you happen to know this director's name?''

"Her name is Wendy Singer. She's a white woman. I met
her a couple of times. Very attractive, very smart. But nobody to mess with. I can tell you that.''

"What about Nina's friends? You said she had friends
there.''

"I only know of two. Trini Serrano and Angela Glass.''

Gunner asked her to spell Serrano's name for him, then
asked her to tell him what she knew about either woman.

"I only met Angela once. And I never met Trini at all.

Angela I liked, though I was surprised Nina was so fond of her. Because they aren't—I mean, they *weren't*—anything alike. Angela is very outgoing and animated, where Nina was never like that at all. Angela kind of buzzes around you like a bee, laughing and talking, laughing and talking. She's like a child who's had too much sugar.'' Mimi had to laugh, just thinking about her.

"And Trini?"

"Trini I never met, like I said. All I know about Trini is that Nina loved her work, and that she'd given Nina a camera and was teaching her to take pictures with it. That's one of Trini's photos up on the mantel there. The black-and-white one of Nina, over on the right side there, next to her wedding picture.''

Gunner hadn't noticed it earlier, but there *was* a new photograph hidden among all of Mimi's old ones: a five-by-seven head shot of Nina in a simple black plastic frame. There was a power to black-and-white photography that could often make even the most inept photographer appear ingenious, but this particular photograph was magical. Dark, yet illuminating; beautiful, yet disturbing. A study of Nina that seemed both worshipful and resentful of her at the same time.

Gunner found himself having a hard time putting it down.

"Would you mind very much if I borrowed this?" he asked Mimi. "Just for a day or two? I won't let anything happen to it, I promise.''

Mimi appeared to find the request unreasonable, but all she did was shrug and say, "If you need it, no. I don't mind. But—"

"It might help to have a recent photograph of her I can show people, that's all. If you'd prefer I took another one . . .''

"No, no, that's fine. You can have that one. Long as I get it back, I don't mind.''

Gunner nodded, already slipping the photograph out of its frame. He was putting the empty frame back on the mantel when he noticed the inscription written on the photograph's back. It read:

*For Nina—*
*You are much stronger and more beautiful than you know.*
*Peace and Love*
*Trini*

"Did Nina give you this?" Gunner asked.

"The photograph? Yes, of course. Why do you ask?"

The investigator shook his head. "No reason."

He didn't want to tell her he found it a little strange, Nina giving something away that one would have thought would hold some sentimental value to her.

"Is that it for friends?" he asked. "Just Trini and Angela?"

"Those are the only ones I ever met. Or that Nina ever really talked about."

"What about friends at work? She did have a job, didn't she?"

"You mean, besides the one at the House?"

"Yes."

"She used to have a job, yes. She was working as a secretary at a law firm downtown. Bowers, Bain and Lyle, I think the name was. But that was some time ago, Aaron. She left that job at the middle of last year, maybe even before that."

"How was she getting by? If Michael wasn't helping her . . ."

"*I* was helping her. And she was getting unemployment for a while. It wasn't easy, but she was making out okay."

"If she was getting unemployment, that means she didn't leave her job at the law firm voluntarily."

"Voluntarily? No. She didn't leave voluntarily. That child was fired from that job."

"Fired? Nina? On what grounds?"

Mimi took a long time to answer. "They said she was hard to get along with."

"And that meant . . . ?"

"I really don't like to talk about it, Aaron. No more than Nina ever did. Let's just say it had to do with a personality conflict, and leave it at that. Okay? The whole subject is very disturbing to me."

"Was it a racial thing? Just tell me that, yes or no."

Again, Mimi took an inordinate amount of time to answer, and then said simply, "Yes." Using the word as an exclamation point to her demand that he let the matter drop.

He did.

"One more question and I'll leave you alone," he said.

"Yes?"

"I've left this one for last, Momma Hillman, because, well . . . you're probably not going to care for it much."

"What is it?"

"It has to do with men."

"Men? What about men?"

"I need to know if Nina had any male friends that you were aware of. Intimate, or otherwise. I've heard about all the women in her life, but other than Michael—"

"Nina didn't have any other men in her life," Mimi said sharply, cutting him off. "Michael was enough. He was one too many, in fact."

"Yes, but—"

"Did she have any male friends? Of course she did. What woman doesn't? But that was all they were, friends. Nothing more, and nothing less. And anybody who tells you any different is a liar. You remember that, Aaron, hear? Anybody who tells you any different is a *liar*."

It was another touchy subject for her; two, back to back. He had known she would find his suggestion that Nina might have had a lover insulting, but he had not expected her to suggest in turn that he might hear testimony to that effect from other sources.

"Nobody's told me anything like that yet," Gunner said. "But it sounds like you're telling me somebody might, eventually. Is that right?"

Mimi started to answer, reconsidered, then said, "All I'm saying is, don't believe everything you hear. All right? Especially from Michael. Michael was always accusing her of playing around on him, nobody could tell him she wasn't, so anything he says, you can't rely on. I just want to make sure you understand that.''

It was an admirable job of cleaning up something Gunner was sure she hadn't meant to bring up.

"Okay. A deal's a deal," he said, putting his pen and notebook away. "I promised to ask only one more question, and that was it. Unless yes-or-no's count."

"Yes-or-no's?"

"I need to know if you have a set of keys to Nina's house. And if you do, if I can borrow them for a couple of days, too."

"The keys to Nina's house? What do you want with those?"

"I'd like to go over there, take a quick look around. I won't disturb anything, I promise. I presume that's where all her things are?"

"The police have that house all locked up, Aaron."

"I know, I know. But it'll be okay. Trust me."

She eyed him suspiciously, said, "I don't want you getting in any trouble, now."

"Who, me? Not a chance." He grinned to put her mind to rest, surprising himself with the ease with which he could lie to her.

Mimi finally stood up and went to the back of the house, then returned a few moments later, a small slip of paper and a trio of keys on a chrome-plated key ring in her right hand. "Those are the keys, and the address and phone number you wanted. For Sisterhood House."

"Thanks, Momma," Gunner said, leaning over to kiss her good-bye again.

"Is that all you needed?"

"Yeah, that's it. Unless you'd like to do me one more tiny favor."

"If I can."

"You think you could call ahead for me later, tell that director—what was her name?"

"Director? Oh. You mean Ms. Singer. Wendy Singer."

"Yeah, Ms. Singer. You think you could call and tell Ms. Singer I might be coming out there to see her, either later today or sometime early tomorrow? Just so she'll know I really am a friend of the family?''

''Sure, baby. I can do that.'' Mimi smiled.

It was good to see that she still had a few smiles left.

# e i g h t

GUNNER TOOK ONE LOOK AT NINA'S HOUSE AND DECIDED against breaking in.

The yellow police tape was still wrapped all around the porch, and the front door was sealed and plastered over with huge signs that promised nothing but trouble to anyone who might be foolish enough to force the door open and go inside. None of the signs had Gunner's name on them, but even when viewed from across the street, they seemed to be speaking directly to him. Nobody else, just him.

The voice of Matthew Poole in print.

But Gunner didn't just pack up his bags and go home. He canvassed the neighborhood, talking to every neighbor of Nina's he could, asking if anyone had seen or heard anything of interest the night she died. He worked both sides of the street, twenty-one houses in all.

Eight people weren't home; five claimed total ignorance of Nina and/or her murder; two were vaguely aware of same; five recalled Nina fondly, cursed her husband, Michael, openly, and had little else to add; and one teenage boy said he'd seen a man loitering around Nina's house about two hours before she died, he couldn't tell who.

Twenty-one neighbors, one witness. Sort of.

"You didn't see the man's face?" Gunner asked the kid.

"No. I didn't see his face."

He'd been mowing the lawn when Gunner found him, six houses down and across the street from Nina's place; sixteen, seventeen years old, tall and lanky and covered with sweat.

"But you know it was a man."

"Yeah. It was a man."

"Did it *look* like her husband?"

"It looked like him a little." He shrugged.

He'd been taking out the trash around nine, ten that evening when he saw the guy walk around the side of Nina's house to the back. End of story. A five-, six-second glimpse of a moving figure, that was it. Standing now less than a few feet from where the kid said he'd been standing at the time, Gunner figured he couldn't have seen much in the way of physical details even in broad daylight. That late at night, from this distance, he would have been lucky to see anything at all.

But at least he *thought* he'd seen something. None of Nina's other neighbors could—or *would*—say even that much.

Everyone else Gunner spoke to, of those who admitted having known the murdered woman, could only bend his ear with words of admiration for her, and condemnation for the louse she'd been married to.

"That was the sweetest child on earth," one woman said. A middle-aged, overweight, and gregarious woman named Florence Gatewood, who lived across the street and three doors down from the Pearson home. "I couldn't believe it when I heard what that animal done to her. I just seen her the day before, she come over here to bring me some mail they left over her place by mistake, an' she was just smilin' an' laughin'. Like she always was. If I'da known what was gonna happen to her . . ." She shook her head, not knowing what else to say.

"I know," Gunner said.

Not knowing what else to say either.

"Errol Flynn used to party here," Wendy Singer said.

"Is that right?"

"It was back in the mid-forties, of course. When the house was owned by Malcolm Lund. Are you familiar with Malcolm Lund?"

"I can't say that I am, no," Gunner said.

"He was a very prolific producer at the time. He didn't make any great pictures, but he made a lot of good ones. A *lot* of good ones. And a few bad ones, too, of course."

"Of course."

She was still escorting him into the house.

They had buzzed him in right away, fully expecting his visit. The building was a huge, two-story French Colonial affair that time had dealt an unfair hand; what once had been majestic was now only unwieldy. Like many of the homes that populated this mile-and-a-half segment of Adams Boulevard, once but no longer commonly referred to as Fremont Park, it was a palatial shadow of greatness past, a monument to money that had long ago departed the premises. The wealthy white men who had once lived here had fled the scene generations ago, seeking the higher ground of Bel Air and Beverly Hills, leaving no trace of their power and influence but the giant walls behind which they had exercised them. Today, those walls housed mostly black people, and for the most part, they were as clean and freshly painted as they had been at birth. But they were the walls of ghosts all the same.

Tall, proud, circular, carported *ghosts*.

Singer, on the other hand, was very much among the living. She seemed to be aging gracefully, even if the house in which she worked was not. Were it not for the liberal sprinkling of gray in her sandy brown hair, and a fullness to her hips that was almost imperceptibly excessive, she could have easily passed for a woman in her late twenties or early thirties. She had the smooth, cherubic face of a Girl Scout troop leader, and bright blue eyes that shone and flickered like candles on a birthday cake. Unlike the formal black attire Gunner now remembered seeing her in at Nina's funeral three days ago, her dress today was casual—khaki pants, tennis shoes, and a large, green pullover sweater—but her manner was strictly professional. Mimi had said she was no one to mess with, and Gunner could see now what she'd meant. The Sisterhood House director was hospitable enough, as her story about the House's origins clearly indicated, but she was about as warm and charming as a parole officer.

Gunner was still waiting for her to show him a real smile.

He had parked his prized Cobra under the shade of a giant avocado tree out front, once the perimeter gate had closed behind him and Singer had come out to greet him personally. Now they were entering the building, beyond two immense doors that led onto one of the most intimidating foyers the investigator had ever seen. Polished wood was everywhere; dark, red, glistening. The arms and legs of chairs and tables, the flooring beneath his feet, all the bookcases and armoires lining the walls—and the railing along both sides of the central staircase around which the entire room revolved. Only in the movies had Gunner seen a staircase like it. Halfway up to the second floor, its carpeted steps stopped at a wide landing and split in two, becoming a snake with two heads coiling east and west, respectively. It was a staircase made for grand entrances.

"Yes, I know," Singer said, watching Gunner drink in the room with open amazement. "It is special, isn't it?"

Gunner grinned, caught off guard. "I was staring, wasn't I?"

"Of course. Everyone does, the first time they visit us. How can you not?"

Finally. A real smile.

A young woman entered the room from somewhere off to the left, but only glanced at them briefly before disappearing again through an open archway on the right. Gunner could hear the voices of other women echoing throughout the house, but he couldn't tell which direction or floor they came from. He could also hear a piano being played somewhere; a light, classical riff, almost childlike in execution, like wind chimes singing on a seaside porch.

Singer led him up the stairs to the second floor.

Her office was at the west end of the house, past a small solarium with window seats all around, the woman playing the piano—an older, heavyset white woman in a floral dress—and a room filled with office equipment. Passing by, Gunner spotted a middle-aged black woman standing before a copying machine and a younger, short-haired blonde tapping away on a computer keyboard. Neither woman saw him.

The pale-skinned, twentyish brunette he and Singer met in the hallway upon their arrival at the latter's open office door was not so unobservant, however. She noticed Gunner right away. She was a ponytailed beauty wearing black denim pants and a burgundy sweatshirt with the USC logo emblazoned across the front, and the sight of Gunner had stopped her in her tracks like the horn of an onrushing semi.

"Hello, Alex," Singer said, with considerable trepidation in her voice.

Gunner was not surprised, then, when the girl reached out and slapped him hard across the right side of his face, filling his eyes instantly with tears. He was stunned, but not surprised.

"Alex! Oh, my God, Mr. Gunner, I'm so sorry," Singer said, belatedly stepping forward to restrain the younger woman.

Not that any restraint was necessary, now. One blow was all the girl had ever intended to strike; that much was clear from the satisfied expression she now wore on her face.

Gunner imagined one blow was all she *ever* hit a man with.

As she continued to glare at him, wholly unrepentant, he rubbed the sting from his cheek and said, "Nice right hand."

"Thanks," Alex said. She seemed to genuinely appreciate the compliment.

"But I'd like to make a suggestion."

"Yeah, I know. Don't ever use it on you again. That's what they all say." She turned to Singer. "I'm going to my room now, Wendy. We can talk in there whenever you're ready. Okay?"

Without waiting for Singer to answer, she walked off, leaving them to watch her vanish down the hall.

"Are you all right?" Singer asked, after a short but uncomfortable silence had passed between them.

Gunner shrugged and tried to smile. "I think so. Forget about it."

"Are you sure? Would you like a cold towel, or something?"

"No. Really. I'm okay."

"I really am very sorry. I saw that coming, but . . . well, it's been a long time since Alex has done something like that, and I guess I just wasn't prepared for it."

"Like I said. Forget about it."

They finally entered Singer's office and sat down. There was a wide-angle window to the left of her desk that afforded her a fine view of the backyard, where an elevated cement patio and an empty swimming pool were the only things worthy of her own or anyone else's attention. Her desk was solid oak, topped with a sheet of glass and laden with paperwork, and her chair was a high-backed wing chair in red, well-worn leather. Gunner's was identical.

Singer asked him if he'd like something to drink, he said no, then they got down to business.

"I know you're probably anxious to drop the subject, Mr. Gunner, but I'd just like to say one thing before we do," Singer said. "And that is that Alex is not representative of the women we have staying here at Sisterhood House. She's a special case."

"I'll bet she is."

"If you knew something about her background—"

"Please. No explanation is necessary. If the young lady likes to slap strange men around, I'm sure she has her reasons."

"She does. Believe me."

"Then there's really no need to discuss the incident any further. Is there?"

He was being polite, but direct: *Let's move on.*

"So Mimi says you were a friend of Nina's," Singer said.

"Yeah. I was."

"A very good friend, from what I understand."

"We were engaged once. A long, long time ago. I hadn't seen very much of her in recent years, but I still considered her a close friend. Nina and Mimi both."

"Of course. I remember seeing you with Mimi at the funeral."

"You do? I'm surprised."

"Surprised? Why?"

"Because I wouldn't think you could make the connection. Between the man you saw then, and the one you see now, I mean. I was in pretty bad shape last Saturday."

"Were you? I didn't notice."

"I think you're being kind."

They smiled at each other for a moment; then Singer turned serious and said, "Mimi also said you're a private investigator."

Gunner nodded.

"Would you mind very much if I asked to see some identification? It's not that I don't believe you, but . . . I'd just feel more comfortable talking to you if I could see something in writing. I hope you understand."

"Sure. No problem." Gunner pulled out his wallet, opened it to his PI license, and passed it over for her inspection.

When she had passed it back to him, she said, "You're looking into the circumstances of Nina's murder?"

"That's right."

"But not for Mimi."

"No. Not for Mimi."

"Then . . . ?"

"I'm doing this on my own, Ms. Singer. Nobody's paying me to be here. I want to find out for myself how Nina died, rather than take someone else's word for it. Call it force of habit."

"By 'someone else,' you're talking about the police?"

"I'm talking about whomever."

Singer fell quiet for a moment, then said, "I wasn't aware there was any question about how Nina died."

"There is for those of us who weren't there. You weren't, were you?"

"At Nina's when she was killed, you mean? No, I wasn't."

"Then—"

"I didn't have to be there to know how or why Nina was

killed, Mr. Gunner. None of us here at Sisterhood House did.''

"No?"

"No. Sad as it is to say, what happened to Nina was not entirely unexpected. At least, not to those of us who were familiar with her history of abuse. Her husband had come close to killing her on a number of occasions before, you know.''

"Did he?"

"Oh, yes.. Michael had put Nina in the hospital at least twice before over the last three years. Once with a concussion, and once with three broken ribs and a punctured lung. Have you ever had a broken rib, Mr. Gunner?''

His mind immediately turning to his recent sparring match with Russell Dartmouth, Gunner said, ''I'm sorry to say that I have, yes. It's not much fun.''

"No. It isn't. Nothing about being married to a man like Michael ever is.''

"Which is to say, there's no doubt in your mind that Michael killed her.''

"That is correct. Why is there a doubt in yours?''

Despite himself, Gunner hesitated before answering. ''Because I have reason to believe he may have been elsewhere at the time of Nina's murder. I can't prove that yet, but—''

"But you'd *like* to prove it.''

"No, I—''

"What is it about some people that they can never believe the inevitable when it finally occurs, Mr. Gunner? Can you tell me that? Why must there always be some answer to a question other than the most obvious one?

"A man tortures a woman for years, his treatment of her is documented throughout, but when she turns up dead, no one can accept the fact that he killed her. That would make too much sense.''

"I think you misunderstand my purpose here, Ms. Singer. I'm not out to vindicate Michael Pearson, I'm out to find out who killed Nina, and why. There's a difference.''

"Is there?''

"Absolutely.''

"And that difference is . . . ?"

"The difference is, Pearson wasn't my friend. Nina was. I thought I'd made that clear."

Singer stared at him, cognizant of the fact that he was essentially demanding an apology from her.

"I'm sorry, Mr. Gunner, but you pushed a button of mine. By even daring to suggest that Nina might have been killed by someone other than the man who'd been *trying* to kill her for almost a decade, I mean. Because I hear such suggestions all too often around here, I'm afraid. Especially from the authorities. And it just drives me up the wall after a while, it really does."

"I understand," Gunner said.

"No. No, you don't. You couldn't. You'd have to work here for a year or so to even *begin* to understand what I'm talking about."

Gunner shrugged, having no desire to argue the point with her. "Okay."

"The men who drive women to homes like this one do not deserve the skepticism with which people so often view their brutality, Mr. Gunner. Their records should be allowed to speak for themselves. When someone acts surprised that a man who's been beating women all his life has finally gotten around to killing one, as if he were no more inclined to do such a thing than you or I, I can't believe it. I *can't*. The writing is there on the wall for everyone to see, why can't anyone ever *see* it? *Why*?"

"I can't answer that," Gunner said. "Except to say that this is a country that bends over backward to give people the benefit of the doubt. Even those who don't particularly deserve the courtesy."

"Like Michael, you mean."

"Yes."

"You really believe he might be innocent?"

"With the emphasis on the word 'might,' yes, I do."

"Why? Have you talked to him? Did *he* tell you he was innocent?"

"Well, as a matter of fact, yes. He did. But that's not—"

"You've seen him? You know where he is?"

Gunner told her about Pearson's little accident, and where it had landed him. She was just as broken up to hear it as Mimi Hillman had been earlier.

"Good for him," she said.

"Yeah. That's the reaction I've been getting from everybody," Gunner said.

"Still—"

"Look. Let's not beat this thing into the ground, all right? I believe there's an outside chance Nina's husband didn't kill her, and I have my reasons for feeling that way. None of which I'd care to go into here. Now, if that somehow makes me circumspect—"

"Have you ever abused a woman, Mr. Gunner?" Singer asked abruptly.

"Excuse me?"

"Have you ever abused a woman? Ever slapped one around because she gave you some lip, or twisted her arm to make her turn down the radio? Ever done anything like that?"

"No."

"Never?"

"Never."

"But you've felt like it, I'll bet." Singer smiled. Gunner shouldn't have found much solace in the gesture, but he did.

"Tell me how I can help you," she said.

"Mimi says Nina had been living and working here for the last five months, up until about three weeks ago. Is that right?"

"Yes." Singer nodded.

"Mimi described her as your aide."

"She was my aide, yes. My assistant, my aide . . ."

"For how long? When did she start?"

Singer thought about it. "I'd say I took her on around the first of the year. In January. If you need the exact date, I can look it up for you . . ."

Gunner shook his head. He had his notebook out again, and made a brief entry in it before asking, "Can you give me a rough idea of what her duties were? Was it secretarial work, or . . ."

"It was mostly secretarial work, yes. Some dictation, some file keeping. Things like that. But she had to do some work in the field, too."

"In the field?"

"Yes. Very often, Mr. Gunner, the women who need our help here at Sisterhood House can't come to us directly, for a variety of reasons. So we try to come to them. To their homes, their places of employment . . . wherever they suggest. That's working in the field."

"I see."

"Nina didn't do very much of that on her own. Mostly she just went along with me, when I thought it might be wise to go with someone. But there were occasions when she went by herself. Not many, but a few."

"Anything memorable about any of them? Any ugly confrontations with a husband or boyfriend, something like that?"

"I imagine she had a few of those, certainly. We all do, sooner or later. Coming to the rescue of battered women can be a dangerous business, Mr. Gunner. Especially if you're alone."

"But nothing specific comes to mind?"

"Involving Nina? No." Singer shook her head. "Nothing I can recall at this moment, anyway."

"Would Nina have told you if something like that had happened to her, do you think? Or might she have just kept it to herself?"

"That's hard to say. If it shook her up badly enough, she would have mentioned it to me, I'm sure. But if not . . . she might not have said a word. Because she didn't like to appear incapable of handling the job, you see. She was always worried I'd decide it was too much for her and let her go."

"What about her friends? Would she have told her friends, if she didn't feel comfortable telling you?"

"You mean, her friends here at Sisterhood?"

"Yes."

"Again, that's hard for me to say. You'd have to ask her friends."

"And her friends here were . . . ?"

"Well, Nina had quite a few friends here, of course. She got along well with everybody. But if you're talking about who she was particularly close to, I'd have to say only two people come to mind: Shirley Causwell and Angela Glass. Of all the women she knew here, I'd say she spent the most time with them."

Gunner put Causwell's name down in his book, wondering two things at once: why Mimi Hillman hadn't mentioned Causwell earlier, and why Singer wasn't mentioning someone else right now.

"What about Trini Serrano?" he asked.

"Trini? What about her?"

It seemed to Gunner that she had stiffened, but he couldn't be sure.

"Mimi says she and Nina were friends as well."

"Oh. Well. I suppose they were, yes." She started playing absently with a pencil on her desk. "But when you asked me about Nina's friends . . . I assumed you were talking about her friends among the *residents* here. And Trini's not a resident, she's just a frequent guest of ours. Or was, up until recently."

"By 'guest,' what do you mean?"

"Well, she's a photographer. A photojournalist, actually. She specializes in documentary photographs of abuse victims and their abusers, she's made an entire career out of it. Perhaps you've seen her work in *Time* magazine, or *Life*."

Gunner shrugged, unable to say whether he had or not.

"She's also a major activist for the cause. She's published several books on the subject, and is widely known on the lecture circuit. She's welcomed in homes like ours all over the country, but as she lives right here in Los Angeles, she's been spending the majority of her time here with us."

"But she doesn't stay here anymore. Is that what I heard you say?"

"That's correct. We won't be seeing Trini here anymore."

"And why is that?"

She glanced at the pencil her hands were still fiddling with, then looked up again. "I don't really know. She just decided to stop coming by."

"She what?"

"She just stopped coming by. I suspect she just became too busy to come anymore, that's all. It was surprising she was able to make time for us as long as she did, really."

There was nothing wrong with what she was saying—or how she was saying it—but Gunner didn't believe her. He didn't know why. He just had the sense that nothing would make her happier than to see him check these questions about Trini off in his little notebook and never ask them again.

He didn't oblige her.

"How long has it been since she stopped coming around?" he asked.

"Excuse me?"

"When was her last visit here? Last week, last month . . ."

"Oh. We last saw her about two weeks ago, maybe. Give or take a day or two."

"And Nina went home when?"

"Nina? Nina went home last month some time. Around the eighteenth or nineteenth, something like that. Why—"

"I was wondering if there was any connection. Between the time Nina went home, and the time Trini lost interest in coming by the house here."

Singer paused before answering, as if she'd been dreading the question. "Why should there be a connection?"

The black man shrugged innocently. "No reason. I was just wondering." He kept his eyes on her a while, then said, "If Trini stopped coming by about two weeks ago, and Nina went back home around the eighteenth of February . . ."

"Yes?"

"Then there would have been about a week in between the two events. Correct?"

"I suppose so, yes."

"That just a coincidence, you think?"

She shrugged. "I don't know what else it could have

been. The two things were totally unrelated.''

"Trini had no objection to Nina's going home? She wasn't disappointed or upset by it in any way?''

"Any more than any of the rest of us were, you mean? No. She wasn't.''

"*You* were unhappy to see Nina leave?''

"Me? Oh, yes. Definitely.''

"Do you mind if I ask why?''

"Because I thought her timing was bad. We all did. Nina had just served her husband with papers two weeks before, and here she was going back home where he could reach her, before he'd had any real time to cool off. It was suicide.''

"Suicide?''

"That's right. It was suicide. She should have stayed with us here another week, at least, and I told her that. But . . .''

"But she left anyway.''

"She wasn't afraid of Michael anymore, she said. She'd learned so much here, become so much stronger . . .'' She shook her head wistfully at the sheer depth of the dead woman's foolishness. "There was just no talking her out of it. She'd made up her mind she was going home, and she went. She had that right.''

"You sound more than a little angry at her,'' Gunner said.

Singer eyed him evenly, determined not to rush her reply. "Working here is not all that different from working in a drug rehabilitation center, Mr. Gunner. The disappointments, the heartbreak are the same. You take a wounded, addictive human being under your wing and nurse her back to health. You educate, encourage, and empower her, until her self-esteem is once more intact. And then you send her back out into the world and watch her destroy herself all over again. In the exact same manner. Just like *that*.'' She snapped her fingers. "Like she's on a string he just has to pull . . .'' She nodded her head. "Yes, it makes me angry. It makes me very angry, sometimes. I wouldn't be human if it didn't.''

She looked off to her left at the clock on the wall, being careful to make sure Gunner noticed the gesture. Either tired of answering questions, or afraid of the direction they were taking.

"Tell me about Nina's enemies," Gunner said, refusing to take the hint.

"Her enemies?"

"Is that too strong a word, 'enemies'? Okay, how about 'people she didn't get along with'? There must have been a few of those."

"Here? I'm afraid not. Nina had *words* with some people from time to time, certainly. She had words with me, on occasion. But—"

"What kind of words? Words about politics, religion, race . . . ? What?"

The look on Singer's face told him he'd just hit on something else she had hoped would not enter into their discussion.

"You and she had words about *race.* Is that it?"

"Not Nina and I, no. But . . ." Singer was having difficulty making her mouth move. "There was a woman here who used to . . . use a certain word that Nina didn't care for. And she and Nina would get into it about it every now and then."

"A word for black people."

"Yes."

Gunner didn't ask her which word it was; he had seen Nina go ballistic at the mere utterance of the word "nigger" too many times to ever forget the effect it had on her.

"Who was this woman?" he asked Singer instead.

"She's not here anymore. She left in late January."

"What was her name?"

"Agnes. Agnes Felker."

"If I wanted to talk to Ms. Felker, would you know where I could find her?"

"I suppose so. Her address is in our files. But why would you want to talk to her?"

"Because it sounds like it would be stupid of me not to. Not all bigots are murderers, of course, but—"

"Bigots? Agnes wasn't a bigot," Singer said.

"No?"

"No. She couldn't have been. Agnes is a black woman herself, Mr. Gunner. If using that word she's so fond of makes her a bigot, she's the strangest one I've ever seen."

Now Gunner was the one who couldn't get his mouth to move.

"All the same," he said finally, "I'd better have a talk with her. Just to see how deep her problems with Nina really ran."

Singer shrugged. "Of course. I'll give Ginger instructions to provide you with whatever information you need." She glanced up at the clock again. "Will there be anything else, Mr. Gunner? Or—"

She was interrupted by a loud, baleful cry, the latest and most insistent of several she and Gunner had been trying to talk over for some time now. It sounded like it was coming from somewhere just outside the building's perimeter.

"What in heaven's name . . . ?" Singer said.

"It sounds like somebody calling out for someone named Sidney," Gunner said.

Recognition lit up Singer's face. "Oh, no. *No!*"

The next thing Gunner knew, he was sitting in her office all alone.

"Don't come any closer," Leo Cagle said.

He was on the outside of the fence, and Gunner was on the inside, but Gunner did as he was told, anyway. The gun in Cagle's left hand had a lot to do with that.

"Is she coming out?" the baby-faced white man asked, tears streaming down the rosy red flesh of both cheeks.

"She" was Sydney Cagle, Leo's wife. And the answer was no, she wasn't coming out. She didn't care how loudly he screamed her name, or threatened to commit suicide out there on the sidewalk for all the world to see; she and Leo were through, and she had no intention of leaving the building to talk to him. Which was fine by Wendy Singer. Leo had a gun, and Singer felt that men with guns were best disarmed by officers of the law, not the men's ex-wives. Even when they were relative teddy bears like Leo Cagle. She wanted to call the police.

"I don't think that's a good idea," Gunner had said.

The downside to calling the cops, he told Singer and Leo's disaffected, pleasingly plump ex-wife Sydney, was that the very sight of a black-and-white *could* set him off. If somebody else had a talk with him first, maybe he'd lose interest and just go away, without hurting himself or anyone else. It was worth a try, wasn't it?

Singer thanked him for volunteering his services and walked him to the door. Sydney didn't even get up out of her chair.

So here Gunner was now, standing less than ten feet away from the distraught Mr. Cagle, trying to determine how serious the white man was about doing himself harm. And how he would take the news that his ex didn't care if he blew his brains out or not, she just wanted to be left alone. Forever.

"She's afraid to come out," Gunner said, starting things off right with a lie. "It's the gun. She said if you gave it to *me*—"

"I'm not going to hurt her! The gun's for me, not her! *Sydney*!"

"Come on, Leo. Take it easy. Let's talk about this for a moment . . ."

Cagle put the nose of the revolver to his head, shaking like a leaf. Gunner had seen his kind before. The fool who'd just learned the hard way that a woman never says good-bye until she's already gone. "That's what I'm *trying* to do, talk," Cagle said. "But not with you. I didn't come here to talk to *you*. I came here to talk to Sydney!"

"I understand that, but—"

"Who the hell are you, anyway? Security?"

"No, I'm—"

The white man was suddenly sobbing, both eyes squeezed tightly shut. "You do everything right. Everything they ask you to do. And it's still not enough . . ."

He was starting to get some attention on the street. That was bad. Too many onlookers around could make him panic, push him straight over the edge.

Gunner didn't know what to say to the man.

"I don't understand," Cagle said, opening his eyes again.

His gun was still pressed against his left temple, though he didn't seem to notice.

"Nobody understands, Leo," Gunner said. He really felt sorry for the poor bastard.

"I haven't put a hand on her for four years. Four years! But she won't forgive me. No matter how I try to make it up to her. No matter what I do to change . . ." His voice trailed off. "It's just never enough."

Gunner took a couple of steps toward him.

"Being a good man's supposed to count for something, isn't it? Isn't being a good man supposed to *count* for something?"

And just like that, he was angry now, glowering and spitting like a man possessed. Gunner could see that the hammer on his revolver was cocked to fire.

"Give me the gun, Leo," the black man said, thinking how easy it would have been to just let the cops handle this, if he hadn't had such a big mouth.

"You bust your ass to become what they want! You make every single sacrifice!"

"I know, man, I know."

Gunner took another step forward. Two or three more and Cagle would be close enough to touch.

"It isn't fair," Cagle said, his mood shifting back to melancholy again. His eyes were filled with fresh tears. "Am I weak? Is that my problem?"

"Weak? No, man, you're not weak. You're just in love with the wrong woman." He had the gun out of Cagle's hand before the man even knew he was reaching for it. Cagle didn't say a word.

"It happens," Gunner told him. "To all of us. Suck it up and move on, Leo. Your Sydney's old news."

Cagle nodded his head slowly, knowing it was true, then turned and ran away.

# n i n e

"THAT WAS NICE WORK," SINGER SAID.

She had watched the whole thing from the open front door, a small flock of the women in her charge encircling her. They all seemed quite impressed.

"Thanks," Gunner said. He couldn't help but notice that Sydney Cagle was not among the curious onlookers.

"Tell me that thing wasn't loaded," Singer said, eyeing the gun the investigator had just taken from Leo Cagle.

It was a .38-caliber Charter Arms, with a two-inch barrel and a silver finish. Gunner flipped open the cylinder and turned the weapon over, dropping six live shells into the palm of his left hand.

"My God," somebody behind Singer said.

"Yeah," Gunner said. "I was thinking the same thing myself."

Shirley Causwell wouldn't see him alone, so he had to interview them together. "Them" being Causwell and Angela Glass, the two Sisterhood House residents Singer had identified as Nina's closest friends. She'd been ready to get rid of him only minutes ago, before Leo Cagle had shown up, but now of course she felt obligated to grant his every wish. Hence the interview he was about to conduct now.

Singer hadn't told him what Causwell's problem with being alone with men was all about, and he didn't ask. Maybe later it would help to know, but right now, it was unimportant. Right now, Gunner just wanted the lady to talk to him.

Not that one-on-two's were his arrangement of choice. Interviewing multiple subjects simultaneously created all kinds of problems—from the simple matter of keeping track of who said what, to the reluctance some interviewees had to being frank and forthcoming with their answers when someone else was around to hear them—but it was the only way this would work. He either did them together, or imposed on Singer even further by asking her to sit in on his conversation with Causwell.

He elected to do them together.

This time, the interview took place outside the house, out on the patio he had caught a glimpse of earlier through Singer's office window. They all sat in white plastic deck chairs around a white plastic table, an open patio umbrella over their heads and a light, uninspired breeze in their faces. Glass sat to Gunner's left, Causwell on his right, the latter so far removed from the table that she hardly seemed to be with them at all.

The black women were strikingly dissimilar. Glass was fair-skinned, Causwell dark; Glass tall and rather dumpy-looking, Causwell short and petite; Glass wore a jagged Afro, Causwell's hair was straight, long, and raven-black.

And Glass knew how to smile. Causwell apparently didn't.

"Don't mind Shirley," Glass said, reaching out to pat Gunner's knee. "She's just a little gun-shy, that's all. She'll warm up in a minute."

"Fuck you," Causwell said. Not amused, not angry . . . As near as Gunner could tell, not *anything*.

Glass just smiled at her, then said to Gunner, "Or maybe she won't."

Whatever her experience with domestic violence, it hadn't cost her her cheery disposition. Or perhaps more accurately, her ability to artificially effect one. She was as unrelentingly ebullient as anyone Gunner had ever met.

"So you were a friend of Nina's," she said. Like that automatically made him all right.

"It looks like we have that in common, yes," Gunner said. Then, to Causwell: "All three of us."

Causwell didn't say anything.

"You know, the idea of having Angela here with us was to make you feel more comfortable."

"I'm comfortable," Causwell said.

"You don't act like it."

"How would you like me to act?"

"Well, for starters, it'd be great if you could act like you don't know me. As opposed to treating me like someone who killed your dog and torched your village in a past life, or something."

Glass thought that was pretty funny, but Causwell just said, "Maybe you did." As deadly serious as she could be.

Sighing, Gunner said, "Okay. I'm a devil. You don't want to tattoo my name on your left breast, and you don't want to have my baby. Fine. Now that you've made that clear to me, we should be free to talk about Nina."

"Nina's dead," Causwell said.

"I'm aware of that. That's why I'm here. Didn't Ms. Singer explain—"

"She told us you're a private detective," Glass said. "And that you came here to talk to us because you think somebody here killed Nina. That isn't really true, is it? Because if it is—"

"You're wasting your fucking time," Causwell said.

"Nina's husband killed Nina. Nobody else. He *told* her he was going to kill her, and he did. It's as simple as that."

"Damn right it is."

"When the cops catch up with him, you'll see. He'll cop a plea, go to jail, and be out on the street again in five years. Maybe three."

"The cops have already caught up with him," Gunner said. "But he's in no condition to cop a plea. Right now he's got his hands full just trying to stay alive."

He told them where Pearson was, and how he had come to be there.

"*You* shot him?" Glass asked.

"Reluctantly," Gunner said.

"My hero."

"I appreciate the sentiment, but I think you're missing the point."

"What point?"

"The point that the man might not be guilty as charged."

"Shit. He's guilty," Causwell sneered.

"And if he's not? What then?"

"Then we only celebrate half as hard." She smiled.

"But if somebody else killed her—"

"There *is* nobody else," Glass said.

"And even if there was, you wouldn't find 'em here," Causwell said. "Only people you're gonna find here were Nina's friends. The kind of friends men don't have. It's not in your nature."

"Is that right," Gunner said sarcastically.

"Yeah, that's right. The name of the house is Sisterhood for a reason, brother. We're all sisters here, and we treat each other that way. Every single one of us."

"Including Agnes Felker."

"Agnes? Agnes was crazy."

"Crazy or not, she didn't like Nina. And she was a 'sister.'"

"Agnes didn't like a lot of people. So what?"

"So maybe Agnes wasn't the only crazy lady living here. That's what." He gave the two women a moment to dispute that, then went on. "Look. I understand this is a very special place for you people. That you all share a certain life experience that bonds you together like nothing else could. But all of your talk about sisterhood aside, this is not a monastery. You're not all monks, and you're not all angels. So you get on each other's nerves and you piss each other off, and when one of you gets pissed off bad enough, you do something about it."

"Do we get in each other's faces? Is that the question?" Glass asked. "Sure we do. All the time. But it never amounts to anything. Wendy would make us leave if it did."

"Like she did Agnes?"

"Man, we *told* you: Agnes was crazy. She and Nina got into it, sure, but that's only 'cause Agnes got into it with *everybody.* She didn't have anything against Nina in particular.''

''But Nina had something against her.''

Glass just blinked at him. ''I don't—''

''Agnes had a bad mouth,'' Causwell broke in, showing some impatience with the way Glass was dealing with the subject. ''Some of the language she used, Nina didn't like much. A lot of us didn't.''

''Oh. Is that what he's talkin' about?'' Glass asked.

''Most of us would just ignore it, but Nina wouldn't. Nina would call her on it. She was just very sensitive about that sort of thing. She didn't *hate* Agnes or anything.''

''The two never got physical with one another?''

''No.''

''No pushing and shoving, no pulling each other's hair . . .''

''No. Never.''

''Never?''

''No. They . . . I mean . . .'' Glass threw a quick glance at Causwell, then gave up a tiny shrug. ''There was this *one* time, at dinner. Only time I can remember anything like this ever happenin'. Agnes called somebody a nigger, I forget who it was, and Nina came over and . . . and Agnes started saying it over and over again. *Nigger, nigger, nigger* . . . Just to piss Nina off.''

''That's how Agnes could be,'' Causwell said.

''And?'' Gunner asked.

''And Nina had to slap her. Just once,'' Glass said.

''Was it a hard slap, or just a love tap?''

Glass took a while to answer. ''It was hard. I told you, Agnes was askin' for it. If Nina hadn't slapped the shit out of her, somebody else would've.''

''*I* would have,'' Causwell said.

Gunner looked at her. ''I take it Agnes wasn't around long after that.''

''No. She wasn't,'' Glass said. ''Wendy doesn't take that kind of shit around here, like I said. She'd been puttin' up with Agnes's crap for a long time, but that was the last straw. She sent Agnes packin' after that.''

"And after she left? You ever see her again?"

"No. *I* didn't see her, anyway."

Both she and Gunner looked at Causwell. After a long pause, Causwell shook her head.

"Did anyone else?" Gunner asked.

"Not that I know of, no," Glass said. "Nina said she got a letter from her once, but that was it."

"A letter?"

"Yeah, a letter. I never saw it, but Nina said it was nasty and vulgar. And of course, full of *nigger* this, and *nigger* that. Nina thought it was funny."

"Funny?"

"Yeah. She was laughin' about it when she told me. I thought she'd be angry about it, but she wasn't. I figured she just found it easier to laugh about the fool, now that she wasn't going to have to deal with her anymore."

"Where would this letter be now? Any ideas?"

"I don't think it's anywhere. I think Nina tore it up and threw it away. I mean, it certainly didn't sound like somethin' she was gonna wanna *keep*."

Gunner turned to Causwell, who had been maintaining a stubborn silence for some time now. "Did *you* ever see this letter?"

"No."

"Or hear about it?"

"No."

"Nina never mentioned it to you?"

"No. Nina never mentioned it to me." She was aiming her icy stare at Glass now, rolling her cold coffee cup between her palms like a potter shaping a vase.

He wasn't supposed to notice, but Gunner saw Glass give her a little smile and shrug.

Rather than ask her about it, he just pulled out his little notebook and opened it. "Tell me about Trini Serrano," he said.

"Trini? What about her?" Glass asked.

"I understand she was another close friend of Nina's."

"Yeah. She was. So?"

"So Ms. Singer says she stopped coming by the house

here just a few weeks after Nina went home.''

Glass looked at him expectantly. "And?"

"And I thought the timing of that was a little odd. Maybe I'm wrong."

Once again, both Glass and Causwell just sat there and stared at him, as if neither of them could begin to guess what he was trying to imply.

"She had to go back east to work for a few months," Glass said. "So what?"

"Is that what she told you? That she was going back east to work?"

"Yes. That's what she told everybody."

"Everybody including Ms. Singer?"

"Wendy?"

"Ms. Singer thinks she stopped coming by because she doesn't have time to come anymore. At least, that's what she told me."

Glass shrugged. "So?"

"So I'm wondering why the two explanations."

Glass expected him to elaborate, but he didn't. "I don't follow you," she said.

"I'm still trying to figure out if there could have been a connection between her departure and Nina's."

"Oh."

"I don't suppose *she* ever had a cross word with Nina."

"Trini?"

"Yeah. Trini."

Glass thought a moment, said, "I don't know about any cross words she might've had with her, but . . . I know she wasn't gettin' along too well with Nina when Nina left."

"Yeah?"

"Yeah."

"How do you know?"

"I know because Nina wasn't speakin' to her. Trini was speakin' to *her,* but she wasn't speakin' to Trini."

"And why was that?"

"I don't know. All I know is, Trini didn't want Nina to go. Nobody here did. I just figured it had somethin' to do with that."

"Nina never discussed it with you?"

"What? Why she wasn't talkin' to Trini?"

"Yes."

"No. She never said anything to me about it."

Gunner looked over at Causwell. "What about you?"

"What *about* me?"

"Nina ever tell you why she wasn't talking to Trini?"

"She never 'told' me, no."

That was all she said.

"But?"

"But I've got an idea."

Gunner waited for her to explain.

"Trini went through some of Nina's stuff. And Nina didn't appreciate it," Causwell said.

"She went through some of Nina's stuff? What, here at the House?"

"I guess so. Where else?"

"Why would Trini do something like that?"

Causwell shook her head. "I don't know. Go ask Trini."

"How is it you know about this? If Nina never told you what her argument with Trini was about—"

"I heard them talking about it once. Trini was trying to apologize, and Nina was trying to act like she wasn't there."

"When was this?"

"Like Angela said. About a week before Nina left. Something like that."

"Where were they that you happened to hear the conversation?"

"I didn't hear the conversation. I just heard the tail end of it."

"Okay. So where were they?"

"They were down in the laundry room. I went down there to do some clothes and found them there, talking. They left as soon as I came in."

"Do you remember what specifically was said?"

"No. I just remember what I told you."

"That Trini seemed to be apologizing for having gone through some of Nina's things."

"Yes."

"But you never heard why."

"Why she'd done it? No. I didn't."

"You ever ask Nina about it later?"

"It wasn't any of my business. If she'd wanted me to know about it, she would have told me."

"And she didn't tell you."

"No. She didn't."

Gunner turned back to Glass, who had suddenly taken up Causwell's former role as the silent observer. "I get the feeling you're hearing all this for the first time yourself," he said.

"I am." Another shrug.

"So what do you think?"

"About what?"

"About what she just said. This business about Trini fooling around with Nina's things."

She shrugged. "I don't know what to think about it. Nina couldn't't've had nothin' Trini would've wanted to steal."

"You don't think so?"

"No. Like what?"

"I never said she was trying to 'steal' anything," Causwell said, correcting her.

Both Gunner and Glass turned around, expecting her to explain the distinction.

"I said she was going through Nina's stuff. That's all. She could have just been trying to *borrow* something, or take something back from Nina that Nina had borrowed from *her*. Something like that. She didn't have to be trying to steal anything."

"Except that Nina's reaction would seem to suggest that she was," Gunner said.

"Why? Because she got mad? Hell, I'd get mad too, I found somebody going through my things without my permission. I wouldn't care why they said they were doing it."

"Same here," Glass said.

"That sort of thing happen around here often?" Gunner asked. "People getting into other people's things, I mean?"

"Often? No, it don't happen often. But—"

"Hey, look, this has been a lot of fun," Causwell said,

cutting in, "but enough is enough. I don't want to answer any more questions, I'm sorry."

Gunner looked at her, not quite knowing what to make of her sudden need to stop talking to him. "You don't?" he asked.

"No. I don't. You asked us to talk to you, and we talked to you. Now I'm tired. I want to go back to my room."

The investigator shrugged, pretending not to care, and said, "Okay. Whatever you say." He started fingering through his notes, taking his good sweet time about it. "If you'd just let me ask you one more question before you leave . . ."

"What?"

Gunner flipped over another page in his book, said, "Here it is. I wanted to ask you about Nina's work in the field."

"What about it?"

"I was wondering if she ever talked to either one of you about any bad experiences she may have had. Any run-ins with angry husbands or boyfriends, that sort of thing."

Causwell sighed heavily and shook her head. "Not that I recall."

Gunner looked at Glass.

"She had a girl pull a gun on her once. Is that what you mean?"

"What girl was this?"

"I don't remember her name. It was somebody who left right after I got here. She was just a kid."

"A kid?"

"Yeah. You know, a youngster. Nina said she was still in her teens. She called the House once after she went home, and Wendy sent Nina out to help her. Her boyfriend had taken her car and left her stranded somewhere, I think. It was something like that. Anyway, when Nina got there, the boyfriend was back and the girl was gettin' in the car with 'im. When Nina tried to stop her, the girl pulled a gun on her, Nina said."

"A gun?"

"Yeah. She didn't shoot at anybody, though. Nina said the girl just showed it to her to make her back off."

"And Nina did."

"Of course. She wasn't crazy."

"Did Ms. Singer know about any of this?"

"Wendy? I don't know. She probably did, I guess."

When Gunner started to turn toward Causwell, she said, "No. I didn't."

"Then you wouldn't remember this girl's name either."

"No. Sorry."

She wasn't sorry at all.

"It was somethin' that started with a V, I think," Glass said. "Vicky, or Valerie . . . Somethin' like that."

Gunner wrote the two names down in his book.

"Aren't you going to ask us where were we last Tuesday night?" Causwell asked.

Gunner looked up, smiling. "As a matter of fact, I was. Yes. Where were you?"

"Last Tuesday night?" Glass asked. Then, catching on: "Oh."

Causwell looked at her disdainfully and said, "That's right, Angela. The nice detective wants to know where we were when Nina died. Would you like to start, or should I?"

When Glass didn't say anything, Causwell turned to face Gunner again and said, "I was here at the house. Watching TV and reading, up in my room. I was here all night."

Gunner turned his gaze on Glass. "And you?"

"I was out," she said. Trying to get her own smile back, but missing the mark considerably.

"Out where? For how long?"

"I was at the library." She shrugged. "I was there three, maybe four hours. Tops."

"Which library was this?"

"The one over on Vermont. Near the Coliseum. I like to hang out there sometimes."

"Were you alone?"

"Yeah. I was alone."

"Did you check anything out?"

"You mean a book?"

"A book, a record, a tape . . . Anything you would've had to take up to the counter."

"Oh, no. I didn't check anything out that night."

Gunner nodded his head, like everything she was saying made perfect sense.

"And you got back here around what time? Do you remember?"

She shrugged again. "Ten-thirty, eleven. Somethin' like that."

"The library's open that late Tuesday nights?"

"No. But I had somethin' to eat after."

"Ah." He nodded again, careful to keep his eyes on her the whole time. Then he stood up and put his notebook away.

"Thanks for the help, ladies. You've been very kind," he said.

"Yeah, sure," Causwell said.

Happier to see him go than she had any right to be.

He dropped in on Wendy Singer for a brief minute before leaving. She had to shoo a middle-aged redhead with a black eye and an ankle cast out of her office to make room for him, but she seemed only mildly annoyed to be seeing him again so soon. He had to wonder if that wasn't because she had been expecting to do so, all along.

"That would have been Virgie Olivera," she said, after Gunner had repeated the story Angela Glass told him about the runaway Sister who had once pulled a gun on Nina. No moment of pause or hesitation to mull the story over, just *boom*, Virgie Olivera, like the name had been rolling around in her head all day, just waiting to get out.

"You remember the incident?" Gunner asked her, acting as if he was surprised to hear it.

"All but the part about the gun. Yes," Singer said.

"Nina didn't tell you about the gun?"

"No. Apparently, she didn't."

"Well. That would explain it, then, wouldn't it?"

"Pardon me?"

"I was wondering why you didn't mention it before. When I asked you if Nina had ever been threatened by anyone while working out in the field." He paused to watch Singer's eyes, then said, "But if you didn't *know* . . ."

"I didn't," Singer said sharply.

Again, the black man paused to study her face before saying another word. "Would you know where I could find Ms. Olivera now?" he asked finally.

"Now? No. That was the last time any of us saw or heard from Virgie, to my knowledge. She might be at the same address she was then, but I doubt it. Virgie liked to move around a lot."

"I see."

"Again, Ginger will be happy to give you her address if you want it. But you might be wise to hear one word of warning first."

"And that is?"

"I don't think the gun was Virgie's. If she indeed had one that day, it was probably her boyfriend's. He's got lots of them."

"He's like that, huh?"

"Yes. He's like that."

"What's his name?"

"Ricky something is all I can remember offhand. His last name's in her file, Ginger can get that for you. He's in the Mexican Mafia. Very bad news."

"And Virgie? She bad news too?"

"I'd be lying to you if I said she wasn't."

"Then this incident with the gun—"

"Doesn't completely surprise me, no. She was a violent young woman, Virgie. Very angry and very emotional. We tried to help her overcome that, but . . ."

"She ever pull a gun on anyone here before?"

"No. Absolutely not."

"But she did get into a fight or two."

"One or two. Yes. But none with Nina, if that was going to be your next question. They got along, those two. They weren't friends, by any means, but they got along. Which is more than I can say about Virgie and anyone else who was staying here at the time. I would never have sent Nina out after her alone otherwise."

"But if they got along—"

"Why the gun? That's easy. Because the boyfriend put her up to it. What else?"

"You sound pretty sure about that," Gunner said.

"I know the nature of the beast. Like most abused women, Mr. Gunner, Virgie was a different person around her abuser. She was a violent person under the best of circumstances, as I've already stated, but under his influence, she was capable of almost anything. Nina was probably lucky to get out of that situation alive. No doubt that's why she never told me all there was to tell about it."

"Like her fight with Agnes Felker, you mean?"

"What fight is that?"

"The one that ended with Nina slapping the hell out of her. At dinner."

Singer didn't say anything.

"Or was that something else you were never told about?"

"I knew about that, of course," Singer said.

"Then why didn't you mention it to me earlier? When I asked you if—"

"I was under the impression you were looking for someone who could have held a grudge against Nina, and then killed her over it, Mr. Gunner. Isn't that right?"

"More or less," Gunner said. "But—"

"I don't believe Agnes fits that description. She may indeed have held a grudge against Nina, but she certainly didn't kill her."

"Why not?"

"Because she's harmless. I told you that. She's fifty-seven years old and stands five foot one in her stockinged feet. She's a foulmouthed old woman with a king-sized chip on her shoulder. That's all."

She waited for Gunner to argue the point, but all he did was stare back at her.

"Again, I'd like to thank you for your assistance with Mr. Cagle earlier. You may very well have saved that man's life. But if there's nothing more I can do for you . . ." She stood away from her desk so that he'd know he was being dismissed.

Gunner said thanks and left.

# . ten

"YOU GOTTA GET YOURSELF A BEEPER," MICKEY SAID. "Or a cellular phone."

"I don't think so," Gunner told him.

"Man, I been tryin' to get ahold of you all afternoon! You had a beeper, I could just page your ass once an' forget about it, 'stead'a callin' all over town *lookin'* for you."

He'd met Gunner at the door of the shop and kept right on walking behind him to Gunner's office in the back, like a stray dog the investigator had foolishly petted and now could not get rid of.

"I am not getting a beeper," Gunner said, turning the lamp on on his desk as he threw himself into the chair behind it, exhausted. "End of subject."

"Man, how are you gonna stay in business today, you don't have a beeper or a cellular phone?"

"How are *you* going to stay in business, you don't go back in there where the chairs are and cut somebody's hair?"

"You see somebody in there waitin' to get their hair cut? I didn't."

"Mickey—"

"I bet your competition's got a beeper."

"I bet my competition's got a service bill to pay every month, too. Not to mention a landlord who acts like a landlord, and not a Beepers-R-Us salesman."

"All I'm sayin' is, you had a beeper or a car phone, you would've got these messages a lot sooner."

"Messages? I haven't heard any messages."

"Okay. You don't want my advice, fine. Man named Goody's called you three times. He sounds desperate. That ain't the stereo store guy, is it?"

"The one and only," Gunner said, pinching his eyes shut and grimacing. He had no more time for Goody's nonsense.

"You want the number?"

"No. Did Ziggy call? Or any policemen, maybe?"

"Nope. Just this guy Goody, and Kimmy Renfro. She says Gaylon needs to speak with you."

"Oh. That's right," Gunner said, nodding. "We're supposed to be going to the Laker game Saturday night."

Gaylon Brown was Renfro's seven-year-old son, and Gunner's private little reclamation project. Nobody had asked the investigator to take an interest in the boy, least of all Renfro; he'd just decided it was something he had to do. There was no explaining it. The first time he'd seen Gaylon, just under a year ago, the boy was vandalizing a neighborhood liquor store with two of his knuckleheaded friends, just a bright-eyed little six-year-old who thought nothing his homies told him to do could possibly be wrong. Gunner had tried to put a scare into him, told him if he didn't straighten up and fly right, he was going to throw his little ass off an overpass onto the nearest freeway. The boy had acted like he got the message, until Gunner let him go and he and his two accomplices met back up a safe distance away and flipped Gunner the bird, laughing like he was the biggest fool any of them had ever seen.

Gunner had been a force to reckon with in Gaylon's life ever since.

It didn't make any sense, deciding on a whim to start playing part-time father figure to a child he didn't know and hadn't sired, but he couldn't see his way around it. And it felt good, somehow.

"Oh, and your girl Claudia called," Mickey said.

"Claudia? What did she want?"

"She didn't say. You want me to start askin' women what they want with you when they call, you're gonna have to deputize me, or somethin'. Swear me in, and give me a badge, and shit.''

"I tell you what, Mickey. I'll pay the rent on time this month. How's that?''

"Rent was due a week ago," Mickey said dryly, finally turning to take Gunner's advice and return to the front of the shop. "Who you tryin' to kid?''

Once he was alone, the first call Gunner made was to Kimmy Renfro.

She sounded dog-tired. It was what he imagined all single mothers of four sounded like at a quarter after six, less than two hours after quitting time on a workday.

"Kimmy, this is Gunner. I'm returning your call.''

"Oh, yeah, Mr. Gunner. Gaylon wanted to talk to you. Somethin' 'bout the game this Saturday. You tell 'im you were takin' 'im to a basketball game?''

"The Laker game, yeah. But that was dependent upon him doing that reading I told him to do.''

"You mean from those books you gave 'im?''

"Yeah. He was supposed to spend fifteen minutes each night with one of them. I didn't care which.''

They were little more than picture books, one Disney and two Afrocentric titles, but Gunner just wanted him to get used to the feel of a book in his hands. Developing a genuine affinity for reading would come later.

"He's been readin' 'em," Kimmy said, sounding more than a little proud of the fact. "Every night 'fore he goes to bed. One of 'em he's read three times.''

"Good.''

"So I guess that means he's goin' to the game Saturday.''

"Yeah. I guess he is. Can you put him on a minute?''

Kimmy said sure, and went to get him.

After a few seconds, the youngest of her three sons came on the line. "Hello?''

"Hey, boy," Gunner said. "This is Uncle Gee. What's up?''

That was the name Gaylon had invented for him: Uncle Gee. It made the investigator feel like an aging rapper.

"Nothin'," Gaylon said.

"What do you mean nothin'? I thought you wanted to talk to me."

"I wanted to know if we goin' to the game. Like you said."

"You been reading your books like I told you to?"

"Yeah."

"Then we must be going."

Gaylon asked who was playing.

"Lakers and the Spurs. What's happenin' with Pee Cee? You see him today?"

Pee Cee was Gaylon's eight-year-old mentor from hell, a thug-in-the-making who had been the ringleader behind most of Gaylon's past misadventures, including the liquor store vandalism that had brought Gaylon to Gunner's attention in the first place.

"No. I don't hang with Pee Cee no more," Gaylon said. Telling a lie of the "little white" variety, at the very least.

"He's not your 'boy no more?"

"No."

"Good. 'Cause he's a dummy, like I told you. And you're too smart to be hanging around with dummies. Isn't that right?"

"Uh-huh."

It was a hard thing for a kid to hear, that his best friend in the world was poison to him, but Gunner was weaning Gaylon off the older boy's influence little by little, bit by bit.

"Tell your mother I'll be picking you up around five on Saturday," Gunner said. "Can you remember that?"

"Uh-huh. Round five," Gaylon said.

The next call the investigator made was to Claudia. He had to sit in front of the phone for a full minute beforehand, trying to prepare himself for what she might have to say. Expecting anything and everything but an expressed desire to reconcile.

She didn't disappoint him.

"I came across some of your things here at the house. A couple of books and a few CDs," Claudia said. "I thought you might want to come by sometime this week and get them."

If there was any joy in her life at this moment, her voice did nothing to convey it; as she had for several months now, she seemed detached to the point of insensibility. It drove Gunner crazy.

"Sure," he said. "What time would be good for you?"

"You mean tonight?"

"I thought I'd come by on the way home, yeah."

"Okay. That'll be fine, I guess. See you then."

He didn't realize she was saying good-bye until he heard the dial tone droning in his ear.

When he arrived at Claudia's house, she had his things in a box right by the door, so she could just hand them to him and send him on his way without ever having to ask him to come in. He stood on the porch and took the box out of her hands as day turned to night overhead, a black silk screen falling over a red-washed sky.

"This should be everything," she said. Her casual attire did nothing to blunt the green-eyed beauty that invigorated him still.

"Thanks," he said.

An icy silence followed, until Gunner finally said, "So how have you been?"

"I've been okay. And you?"

"Good."

"How's work?"

"Work's good. A little unsteady, but good."

She nodded to show she was pleased to hear it.

"Have you been seeing anyone?" he asked abruptly.

"Aaron—"

"Yeah, you're right. That was a stupid question, I'm sorry."

Bad timing. That, more than anything, was to blame for this awkward moment, two lovers who had once been good for each other struggling to say a simple good-bye.

They had met almost two years ago in the course of a case Gunner was working. She was a grief-stricken widow, and he was the private investigator trying to prove the innocence of her husband's accused murderer. Drawn to her from the moment he first set eyes on her, he had caught her at the most vulnerable period in her life, and out of need, she had responded to him. It was this inauspicious beginning to their relationship that gave Claudia reason to doubt the validity of everything that came afterward, and it was her doubt that inevitably led him to put an end to the constant series of breakups and makeups their life together had become.

He had little right to be angry, being the one who had actually pulled the plug on their affair, yet Claudia's indifferent reaction to it all made him crazy. To say that their time together was doomed to be wasted was one thing; to shed not one single tear over the fact was quite another.

But that was Claudia. Fortified by the Lord to be impervious to pain.

"I'd better go," he said.

She didn't say a word to stop him.

Three o'clock in the morning, his phone rang. A jarring, nerve-wrenching sound that awoke him immediately.

It was the sound of death calling.

He would have let his answering machine pick up, except that it hadn't been working for weeks. Which had been okay up to now; the only calls he wanted to be bothered with he could just as easily take at Mickey's. Like Roman Goody's calls, for instance.

Jesus, he hoped this wasn't him.

He waited a few seconds, just to see if the ringing would stop on its own, then fumbled around in the dark for the receiver and found it. "Yeah?"

After a long stretch of unnerving silence, someone said, "Get ready to die, motherfucker." And hung up.

The voice had been little more than a whisper, the androgynous rasp of someone breathing into the phone, and not much else. He thought it was familiar, but he couldn't be sure. What he could be sure about was how eerie it had sounded, like something right out of a cheap horror movie, and how well it had gotten its intended job done.

It scared Gunner shitless.

Odds were it was a prank call, just some idiot with the vocal cords of a ghoul who'd chosen Gunner's number at random out of the book.

But it took him a while to fall asleep again, all the same.

The first thing Wednesday morning, he called Ziggy.

The lawyer had nothing new to report about Pearson's condition, and the police still hadn't come calling—yet. Gunner told him about Goldy Cruz, and how he had been spending almost all of his time since his conversation with her.

"You're tellin' me Pearson might not be the guy?" Ziggy asked.

"That's what I'm telling you, yeah. He *might* not be the guy. I don't know if he is or not, yet."

"But you intend to find out."

Gunner didn't answer that.

"I don't like it. These personal matters, they can make a man do some foolish things, he isn't careful. And you're in enough trouble as it is."

"You're suggesting I should let the cops handle it?"

"That's what they get paid for, isn't it?"

"And if Pearson dies? You think they're going to keep Nina's murder case open more than five minutes after he's tagged and bagged?"

Ziggy fell silent, thinking it over. "You can tell me you can do this without getting overly emotional about it, I guess I'm okay with it. But if you can't—"

"Overly emotional? When the hell have you ever known me to get overly emotional?"

"I'm gonna ignore that pathetic attempt at humor and simply tell you to keep in touch. Okay? I don't hear from you every six hours or so, I'm gonna ask our good friend Lieutenant Poole to haul your ass in for your own protection."

"I've got condoms for my own protection, thanks."

"You know what you need? You need a pager. That way I could just page you when I need to talk to you, 'stead of waiting around for you to call."

"You been talking to Mickey?"

"Mickey? Why?"

"It's a fucking conspiracy. That's what it is. You two had your way, I'd never have a moment's peace from either one of you."

"We just wanna know you're okay, kid. That's all."

Ziggy cracked up and got off the phone.

Trini Serrano wasn't in, so Gunner left a message for her on her answering machine, asking for a callback as soon as she could get around to making one. Next, he called to make a noontime appointment with the personnel director at Bowers, Bain and Lyle, the law firm Mimi Hillman had said was Nina's last place of employment before her stint at Sisterhood House. And finally, he dropped in on Agnes Felker. Unannounced.

She lived in a ramshackle apartment building on the northbound side of Martin Luther King, Jr. Boulevard, about six blocks west of the Los Angeles Memorial Coliseum. Only a few feet from her door on the second floor, what looked like a homeless man was curled up in a ball on the floor at the end of the hall, sleeping soundly. Or dead. The sheets of old newspaper draped over his body in lieu of a blanket made it hard to tell which.

Gunner knocked on the door three times before someone on the other side began moving around, betraying their presence inside.

"Who is it?" a coarse, though barely female voice demanded. There was no peephole in the door, so the question was entirely necessary.

"My name is Aaron Gunner. I'm looking for Agnes Felker," Gunner said, shouting to be heard.

"Who?"

"I'm a private investigator. I'd like to ask you some questions about Nina Pearson—"

The door came flying open, without warning. The woman who had thrown it aside stood there at the threshold of the apartment and glared at him, holding the cold metal nostril of a single-barreled shotgun just under his chin.

"Jesus Christ," Gunner said, feeling his bladder threaten to let go.

She was a vicious-looking little thing, a dark-skinned, fiftyish woman with short black hair greased flat against her scalp and shaped into curls framing her face; an angry, masculine, high-cheekboned face that a cosmetic overload did nothing whatsoever to soften. She had a wide, red mouth lined with large, incredibly even teeth, and a small, bony body. And her anger was something that seemed to radiate from her being like heat off a hot stove.

"Come on in here, motherfucker," she said. "Come on."

She backed into the room slowly, and Gunner followed, arms raised over his head, certain each step would be his last. When they were both inside the apartment—a poorly furnished, litter-strewn place surrounded by the world's most disheartening wallpaper—she put another foot of empty space between them and told him to close the door.

"Now, wait a minute," Gunner said. Afraid to argue with her, but more afraid to be alone with her in an enclosed area.

"I said close the goddamn door," Felker told him again.

Refusing to either use his hands or turn his back on her, the investigator stuck a foot out behind him and kicked the door closed.

"I think you've made a mistake," he said.

"No, man. You the fool made the mistake. You an' Otha, both."

"Otha?"

"Nigga can't do his own killin', so he sends you over here to do it for 'im. Goddamn his sorry ass!"

There was that word Nina had disliked so much: *nigga*.

Gunner shook his head, said, "You're wrong. I don't know any Otha. I'm a private investigator, I just came over here to ask you some questions about Nina Pearson."

"That's bullshit."

"No it isn't. It's the truth, I swear it. Put the gun down a minute, and I'll prove it."

"This gun ain't goin' nowhere. You think I'm stupid or somethin'?"

"I think you're going to blow my head off, you keep

aiming that thing at me. Whether you intend to or not. And then you're going to find out what I'm telling you is for real. I don't know this guy Otha.''

He watched as Felker studied him, trying to decide what to do.

''How you gonna prove it?'' she asked him eventually. Keeping the shotgun pointed right at his face.

''I've got ID in my wallet. I'm a licensed private investigator for the state of California.''

''That ain't what I meant. What I meant is, how you gonna prove Otha didn't send you over here to kill me?''

''Only way I can prove that is to have you call some people, ask them to vouch for me. Starting with Wendy Singer, over at Sisterhood House. She'll tell you who I am.''

''Miss Singer? You workin' for her?''

''I'm not working for her, no. But I've talked to her. I was over at the house yesterday, asking about Nina Pearson, like I said.''

''What you wanna know 'bout Nina Pearson?''

''Put the gun down and I'll tell you. Please. Before something happens we're both going to regret.''

It took her a long time to make up her mind. Gunner just stood there and waited, watching her trigger finger wiggle and twitch, wiggle and twitch; all on a weapon similar to the one that had killed Nina Pearson.

''Sit your ass down on the couch,'' Felker finally said. ''On top of your hands, so you can't move 'em.''

''What about the gun?''

''Do what I tell you, nigga, or I'm gonna show you what about the gun. All right?''

Gunner did as he was told and sat down, pinning his hands palm down beneath his buttocks.

''Now. What you wanna know 'bout Nina?'' Felker asked.

''You're still holding the shotgun,'' Gunner said.

''That's right. An' I'm gonna *keep on* holdin' it.''

''How about if you just take your finger off the trigger? Can you do that, at least?''

''No.''

"Look. You want to keep it pointed at my face, fine, that makes you feel more comfortable. But take your finger off the trigger for a minute. So the goddamn thing doesn't go off by accident. You want to shoot me by *accident*?"

After some consideration, she decided she didn't. She pulled her finger out of the shotgun's trigger guard, but otherwise kept the weapon right where it was, aimed roughly at his nose.

"Okay. My finger ain't on the trigger. Now answer my goddamn question."

"I'm talking to people who knew Nina to see if I can get a line on who killed her," Gunner said.

"Who *killed* her? Somebody killed Nina?"

"You didn't know?"

"Know? Man, how'm I s'posed to know? I ain't seen that bitch in two months!"

She didn't seem disturbed to hear the news, just somewhat surprised by it. As if Nina were the last person on earth she would have thought would come to such a terrible end.

"I can see you two were very close," Gunner said.

Felker grunted. "Who? Nina an' me? Shit."

"What exactly was your problem with her, you don't mind my asking?"

"I ain't got no problem with her now, what you say is true. Her old man finally got her ass, huh?"

"It looks that way to the police. But me, I'm not so sure. That's why I'm here."

"Shit. He killed her. Her nigga got her, same as my nigga's tryin' to get me. Same goddamn diff'rence."

"What makes you so sure?"

"What makes me so sure? You all alike, that's what. Every goddamn one of you!"

She had her finger back on the shotgun's trigger, dark eyes suddenly rekindled with rage.

"Okay, okay! You're right, you're right," Gunner said, trying to appease her. Thinking the gang down at Sisterhood hadn't prepared him for her enough, simply describing her as "crazy." Crazy didn't even begin to do this fruitcake justice.

"I don't believe it, what you're tellin' me," Felker said. "I think you're makin' it all up."

"I wish I was. Believe me."

"So what you say your name was again? Gunner?"

"That's right. Aaron Gunner."

"Gunner. Uh-huh. So who you workin' for, then, Mr. Gunner, you ain't workin' for Miss Singer? Somebody gotta be payin' you, right?"

"Nobody's paying me. I'm doing this for myself."

"For yourself?"

"That's right. Look, you've got your finger on that trigger again, and I can't think straight when you do that. Could you please . . ."

Felker put her finger back where it had been, outside the shotgun's trigger guard.

"Thank you," Gunner said.

"You was sayin' you're doin' this for yourself," Felker said, reminding him where he had left off.

"Yes. Nina was a friend of mine, I owed her."

"You ain't workin' for that nigga's lawyer, or somethin'? Tryin' to get 'im off?"

"No. I told you, I'm not working for anybody."

"Then what you tryin' to prove? I don't understand."

"I don't want the cops to make a mistake on this one. That's all. I don't want them to lay Nina's murder on her husband just because the shoe fits."

"No? Then who you think they should lay it on? Hell, that nigga was the only one in the goddamn world didn't treat that bitch like *gold*. Like a angel sent from heaven, or somethin'. Them fools over Miss Singer's house, they like to wet their pants every time she—"

She never finished the thought. Something came snapping into focus for her and stopped her cold, leaving her jaw swinging open like a barnyard gate.

"Oh. Uh-huh," she said. "Now I understand."

"You understand what?"

"I understand what the fuck you doin' here. That's what. You think *I* killed the bitch. Just 'cause I was the only one wouldn't let her tell me what to do, or how to act."

"And how did she want you to act?"

"She wanted me to act *white*. That's how. White, just like her."

"White?"

"That's right. White. She didn't like to hear a black woman talk like a black woman. Every time I opened my mouth, she'd be in my face, right in front of everybody, tellin' me she didn't like my language. *My language,* like it wasn't *her* fuckin' language too! Like I was some kinda *embarrassment* to her, or somethin'!"

"I heard it was just one word in particular that she objected to," Gunner said.

"What, 'nigga'? What the fuck's wrong with that? That's what we are, ain't we? Ain't we all niggas?"

Gunner treated the question like something he hadn't heard.

"Shit. You don't think so neither, that it? You think you're somethin' more'n that, same way she did. Don't you?"

"Let's just say if I had my pick of words to throw out of the English dictionary, that would be my first choice," Gunner said. "Hands down."

"You don't never call nobody a nigga?"

"No. Not if I can help it."

Felker shook her head, amazed. "I don't understand that," she said.

And Gunner knew she never would. Black men and women who threw the n-word around like she did were too short on brain cells to appreciate how they were embracing one of the most powerful and dehumanizing weapons ever used against their own people. They liked to say that the twist they put on the way it was spelled and pronounced made something harmless out of it, but the truth was, it just made them feel better for having bought into the white man's contention that it was a perfectly suitable name for them.

Funny, Gunner thought, but the Japanese never did take to "Jap" that well. Nor the Jews to "kike." Nor . . .

"Let's get back to Nina," Gunner said.

"I ain't got nothin' more to say 'bout Nina. It was on

account'a her I got kicked outta Miss Singer's place, I don't give a shit about her no more.''

"Where were you last Tuesday night? Say, between the hours of seven and twelve midnight?''

"Last Tuesday night? What, that when she got killed? Last Tuesday?''

"Yeah.''

"I was here. With Otha. Watchin' TV. Not that it's any of your goddamn bus'ness.''

"Was anyone else here with you?''

"No. Ain't never anyone else here with us. Otha don't like me havin' no company in here.''

"Even when he's around?''

"Even when he's around. He gets jealous. That's his problem. Anybody comes aroun' me, he starts actin' a fool.'' Tears were welling in her eyes as she thought about it. "I tell 'im I love 'im, an' he tells me he loves me. But when he gets *mad* . . . he don't hear nothin' I say. He just . . . He just starts *beatin'* on me. An' *beatin'* on me. Like . . . like I'm . . .''

She was crying in earnest now, the shotgun roiling around in her unsteady hands like a dinghy on choppy waters. Gunner would have felt sorry for her if he weren't so afraid of dying.

"I'm sorry,'' he said. Trying to lead up slowly to saying good-bye.

The apology brought her back to reality. Suddenly aware of what she'd just done—cried like a baby in front of a strange man who, in all probability, thought what she'd told him was funny—she rubbed at her eyes with the back of one free hand and said, "Shit. What do *you* know 'bout bein' sorry? You don't know *shit* 'bout bein' sorry!''

"Look. I've caught you at a bad time. Maybe—''

"Oh. You wanna leave now, huh? I thought you wanted to talk about Nina.''

"Well, yeah, but—''

"Hell, I ain't got nothin' to hide. What you wanna know? Go ahead an' ask me somethin'.''

Gunner didn't say anything, afraid that if he did, she might never let him leave.

"I told you to ask me a question, nigga," Felker said, the shotgun relatively steady in her hands again.

Gunner gave it some thought, said, "Okay. One more before I go." Laying down the terms of his own surrender.

"Let's hear it."

"Who else could have wanted Nina dead besides her husband? Anyone come to mind?"

He watched the tiny black woman's face change as she thought about it, concentrating for all she was worth. Finally, she shook her head and said, "I don't know nobody would wanna *kill* her. Didn't nobody ever get that mad at her, hardly. But . . . there was one girl I know was, once. I don't know if she was pissed off enough to *kill* anybody, but she was pissed off enough to put some serious foot in Nina's ass. That's for damn sure." The memory brought a toothy grin to her face.

"Who was this?"

"Girl up at Miss Singer's place name' Shirley. Coldest bitch stay up there, you ask me."

"Shirley Causwell?"

"Yeah. That's her. Shirley Causwell."

"She was pissed off at Nina? For what?"

Felker shook her head again, grinning anew, and said, "Ain't my bus'ness to tell you that. You wanna know that, you gotta ask *her*. Or Trini. Trini knows."

"The photographer?"

"Yeah. The photographer. White girl always up there takin' pictures of everybody, an' shit. Her. She knows."

"How long ago was this?"

"You say you only gonna ask one question. An' you asked it. I think you better raise on up outta here, now. Get the hell outta my face."

"I think you're right," Gunner said.

Without either of them saying another word, he edged his way out of the apartment and started for the stairs, never looking back. His sense of relief was so intense he could barely walk.

Outside on the sidewalk, a bearded black man with a do-rag on his head and a cigarette pinched between his teeth stormed past him, heading into Felker's building as Gunner was going out. Forty, maybe forty-five, he was wearing a grungy old pair of overalls, the kind auto mechanics always wore, and both of his hands were rolled into fists that looked to Gunner's eye like something a man could use to pound tent stakes into the ground.

Otha. It had to be.

Gunner went to his car and jumped in, praying to God he could get out of there before Agnes Felker's shotgun could go off—or worse, be turned meekly over to her old man the way it likely always was.

A peace offering that never seemed to buy her a thing.

# eleven

THE PERSONNEL DIRECTOR AT BOWERS, BAIN AND LYLE wouldn't tell him *squat*.

She was a courteous but stiff young woman named Olivia Ishimura, and she sat behind the desk in her office like a Marine private dressed for full inspection, offering Gunner nothing but vague inferences and sweeping generalizations regarding Nina Pearson's employment history at the firm. Not because she didn't want to be helpful, she said, but because so much of the information contained in Nina's file—or any employee's file, for that matter, past or present, alive or dead—was confidential.

"You understand, I'm sure," she said.

Nothing Gunner tried would make her more conversant. Neither overplaying the "official" nature of his inquiry, nor appealing to her sympathies as a former co-worker of a brutally murdered young woman. She had one thing to tell him, and one thing only: that Nina's work had been substandard, her reviews steadily declining, and therefore the head of her department had been forced to let her go. That was all there was to it.

Her termination couldn't possibly have been racially motivated? Gunner asked her.

Ishimura's answer was a flat and emphatic *no*. Then she really clammed up.

Gunner thanked her for her time and left.

He didn't realize the receptionist out front was not the

same one he'd seen coming in until he reached the main
lobby of the building downstairs. He stepped off the elevator
and there she was, the original Bowers, Bain and Lyle receptionist, standing around watching all the elevator doors
like somebody waiting for a lunch date. A tall, very prim
and proper black woman in her late forties, if appearances
weren't deceiving, she closed on Gunner quickly and said,
"Mr. Gunner, hello. May we talk? Please?"

She took his arm, leading him around the corner, and said,
"I'm Allie. The receptionist who signed you in upstairs. Remember?"

"Sure," Gunner said. "What—"

"I'm sorry, but we can't talk here. If I'm seen, I'll lose
my job for sure. Is your car parked downstairs?"

"Yes. But—"

"I'll walk you down. This won't take long."

They rode the parking elevators down to Gunner's level
and found the red Cobra where he had parked it. They'd had
to share the elevator car with two other people, so the ride
down had been a silent one, even though Gunner was quite
obviously the only one in the car the receptionist had ever
seen before.

"Oh, my. It's a convertible," she said, eyeing the topless,
two-seater Cobra with unabashed disappointment. Apparently, a panel van with tinted glass would have been much
more to her liking.

"I think we're safe down here," Gunner told her, in a
hurry to hear what she had to say.

She had to survey the four corners of the entire parking
level before she could bring herself to agree with him. Then
she said, "You're a lawyer, right? Somebody Nina's family
hired?"

"Actually, I'm a private investigator. But—"

"I was taking somebody a note and passed by Olivia's
office and heard you talking. It sounded like you were trying
to find out why she was fired."

"That's right. I was."

"But Olivia wouldn't tell you anything. Would she?"

"She told me Nina had been a substandard worker. Beyond that, no. She wouldn't tell me anything.''

"And you believe that? That Nina was a substandard worker?''

"Can you think of any reason why I shouldn't?''

"Yes. I can.'' She studied his face intently, looking for some form of proof that he could be trusted. "Nina got fired for blowing the whistle on Mr. Stanhouse. Her boss.''

"Let me guess: Because he was a racist.''

"A racist?''

"I'd heard somewhere her firing may have had something to do with her being black.''

The receptionist shook her head, said, "No. It didn't have anything to do with that. Nina got fired for claiming Mr. Stanhouse was sexually harassing her. He kept coming on to her, so she reported him to Mr. Bowers. But instead of firing *him,* they fired *her.* It was very, very unfair.''

"Stanhouse was sexually harassing her? How?''

"I don't know, exactly. Nina never talked to me about it, directly. But what I heard is that he'd follow her home sometimes, and call her there after hours. Things like that. It wasn't the physical kind of harassment. It was just . . . well, an obsession with him, I guess. He liked her, and he wanted her to like him. Only Nina wasn't interested.''

"And she told him so.''

"Of course. Many times. But he wouldn't get the message, so she went to Mr. Bowers. And that's when she got fired. It didn't have anything to do with her work performance. It was just office politics. *Sexual* politics.''

"Is this Mr. Stanhouse in today, by any chance?'' Gunner asked.

"Yes. But you're not—''

"Going back up there to see him? No. I'm not. But if you can tell me what kind of car he drives, and what level employee parking's on in this building . . .''

Allie said she could do that, no problem.

And she did.

Stanhouse drove a late-model Acura. The muscular 3.2TL four-door sedan, in jade green with gleaming chrome wheels and gold accents. It suited him perfectly. Like the car, the thirtyish black man exuded style and refinement, yet was somehow physically unextraordinary. His designer suit was impeccably tailored, and the shine of his shoes was almost mirrorlike, but his hair was wiry and uncooperative on the sides, and his face was that of a favorite uncle, round and soft and wholly without menace. Exactly what the receptionist at Bowers, Bain and Lyle had told Gunner he would be: a sheep in wolf's clothing.

Gunner watched him get off the elevator at the employee parking level, then followed him over to the Acura, the car all but proving without question that he'd latched on to the right man. Stanhouse's approach to the Acura was cautious, as if he'd been expecting to find another vehicle in his parking place in its stead. Frowning, he stood away from the car and thumbed a key chain control three times. Testing his car alarm.

He had opened the driver's-side door to take a look inside when Gunner finally made his presence felt.

"The car's okay," he said, walking up to where the attorney could easily see him.

Stanhouse turned around, only slightly startled, and said, "What's that?"

"I said the car's okay. No need to be concerned."

Stanhouse pulled his head up and out of the car to stand up and face him directly. "I got a call upstairs that the alarm was going off," he said. "One of the attendants here—"

"Yeah, I know. That was me," Gunner said, stepping forward with his ID open in his right hand, holding it out so the other man could get a good, clear look at it.

"I don't understand," Stanhouse said.

Gunner explained it to him, leaving Allie the receptionist out of the picture, as he had promised he would.

"Her mother sent you over here, didn't she?" the attorney asked afterward, clearly agitated.

"Who, Mimi?"

"I think that was her name. This was her idea, wasn't it? Dredging all this crap up again, even after Nina's death."

Gunner shook his head, said, "She's not the reason I'm

here, no. But I'm curious as to why you would think she might be.''

Stanhouse shook his own head and said, "It doesn't matter. I've got nothing to say to you. Or her. Not now, not ever."

Gunner shrugged. "Okay. Lock your car up and come on, we can ride back up to your office together.''

Stanhouse just stared at him.

"You don't want to talk to me, it's cool. I'll talk to Mr. Bowers. Or Mr. Bain. Or Mr. Lyle. One of those fine gentlemen should be able to give me a moment of their time, don't you think?''

"I can't speak for Mr. Bowers. But seeing Mr. Bain or Mr. Lyle would be quite a trick. They've both been dead for over ten years now.''

"Really?''

"Really. And as for Mr. Bowers, even if he did agree to speak with you, I'm sure he'd only tell you what I'm about to tell you now. Which is that Nina was a very disturbed young woman whose allegations against me were completely false. Not only that, but they were the exact opposite of the truth.''

"Meaning what? That *she* harassed *you*?'' Gunner had to grin at the very idea.

"That's right. She did,'' Stanhouse said.

Gunner started to laugh.

"You can laugh if you like. But that's how it was. It was a classic case of the secretary having a crush on the boss. Only Nina took it too far. When I refused to go to bed with her, she tried to have me fired, claiming *I* was the one pressuring *her* for sex. And it might have worked, too, if Mr. Bowers hadn't known me as well as he does.'' He closed his car door, reactivated the alarm, and said, "Now, if you'll excuse me, that's all I've got to say about the matter. You want to talk to Mr. Bowers about it, you're welcome to try. But don't hold your breath.''

He started forward, intending to march right past Gunner for full dramatic effect, but the investigator held his ground, barring his path.

"Let me by," Stanhouse said. He looked like a man who might spontaneously combust if he was forced to talk about Nina another second longer.

"When we're done," Gunner told him.

Gunner thought the attorney's first move would be a push of some kind, a hand on his shoulder or in the middle of his chest, but to Stanhouse's credit, he threw a right hand at Gunner's left eye instead, getting right down to business. No girlish preliminaries for him. It was a good right hand too: quick and straight and full of bad intent. Gunner had little choice but to admire it as he feinted left, ducking under it, and drove a right hand of his own into the other man's midsection, hard, instantly reducing him to a doubled-up noncombatant choking for air.

"That's assault," Stanhouse gasped, falling to his knees.

"Actually, that's self-defense," Gunner said, glancing about briefly to see that they were still all alone on this parking level. "Assault is when I attack you first. Without provocation. You can look it up when you get back upstairs, you don't believe me."

He gave Stanhouse a few more seconds to gather himself, then crouched down to be at eye level with him again and said, "Look. Let's not get crazy, all right? I brought you down here to talk to you, not ruin your suit. Answer a few questions for me, and I'll be on my way. You can do that, can't you?"

Stanhouse struggled to his feet, slapping away Gunner's attempts to help him. "I've already told you everything you need to know," he said, brushing himself off. "I didn't sexually harass anybody. Nina—"

"I tell you what, Stanhouse. You don't hand me any more of this shit about Nina being madly in love with you, and I won't laugh in your face anymore. What do you say?"

"You don't think she *could* have loved me. Is that it?"

"She could have loved you, sure. Anything is possible. But to the point of obsession? To where it was affecting her work and jeopardizing her employment? Not a chance."

"How the hell would *you* know? You didn't know her."

"Actually, I did. She and I were good friends, once. Very good friends."

He'd said it just to see how Stanhouse would take it, this not so subtle implication that he and Nina used to be lovers, and for the most part, he got the results he had thought he might: Stanhouse seemed shaken.

"But that's neither here nor there," he went on. "Who Nina was or wasn't in love with isn't nearly as important to me as who killed her, and why. As it must be to you, I'm sure."

"Who killed her? What are you, nuts?" Stanhouse asked. "That sonofabitch she was married to killed her. Who else?"

"That's exactly what I came here to find out: the who else."

"Jesus. You think *I* did it? Is that what you think?"

"Well, put yourself in my shoes for a minute. You're telling me she was a mentally disturbed woman under your direct supervision whose constant sexual advances were making your life a living hell, and whose baseless charges of sexual harassment almost cost you your job. That doesn't sound like a motive for murder to you?"

"No!"

"It doesn't?"

"No! You're out of your mind to even suggest such a thing. I could never have hurt Nina. Never!"

"Because you were in love with her."

"No! I mean—" He stopped himself, the words to come catching in his throat like a vulgarity he was not allowed to speak.

"What *do* you mean, Mr. Stanhouse?" Gunner asked.

The attorney shook his head and said, "I'm all through answering questions. You want to talk to me again, you're going to have to do it with my attorney present. My secretary will be happy to give you his number."

He paused a moment to see if Gunner had anything to say about that, then said, "Now—I'm leaving. Same way I came down here. You want to stop me, let's go." He waved Gunner forward playfully. "Maybe this time I can fuck *your* clothes up a little."

Gunner had to grin, so impressive was the other man's pluck. "Relax, counselor. I'm through with you. For now." He made a show of stepping aside to grant Stanhouse passage, and Stanhouse took advantage of it, striding slowly past him like a one-man victory parade, chest puffed out and chin held high.

Gunner didn't laugh out loud until he was long gone.

"You got to call this guy Goody," Mickey said, "before he drives me to an early grave."

Gunner had called him from the Tommy's Original hamburger stand on Beverly and Rampart downtown, where he was eating lunch, right after he'd left a message for Matt Poole out at Southwest. He was fairly certain Poole wouldn't tell him what he wanted to know—what ballistics had determined about the make and model of shotgun that had been used on Nina—but he thought it was worth a try anyway. The one Agnes Felker had been waving around looked like a twelve-gauge Browning. If Nina had been killed with something like that . . .

Well, coincidences just didn't come that big.

So he gave Poole a call and left a message, then called Mickey afterward, and that was what he heard the minute the barber answered the phone and realized who was calling: "You got to call this guy Goody."

"Forget about him. I'll call him later," Gunner said. "What about Trini Serrano? She call me back yet?"

"Yeah, she called. She said she'd be available to see you anytime after one, you wanna come by her place. She gave me the address, in case you didn't have it. You want it?"

"No thanks. I've got it. Anything else?"

"Nothin' except this guy Goody. He's called this mornin' *twice.* First at eight, then eight-thirty, mad as hell 'cause you ain't called 'im back yet. I know you say it's nothin', man, but it don't sound like nothin' to *me.* Sounds to me like this man's ass is in some serious trouble, he don't get ahold of you soon."

"Goody always sounds that way," Gunner said, trying to finish his chiliburger and talk on the phone at the same time.

"Yeah, well, I'm just tellin' you what he sounds like to me. So if somethin' happens later, you can't say I didn't warn you."

"Jesus. The man's just trying to get me to do a job for him, Mickey. That's all. He offered it to me once, and I turned him down, so now he's trying to *hound* me into taking it. He's one of those people who don't know how to take no for an answer."

"Okay. Whatever you say."

Mickey still sounded concerned.

"All right, all right. I'll go see the sonofabitch right after I talk to Serrano. That okay with you? Will that make you feel better?"

"I'll feel better when you start payin' me for this shit. That's when I'll feel better. Doin' this mess for free is gettin' old, I swear to God."

"One day, I'll make it all up to you, Mickey. I promise," Gunner said.

But Mickey had better sense than to believe him.

# twelve

TRINI SERRANO'S STUDIO WAS IN HOLLYWOOD, ON MEL-
rose Avenue between Kenmore and Edgemont, not far from
the campus of Los Angeles City College. It was a ground-
floor storefront in an old, two-story brick building, with a
large display window and a half-glazed door to match. There
were no markings out front, but a mannequin occupied the
display window; a nude female, posed in a crouch, hands up
to guard its face, like someone cowering under the blows of
an ongoing beating. The prototypical abused woman: naked,
helpless, her shame exposed for all the world to see.

Beyond the grimy glass pane of the door, Gunner could
see someone working inside; a Caucasian woman, medium
height and weight, dressed in a crisp white blouse and dark
slacks, arranging photographs on the west wall. He knocked
on the door and she turned around, a mop-topped brunette
with a kind face and plenty of gray around the ears. Old
enough to be somebody's grandmother, maybe, but still more
attractive than some women would ever live to be.

Another vaguely familiar face from Nina's funeral last
Saturday.

Without waiting for her to do the honors, Gunner let himself in through the unlocked door and said, "Hi. I'm looking
for Trini Serrano."

Moving to greet him, right hand extended, the brunette
smiled warmly and said, "You must be Aaron Gunner. Welcome." She shook his hand. "Wendy Singer told me I'd

probably be hearing from you. Come in please, make yourself at home.''

She ushered him further inside and watched with some
satisfaction as he took a look around, admiring the place.
Her photographs were everywhere. Black-and-whites of assorted sizes, mounted in double rows on opposing walls. A
graphic litany of women riding the emotional roller coaster
that was life with an abusive partner; women of all colors
and all ages. Laughing during the deceptive lulls between
bad times, crying when the bad times inevitably returned.
Bruised and battered, ducking away from punches and clawing at hands clamped around their throats, hiding behind
locked bathroom doors and shivering under the covers of
unmade beds. And here and there, their mates, the lethal
monsters, almost all of them men, to whom they owed their
unenviable existence: faces contorted by rage, spittle flying
from open mouths, hands clenched tight around anything that
could be used as a weapon. Broomsticks, leather belts, hiking
boots, and pool cues . . .

''It's not a pretty sight, is it?'' Serrano asked.

Gunner turned, startled. Without realizing it, he'd been
staring in silence now for a full minute.

''What some of us do to the people we claim to love, I
mean,'' Serrano continued.

''Oh. No. It's not,'' Gunner said, his eyes drifting back
to the photographs on one wall as if of their own accord.
''It's not a pretty sight at all.''

''I guess you wonder why I do it. Spend all my time
taking pictures like these.''

Gunner faced her again and said, ''I imagine you do it
because you think it's important.''

Serrano smiled, making the crow's-feet at the corners of
both eyes widen beautifully. ''That's part of it.''

''And what's the other part?''

''The other part is that it pays better than wedding pictures.'' She smiled again, enjoying herself, but Gunner
couldn't bring himself to do the same. ''Come on, Mr. Gunner. It's just a joke. I take my work very seriously, I assure
you.''

"I'm sure," the investigator said.

"I was just putting some new prints up when you came in. We can talk out here while I finish, or we can go back to my office and talk there, if you prefer. Whatever makes you feel more comfortable."

"Out here is fine," Gunner said.

"Wendy tells me you were an old boyfriend of Nina's," Serrano said, after he had declined her offer of something to drink. She was peeling yet another photograph off the west wall as she spoke. "Do you mind if I ask what happened? That is, why it is you two never got married?"

"I'm afraid that's a long story."

"You couldn't make a short one out of it? Just this once?"

"I suppose I could. You don't mind telling me first why you're interested."

"I'm interested because I think it might tell me something about you I should know. Like whether you're a good guy, or a bad guy, for instance. If you're a good guy, I can talk to you freely, without worrying about what you might do with the information I give you. But if you're a bad guy . . ."

"I'm not a bad guy," Gunner said.

"Good. But tell me what happened between you and Nina anyway."

"Well, like I said, it's a long story. But the short of it is, I walked away from her. Thinking I could do better."

"And did you?"

"I haven't yet. And I probably never will. One of life's little lessons learned in retrospect."

"Ah. I'm sorry."

"Don't be. It's a waste of energy, being sorry."

"Yes. I've noticed that." She turned away from her work to smile at him again. "Okay. Your turn."

Gunner asked her what, exactly, Wendy Singer had told her about him.

"Just that you're an old friend of Nina's who's investigating her murder. Because you aren't completely certain it was her husband who killed her."

"And your feelings about that are?"

"What? That you aren't certain her husband killed her?"

"Yes."

"I don't have *any* feelings about it. I'm not so sure he did it either."

It wasn't what he had expected her to say, and his face must have shown it.

"Does that surprise you?" Serrano asked.

"Just a little," Gunner said.

"Why? I'm not the first person to say something like that, am I?"

"As a matter of fact, you are. Everyone else I've spoken to so far not only believes her husband killed her, but that he was the only one who could have possibly had a motive for doing so. They say Nina was too well loved to have been killed by anyone else."

"Oh, she was certainly well loved," Serrano said. "And deservedly so. Nina was a beautiful human being. But that doesn't mean there weren't people in this world who might have wished harm to her."

"Such as?"

"Such as Shirley Causwell. Another resident over at Sisterhood House who was there while Nina was. And a man named Gary Stanhouse. Her ex-boss, works at a law firm Nina used to work for downtown. Is that a straight enough answer for you?"

"The straightest I've had all day," Gunner said.

Serrano put down the photograph she was holding and lowered herself into a nearby chair, no longer willing to divide her attention between Gunner and her work. "Have you spoken to Shirley yet? Is she still there at the house?"

"She's still there. And I spoke to her while I was there yesterday, yes."

"And what did she say?"

"She said the only two people she ever saw Nina have words with were Agnes Felker and you."

"Me?"

"Yes. Both she and Angela Glass told me Nina wasn't speaking to you the last few days of her stay there, and Shirley said she thought she knew why. Seems she heard part of an argument you and Nina had in the laundry room once, over you going through Nina's things at the house without clearing it with Nina first.'' He waited for Serrano to deny it, but she didn't say a word. ''You have any idea what she was talking about?''

''You mean, do I recall the conversation she was referring to? Yes. I remember it. But I also remember that Shirley couldn't have caught more than the last ten or fifteen words of it, so how she can say she knows what it was about is beyond me.''

''It wasn't about you going through Nina's things without her permission?''

''No. Not really.'' Serrano hesitated. Either to formulate a lie, or to decide how much of the truth he needed to hear. ''What we were really talking about was a bracelet I gave her. Nina had taken the inscription I'd put on it the wrong way, and wouldn't wear it. So I'd gone through her things to find it, just to make sure it was still there. I was afraid she'd thrown it out. That day down in the laundry room, I was trying to explain to her one more time what the inscription meant. I was apologizing for not having made my meaning more clear.''

''What was the inscription?''

''I'd rather not say. I'm sorry.''

''Was it something along the lines of 'For Nina, you are much stronger and more beautiful than you know'?''

Again, Serrano hesitated, clearly surprised to hear her own words recited back to her so accurately. ''You've seen the photograph,'' she said.

''Yes. It was at her mother's. A beautiful piece of work. You captured Nina perfectly, I thought.''

He wasn't going to tell her he actually had the photograph they were talking about with him now, in the inside pocket of his coat. He didn't want to take the chance that she would ask for it back.

''Thanks. I always thought so too,'' Serrano said.

''But we digress. I was asking if the two inscriptions were similar. The one on the photograph, and the one on this bracelet you say you gave her.''

Serrano remained silent.

"I tell you what. It's a personal matter, I can see that. That's why I'm not asking for any specifics, you don't want to give me any. All I'd like to know is whether the inscription on the bracelet was as suggestive as the one on the photograph. A simple yes or no will do."

"Define what you mean by 'suggestive,' Mr. Gunner."

"I mean something that could be interpreted by some as having a sexual or romantic undertone to it, Ms. Serrano. As would something you might write to your lover, for example."

"My 'lover'? You think Nina was my *lover*?"

"I think that's one way to read the inscription you wrote on the back of the photograph. Yes. You can't see that?"

Serrano was shaking her head emphatically, stung by the accusation. "I don't believe this," she said.

"You don't believe what?"

"I don't believe you're just as small-minded as she is. That's what. I knew she'd tell you, of course, but I thought you might be sharp enough to see that there's nothing to what she says. Nothing whatsoever."

"Who?"

"If anyone's to blame for what happened to Nina, it's her. She was the one who drove Nina to leave that house as abruptly as she did. If she'd just left us alone—"

"You're going to have to forgive me, Ms. Serrano, but I don't have the slightest idea who you're talking about," Gunner said.

"Please, Mr. Gunner. I think you know very well who I'm talking about."

"It's your privilege to think whatever you like. But the fact remains I don't."

Serrano didn't say anything for a long time, looking for either the glimmer of truth or deceit in his eyes. "I'm talking about Wendy," she said. "Who else?"

"Wendy Singer?"

"Yes. Wendy Singer. What other Wendy do you know?"

"She thought you and Nina were having an affair? Is that what I hear you saying?"

"She didn't just think it. She was convinced of it. She didn't tell you that when you talked to her yesterday?"

Gunner shook his head.

"If that's true, I'm surprised," Serrano said. "I thought sure that's where you'd gotten it, this idea that Nina and I were anything more than just friends."

"No."

"That's why I'm no longer welcome there, you see. She thinks I'm some kind of lesbian Lothario. That my photography is all a front for my activities as a predator of tender young girls like Nina."

"And it's not."

"No. It's not. First of all, because my work is not a front for *anything*; to suggest that it might be is gravely insulting. And secondly, because a person's sexuality is nothing to be ashamed of. If I *were* the lesbian seductress Wendy thinks I am, it wouldn't be a secret to anyone, I assure you. I don't believe in that kind of duplicity."

"Then what makes Singer think you and Nina were sexually involved?"

"I couldn't tell you that. No more than she could tell me. I think the woman's just a prude, and she's very over-protective of the women she takes in. Which is understandable, considering how fragile and vulnerable they often are. But you put those two things together—a prude's sensibilities and a mother hen's overprotectiveness—and that's what you get. A homophobe with an overactive imagination."

"Still—neither of you gave her any concrete reason to think something was going on between you?"

"We were close, Mr. Gunner. Very close. I liked Nina, and she liked me. Naturally, we spent a great deal of time together. She wanted to take up photography, and I was showing her the ropes. I even gave her a camera to help her get started. I guess seeing us together all the time gave Wendy the idea that we had to be doing more than just taking pictures together, I don't know. And my being such a tactile personality must have caused her to wonder too, I suppose."

"Your being a what? A 'tactile—'?"

"Personality, yes. Which is just a more clinical way of

saying I'm touchy-feely. Not with people I just met, you understand, but with people I feel particularly close to, or comfortable with. There's almost never anything sexual about it, but I admit some people take it that way.''

"There's no chance Singer saw this bracelet you gave Nina? Or the photograph you inscribed for her? Anything like that?"

"Anything like what? I don't understand what you're asking."

"Anything else you might have given to Nina bearing a personal message of some kind. Like another piece of inscribed jewelry, or a card, or a letter . . .''

"Oh. No." Serrano shook her head. "There was really very little of that sort of thing for her to see. The bracelet and the photograph, that was about it.''

"And you're sure Nina never showed her either one?"

The question seemed to throw Serrano off balance a bit. "Why would she have? I don't—"

"I thought maybe Nina had the same problem with interpretation Singer did. You did say she'd taken the inscription you put on her bracelet the wrong way earlier.''

"Yes, but—"

"What, wasn't that what you meant? That she'd mistaken it for an expression of love, rather than one of friendship?''

"I didn't say that, no. She . . .'' Whatever she was going to say, she held back, suddenly being careful with her choice of words.

Gunner didn't push her.

He waited a few seconds, then asked, "When was the last time you saw Nina, Ms. Serrano? Was it before she went home, or after?''

His patience had given her time to regroup. No longer looking afraid to say what was on her mind, she said, "It was before. I never saw Nina after she went home."

"Never?"

"No. Never."

"I thought you two were so close."

"We were. But as you've so cleverly surmised, Mr. Gunner, we did grow apart near the end. And yes, it was because

Nina, too, came to have doubts about my intentions. Though she had more reason to doubt them than Wendy did, certainly.''

"And why is that?"

"Because she was afraid. Someone had *made* her afraid."

"Afraid of whom? You?"

"Not of me, no. She was afraid of *herself.* Or more accurately, of what she thought she was becoming."

"You're losing me," Gunner said.

"She was afraid of becoming a lesbian, Mr. Gunner. All right? She'd had one homosexual experience, just one, but the woman she'd had it with was trying to convince her it was evidence of her true sexual identity. That wasn't true, of course, but Nina was starting to believe it, all the same."

Gunner was silent, and somewhat numb. Trying to get a handle on his feelings about it, this allegation that Nina had once been with another woman. Mimi's daughter, and his former fiancée, naked in the arms of . . .

"Shirley Causwell," he said. Taking a not so wild guess.

"Yes." Serrano nodded. "She was the one in love with Nina, not me."

"How do you know that?"

"Because Nina told me. We were friends, remember?"

Gunner was suddenly reminded of how Agnes Felker had behaved just a few hours ago, when he'd asked her what reason Causwell could have had for wanting to "put some serious foot in Nina's ass." Like she knew a secret she was dying to tell, but couldn't.

*Ain't my bus'ness to tell you that,* she'd said. *You wanna know that, you gotta ask* her. *Or Trini. Trini knows.*

"But if she was the one Nina was involved with—" Gunner said now.

"Why did Wendy come down on me, instead? Simple. Because she didn't know about Shirley. No one did. Shirley and Nina were only together once, like I said, and Nina never told anyone about it but me. She didn't *want* anyone else to know."

"She was ashamed."

"Yes. That, and confused. She didn't know what it meant, or why it had happened."

"Was it . . ." he started to ask, then changed his mind, deciding on an alternate way to ask the same question. "Was she taken advantage of in any way? Did she . . ." Again, he broke the question off, not caring for the way it sounded, even in his head.

"You want to know if it was consensual," Serrano said. "Is that it?"

"Yes."

"For the most part it was. Yes. Shirley simply put her in a position to be tempted and"—she shrugged—"Nina gave in to it. It happens like that, sometimes."

Gunner nodded his head, not really caring to hear much more about it.

"But that wasn't what you wanted to hear, was it? You'd been hoping I could tell you she'd been raped, of course."

"Raped?"

"Because that would have made you feel so much better about her, I imagine. To know that such a horrible thing had been forced upon her, rather than entered into of her own free will. Isn't that right?"

Gunner just stared at her, wondering what the hell she was going off about.

"It was sex, Mr. Gunner. That's all. No oaths were taken, no blood was spilled. It wasn't a pagan ritual."

"I never said it was."

"No. But your face leaves little doubt how much you approve of the concept."

"It's a little late for me or anyone else to be approving or disapproving of anything Nina did in life, don't you think?"

"Still. It's obvious how you feel about it."

"Obvious to you, maybe. But not to me. Near as I can tell, I'm just surprised, not revolted. I don't care what you think my face tells you."

Serrano took a few moments to think about that, the validity of her powers of intuition being called into question.

"So. Maybe I was wrong," she said eventually.

"Yeah. Maybe you were," Gunner agreed.

"It's just . . . I can't stand the way some men react to it, that's all. The thought of their women finding comfort with other women. As if they'd be better off dead, or something." She shook her head sadly, said, "Life is too goddamn short! You want to get through it in one piece, sometimes you've got to take love where you can find it. No matter what other people think."

She looked up at the photographs on the wall behind her and went on. "I've seen too many women die to ever give a damn again who someone's found to love them, or why. What's important is life without pain, Mr. Gunner. Nothing else. Whatever one has to do to find some peace and joy in their lives is all right with me."

"I believe you," Gunner said.

"But you don't feel the same way."

"I feel a person should be free to pick and choose whom to love, and how to love them, yes. But I don't think love is something you take from just anyone, simply because it's being offered to you. I think you have to be a little more selective than that."

"And what if being selective isn't an option? What if a person only finds one offer on the table?"

"Then that person has to decide whether or not they deserve better. If the answer's yes, they wait; if it's no, they take what's available and try to make do."

"You make it sound so simple."

"It isn't simple. It's just the way it is. You either believe what you need is in the cards for you, or you don't. Nobody compromises on anything without losing faith in what they really want first."

"And that's why you're so happy today, right? Because you kept the faith and decided you could do better than Nina."

"No. That was a mistake," Gunner said.

"But you just said—"

The investigator waved her off, said, "Look. We're straying a bit far afield here. Whatever mistakes I made with Nina have nothing to do with what we're talking about right now, which is the one-night stand you say Nina had with Shirley Causwell.''

"It's not the one I *say* she had with Shirley. It's the one she *had*," Serrano said, correcting him. "I've got no reason to lie about something like that."

"All right. The one she *had*. You're saying Nina regretted it afterward, but Causwell didn't. That right?"

"Yes."

"And that that was the reason Nina eventually distanced herself from you. Because she was afraid your intentions were the same as Causwell's."

"Yes."

"It had nothing to do with you rummaging through her things, or anything like that."

"No. I told you. I went through her things, yes, but only to find her bracelet."

"And you never did, I take it."

"No. I never did. She told me she'd given it away."

"Given it away to whom?"

"She wouldn't say. I always felt she was lying, in any case. I think she still had it, she just couldn't bring herself to wear it anymore. She was convinced I'd meant it as a token of my love for her, and nothing I ever said could change her mind about it. Nothing."

"And you blame Causwell for that."

"Yes. Her and Wendy both."

"What else do you blame Causwell for? Nina's murder, maybe?"

"Nina's murder?"

"That's right. You said Nina's husband wasn't the only one who might have wished her ill. Remember? You said both Causwell and Gary Stanhouse could have, as well. I took that to mean you felt they each had a *motive* for killing her, if nothing else. Wasn't that what you were trying to say?"

"Yes, but . . . to my knowledge, that's *all* they had. A motive."

"And Causwell's motive would have been what? Revenge?"

"I don't know. I guess that's what you'd call it, revenge. She was a spurned lover. Spurned lovers kill to enact revenge on the person who rejected them, right?"

"Sometimes. Sometimes not. They kill out of jealousy from time to time, as well."

"Jealousy?"

"Sure. She could have been jealous of somebody else Nina was seeing, or somebody she *thought* Nina was seeing. Couldn't she?"

"I suppose. But—you don't mean *me,* do you? You aren't suggesting she was jealous of *me?*"

Gunner shrugged, said, "Why not? If Singer could get the wrong idea about your relationship with Nina, why couldn't Causwell?"

"Because Shirley's a lot smarter than that, I think. Wendy's excuse is that she's paranoid about such things, like I said. But Shirley isn't. Shirley can tell the difference between what's real and what's imagined."

"Okay. So jealousy's out. Her motive was revenge, in your opinion."

"Yes."

"And Stanhouse? What about him?"

"The same. Revenge. He was in love with Nina too."

"And Nina rejected him."

Serrano nodded her head. "Yes. He was her boss, like I told you earlier, but he wanted to be more. He kept trying to get her to go out with him, and she kept telling him she wasn't interested. When she couldn't get him to leave her alone, she reported him to his supervisors, but all that succeeded in doing was getting her fired. *He* was stalking *her,* but she was the one who lost her job. It often works out like that, I'm afraid."

"She told you he'd been stalking her?"

"Yes. At least, she said he'd followed her home a couple of times. And would call her there, every now and then. That sounds like stalking, doesn't it?"

"You know if he ever got violent with her?"

"Violent? No." Serrano shook her head. "I never heard

about anything like that. But that doesn't mean it didn't happen.''

"Did Nina have any plans to sue over her firing? Or file a complaint with the EEOC, at least?''

Serrano shook her head again, said, "Not that I was aware of. She probably figured she couldn't win, so why bother?''

"Did Stanhouse ever show up at Sisterhood? Either while you were there, or at some other time when you weren't?''

"If he did, no one ever told me about it. Ask Wendy, she'd know better if he'd ever been there than I would.''

The investigator nodded, acknowledging the merit of the suggestion. "Now tell me about Nina's photography,'' he said.

"Her photography? You mean the stuff she did with the camera I gave her?''

"Yes.''

"What do you want to know about it?''

"Not much, really. Just what kind of photographs they were, and who or what was in them. That sort of thing.''

"Why?''

"Let's just say I'm curious.''

"Well, most of what she did was similar to my work, as you might imagine. They were character studies, of people at the house primarily. Some candid, some posed. All black-and-white, all rather crude and childlike. But good. Some even very good.''

"Where are these pictures now? Do you know?''

"I have a few of them here. I was the one who developed them, of course. But the majority of them were with her, I wouldn't know where they are now.''

"Would it be possible to see the ones you have? If they're somewhere close at hand?''

"I don't see why not. Hold on, I'll just be a minute.''

She disappeared toward the back of the room, through a door Gunner suspected led to the office she had alluded to earlier. She was gone longer than the minute promised, but not by much. Gunner had just started leafing through the stack of new photographs she'd been mounting on the walls, when she returned, a large manila folder in her right hand.

"Here they are," she said.

There were five of them. All black-and-white eight-by-tens, shot in what appeared to Gunner to be various parts of Singer's Sisterhood House. Two of the subjects he recognized; the other pair were strangers. As Serrano had warned him, the photos were technically crude, but not without promise. Still lifes of women Nina had once shared living quarters with.

An unidentified black woman covering her face with both hands.

A Hispanic woman, also unidentified, kneeling at the side of a double bed, head bowed down in prayer.

The same woman, sitting at a crowded dining-room table, laughing.

Agnes Felker tearing pages out of a magazine, her face an iron mask of devious concentration.

And a blond woman sitting cross-legged on a hardwood floor, watching TV. The same one who had slapped Gunner silly in front of Wendy Singer's office door the previous afternoon; he couldn't remember her name.

Alex Schumacher, Serrano said it was.

"You know her?" Gunner asked.

"Not well, but I know her. Sure."

"She really as crazy as she pretends to be?"

"Oh. I guess you got the treatment yesterday, huh?"

"If getting your face slapped into next Tuesday is the treatment, yeah. I did."

"She say anything to you afterward, by any chance?"

"Not much. Does she usually?"

"Sometimes she recites a riddle, or a rhyme. Sometimes both."

"I didn't get a riddle or a rhyme. Just a smile."

"Good for you. She didn't rub it in. Anyway, in answer to your question, I don't think she's crazy, no. Alex just likes to shock people, that's all. It's her way of getting attention."

"You don't think it goes any deeper than that?"

"No. You'd expect to see it manifest itself in other ways, if it did. But it never does. Slapping a strange man's face every now and then is as aberrant as her behavior ever gets, at least as far as I know."

Gunner nodded as he looked over the five photographs again. Searching for something *significant* in one or more of them; something pronounced, or off center, that might catch his eye and give him some reason to wonder if it wasn't a photograph Nina had taken that eventually led to her death . . .

But there was nothing like that here.

"Well. I think I've taken up enough of your time," Gunner said, handing the photos back to his hostess. "Don't you?"

"I was glad to help," Serrano said, shaking his hand again.

He gave her a business card as she walked him to the door, and told her to give him a call, anything else came to mind she thought he might need to know.

"Oh, and by the way," he said, "I almost forgot to ask."

"Yes?"

"Where were you last Tuesday? Between the hours of seven P.M. and midnight?"

It was something of a cheap shot, waiting until he was walking out the door to ask her the question, but he wanted to see how she'd answer it after being led to believe the subject was never going to come up.

"I was working. Why?"

"Here locally, or somewhere out of town?"

"Out of town? Who told you I was out of town?"

"Nobody. But the ladies out at Sisterhood had said you were doing some work out on the East Coast somewhere, and that was why—" He stopped short, remembering something. "Oh. Wait a minute."

"Yes?"

"I was going to say that that was why you haven't been out to the house lately. Because you've been out of town. But you've already explained the real reason for that, haven't you? About why you haven't been around, I mean."

"Because Wendy thinks I was Nina's lover? Yes, I did," Serrano said.

"Then you haven't been out to the East Coast at all, have you?"

"The East Coast? No. I haven't. I was in Detroit for two weeks back in November, but that was about it."

"Sure."

"It's nice to hear Wendy's made up a cover story for me, though. Better that my friends at her place think I've been out of town than that I'm a camera-wielding lesbian on the prowl for abused, defenseless young women like them. Right?"

She tried to smile, not wanting to appear too bitter about the slight, but it was an effort wasted.

Getting stabbed in the back was something only a fool could learn to smile about.

He was almost home when he remembered his promise to Mickey.

Roman Goody was somebody Gunner had tried to put in his "Never Again, So Help Me God" file nearly one week ago, but the man wouldn't stay in the past. He wanted Gunner's attention at least one more time, and he was apparently willing to call his office number at least two or three times a day until he got it. Gunner wasn't the one taking Goody's calls, so it would have been just fine with him to wait the fat man out, but since Mickey had already lost patience with that approach . . .

Gunner had to go see Goody tonight.

"Shit," he said, turning the Cobra around.

It was a few minutes past five in the early evening, approaching the zenith of L.A.'s rush hour. Somebody had turned the thermostat down on the city, so that all Gunner could see above his head was a gray, somewhat chilly mist that the sun could not seem to burn its way through. It was almost cold, but not quite. Winter in the City of Angels, Gunner thought to himself.

*Brrrrr.*

A full two blocks before Gunner reached Best Way Electronics, he knew he should have called Goody sooner. The red and white Fire Department ambulance and all the black-

and-whites parked out front were a dead giveaway.

He had hell getting through, but eventually he talked the uniforms out front into letting him inside the building, having had to represent himself as a private investigator still under Goody's employ. One of them told him what all the excitement was about, though Gunner had already known. He had only asked to have his suspicions confirmed before he could go inside and find something worse than what he was expecting, though what that could possibly be, he didn't know.

What he was expecting was about all the bad news he could stand.

# thirteen

THEY WERE GETTING READY TO WHEEL THE BODY OUT ON a gurney when he reached Goody's office in the back, lab guys and plainclothes detectives going over the room like paleontologists poring over a dig.

Somebody had beaten Goody to a bloody pulp sometime early that morning and left him in his office to grow ripe. His store had been open for business for more than six hours before one of his employees finally decided he was worth worrying about, and opened his locked office door with a spare set of keys.

The Compton PD detectives working the case were strangers to Gunner, but they treated him decently enough. Their names were Bertelsen and Bunche; white cop, black cop, left shoe, right shoe. Different, yet the same. Once they'd put him through his paces a bit, making him explain and explain again who he was and what he was doing there, they pretty much told Gunner anything he wanted to know. And in return, he gave them a probable name for the perp they were looking for: Russell Dartmouth.

They'd let him take a peek under the sheet covering Goody's body before the men from the coroner's office rolled it away, and he'd told them then that Goody's face—or what was left of it—had Dartmouth's mark all over it. It was what his own face would have looked like had the big man been allowed to finish the job he'd started on Gunner only the week before.

"How can you be so sure it's him?" Bunche asked, his back teeth vigorously pulverizing a mouthful of mini-mints. Every time Gunner turned around, he was working on another fistful of the things.

"Because he's crazy," Gunner said. "I told you."

He lingered around the crime scene for nearly an hour, permitted to look but not to touch. It would have suited him fine to leave as soon as they gave him the okay, but he figured a quick exit might lead them to wonder what kind of investigator he was, not being curious enough to even look the place over. There wasn't much to see, just the mess Goody's killer had made drop-kicking him around, but Gunner went through the motions of examining it anyway, actually more interested in all the cop talk going on around him than anything else. The police photographer telling one of the lab techs a bad joke, something about a nearsighted squirrel and a horny raccoon; Bertelsen and Bunche waxing philosophical about the Endicott homicide, still unsolved and driving them nuts; Bunche and the M.E. arguing over the delay in the Gatewood autopsy; Bertelsen and one of the uniforms raking some cop named Brimmer over the coals for getting caught out of uniform with a hooker named Chip, who, as near as Gunner could tell, was a transvestite. Fascinating stuff, the conversations one could hear taking place at a crime scene. Irreverent, vulgar, and generally trivial to the point of game show fodder—but fascinating.

When the photographer started up another joke, this one dealing with a hippo in a gay bar, Gunner decided he'd been entertained enough.

He gave Bertelsen and Bunche the address in Venice where he and Dartmouth had had their little brawl, and left, Bertelsen suggesting as he walked away that he watch his back for a while. He'd shrugged the comment off at the time, but inside of five minutes, just as he was turning the key in the Cobra's ignition, it inspired him to make a connection between two things he had somehow failed to connect before: Dartmouth and the unsettling phone call he'd received at three o'clock that morning. The memory was too vague now to be sure, but looking back on it, it seemed to Gunner that the caller who had so ominously warned him to "get ready to die" could indeed have been Dartmouth. It was an idea that actually answered more questions than it asked, not the least of which was why Goody might have wanted to spend the last two days of his life trying desperately to get the investigator on the phone. If Dartmouth had been showering him with phone calls similar to the one Gunner had received . . . well, it wasn't hard to see Goody thinking it might be nice to have a hired gun like Gunner around to protect his considerable backside.

*I'm just tellin' you what he sounds like to me,* Mickey had said, when Gunner called for messages earlier in the day. *So if somethin' happens later, you can't say I didn't warn you.* Hell if the sonofabitch hadn't been right to be so concerned.

Gunner knew it would be a long time before he heard the end of this one.

His home was empty, but it took him a good fifteen minutes to convince himself of the fact. He'd come in through the back door and gone from room to room, entering each on catlike feet, not hitting a single light until he was done. The Ruger had been in his hand the whole time, ready to put a bullet in anything that might come at him without announcing itself first.

It was the last thing he needed, the specter of Russell Dartmouth hanging over his head to distract him, what with his investigation into Nina Pearson's murder getting more complicated and impenetrable by the second. A lesbian lover and the mentor who'd been mistaken for one; a blonde who liked to slap strange men around, and an old woman who thought "nigger" was a perfectly acceptable noun; the stalker Nina had once worked for, and the overprotective shelter director whose roof she'd lived under just before her death. Individually bizarre they were, and collectively even more so. But where was the murder case hidden among them? Who deserved Gunner's scrutiny, and who deserved his neglect?

Gunner had no idea.

Which was why he spent the better part of his evening trying to sort it all out, stretched out on his living room couch eating leftover fried chicken out of a cardboard bucket, one Bob James CD after another playing on the stereo. James was a favorite of Gunner's, a soft jazz keyboardist whose music was invariably upbeat and soothing, and sometimes his lushly orchestrated arrangements could put Gunner in a zone of inspired thought and reflection. He was hoping that would be the case tonight.

His first thought was of Michael Pearson.

Nina's husband still had the inside track on most likely suspect, but he was starting to get some company. Shirley Causwell and Gary Stanhouse were in the running for that title too, if what Trini Serrano had said about both this afternoon could be believed. Unfortunately, that was a big if. Much of what Serrano had told Gunner he'd had little trouble accepting, but this business about the bracelet she'd been trying to find when she went through Nina's things didn't quite sit right with him, he wasn't sure why. She struck him as the kind of woman who would make no secret of her desire for Nina, if she had in fact felt any; she seemed far more insulted by the idea that Wendy Singer thought she was a cradle robber than that she was a lesbian. So when she said her love for Nina had been strictly platonic in nature, it seemed safe to assume she was telling the truth.

And yet . . .

She'd made a major mystery out of the inscription she claimed the missing bracelet bore. Why? Why be so tight-lipped about that, and so forthcoming with everything else? If the inscription wasn't somehow shameful to her, or incriminating, why bother withholding it from him?

It didn't make sense.

Finding the bracelet himself would help to explain things, of course, but Gunner wasn't so sure he needed to be making that a priority just now. Not with Causwell and Stanhouse emerging as far more deserving objects of his attention. Even before Serrano had pointed an accusatory finger in their direction, Gunner had pretty much made the pair for what they were: wannabe suitors of the dead woman, emotionally disturbed and potentially violent. Causwell's feelings for Nina he'd merely had his suspicions about, based on the way she'd sometimes said Nina's name, or the open contempt she'd shown for the man who'd been abusing Nina for years—as if she took the abuse personally, like something *she'd* been the target of, and not Nina—but Stanhouse had been an open book to Gunner from the beginning. Both people had loved Nina, and both had been denied her. The challenge for Gunner now was to determine which of the two, if either one of them, had been enraged and/or discouraged enough by losing her to kill her.

Gunner's guess at the moment was Stanhouse.

Then there was Agnes Felker to consider. Being a basket case and a murderer were not always the same thing, but the two roles did intersect with certain regularity. And Felker was most definitely a basket case. A gun-toting basket case, in fact. Which brought to mind the one thing she had that no one else Gunner had talked to over the last two days appeared to: a suitable weapon. A shotgun similar or identical to the one somebody had used to spray Nina's pretty little head all over her kitchen. It was the only thing that really made Felker a viable suspect—having once been slapped by Nina at the dinner table didn't seem to give her much in the way of motive—but until he heard from Poole regarding those ballistics tests, the weapon had to be looked upon as reason enough for Gunner to keep the book on Felker open.

As for Wendy Singer and Angela Glass? They were wild cards. Both had feelings for Nina that seemed to go beyond the norm, but that was it. Singer was worth watching only because she'd been less than candid with Gunner about a number of things, all of them seemingly inconsequential, and Glass's only apparent qualification as Nina's murderer was her alibi. She'd told him she was at the library at the time of Nina's death, and that would have been weak even if she'd said it with some conviction.

Gunner finished off his third bottle of Red Dog beer and opened up a fourth, deciding on the spot to start the next day back at Sisterhood House. Gary Stanhouse was the suspect

he most wanted to pursue, but Stanhouse was going to have
to wait. Because all Gunner knew about the attorney right
now was where he worked and the license plate number of
his car. The latter could be turned into a home address eventually, maybe even as early as Thursday afternoon, but until
then, there didn't seem to be anything Gunner could do with
Stanhouse but harass him down at Bowers, Bain and Lyle
for the second day in a row, a tactic that almost certainly
would buy the investigator nothing more than some kind of
official escort from the building. The way to work Stanhouse,
Gunner knew, was to squeeze him, but not just at work. At
home, at the supermarket, at the health club—even at church
on Sunday. And that was going to take time. And patience.

In the meantime, he'd go back to Sisterhood House and
talk to Causwell. Confront her with Serrano's charges that
she'd been in love with Nina, and see what developed. He
could get her mad enough, she just might tell him more than
she wanted him to know. After that . . .

He never could get focused on the "after that." He became too preoccupied with the odd sensation that something
was eluding him. Something important. It was a feeling he
had often, and sometimes it meant something, and sometimes
it didn't. It was either a significant piece of data trying to
dislodge itself from his brain, or just an imaginary one, like
the itch an amputee feels on a leg that is no longer there.

Gunner swallowed some more beer and waited for the
truth to reveal itself.

But he was waiting in vain.


Hours later, the phone rang twice. First at two A.M., then at
two-thirty.

The first call woke him from a sound sleep, the phone's
shrill ring jarring his nerves the same way it had the night
before. Only this time, he answered it immediately, having
not a doubt in his mind who he'd find on the other end of
the line.

"Dartmouth? That you?" he asked.

"Your turn next, motherfucker," the caller said. Still

whispering into the mouthpiece of the phone like a depraved ghost.

"You come after me, you crazy sonofabitch, I'm gonna have something for you. You hear what I'm saying? Save yourself some grief and turn yourself in."

Silence.

"Dartmouth!"

"You gonna bleed, brother. You like to bleed?"

The line went dead.

Gunner was still trying to decide if the voice had indeed been Dartmouth's, when the phone rang a second time, thirty minutes later. He let it ring for several minutes before he picked it up, not completely convinced the sound was real and not something he was simply imagining.

"Look, you sick fuck—" he started to say.

And then Ziggy said, "Whoa, kid, whoa! It's me!"

"Ziggy?"

"Sorry to wake you, kid, but I just found out myself, and I didn't wanna take a chance on missing you in the morning."

It was just as Gunner had thought, almost twenty-four hours earlier: A ringing telephone at this ungodly hour really *was* the sound of death calling.

He was out of the house by eight the next morning. With Pearson dead, he had to start acting like his next hour of freedom would be his last, because it could very well be. All Poole had to do was decide to hold a grudge, and the DA's office would do the rest. It was like Ziggy had said: Gunner could become a wanted man at any time.

Sticking to the plan he had formulated the night before, he made his first stop at Sisterhood House, intending to have a second go-round with both Shirley Causwell and Wendy Singer. But just as he was trying to pull in, Singer was pulling out of the front gate, looking somewhat harried and disheveled behind the wheel of an old Ford station wagon. She would have driven right past him if he hadn't honked his horn for her to stop.

He got out of the Cobra and walked over to her window, just as she was rolling it down.

"I'm sorry, Mr. Gunner, but this is really a very bad time," she said.

"Trouble?"

"It's Agnes Felker. Have you spoken to her yet?"

"I saw her for a few moments yesterday, yeah. Why? What happened?"

Her voice slightly breaking, Singer said, "She's in the hospital. I was just going out to see her now."

Gunner started to ask why, then realized he already knew the answer. Instead, he said, "You mind if I come along?"

Singer shrugged and waited for him to park his car.

Her doctors did not expect Agnes Felker to live. She was fifty-seven years old, and had suffered enough serious injuries to kill a woman half her age. One of her attending physicians told Singer she had suffered a fractured skull, a dislocated shoulder, four broken ribs, and a bruised kidney. She had also lost four teeth. Asleep in her bed in the emergency ward at County-USC hospital, she looked like a mummified corpse awaiting burial, connected to a panoply of machines by more wires and hoses than either Gunner or Singer cared to count.

The ambulance that had brought her in had actually been called for her boyfriend Otha, who was dead. He was dead because Felker had shot a hole in his chest big enough to put a man's leg through, after he had laid his hands on her for the last and final time. The way it was explained to Singer, the couple's neighbors had first heard the sound of a shotgun blast, then found Otha out in the hallway outside the couple's apartment, bleeding all over the carpet like a stuck pig. The neighbors called 911, but by the time the paramedics arrived, the wounded man was beyond their help. They found Felker in her living room before she could expire, the shotgun she had finally found the nerve to use beside her mangled body. No one in charge of her care would even pretend that they liked her chances of pulling through.

Felker's daughter, Betty, had been the one who called

Singer down, knowing the shelter director from her mother's time as a resident out at Sisterhood House. As big as her mother was tiny, Betty had no patience for Agnes's submissive role as an abuse victim; in fact, she was downright cold about it. As soon as Singer and Gunner had arrived, she'd left them to visit the cafeteria downstairs, showing more signs of annoyance than grief, though she did seem to be finding some satisfaction in Otha's death, which she said had been long overdue.

Singer was far more emotionally distraught. When the doctors would only allow her a look at Felker through the emergency room window, she tried to argue her way through the doors, but her heart just wasn't in it. She was like a grieving mother: too drained and tired to do much more than raise her voice. Gunner watched her suffer and could not help but be impressed; her compassion for Felker was real and deeply felt.

After about an hour, Singer grew tired of waiting for something bad to happen and told Gunner she was ready to leave.

Downstairs in the car, she finally broke down.

It was a long, bitter cry, the end result of something that had been building up inside her for some time. Gunner tried to reach for her, but she waved him off, acting like his touch was something to be avoided at all costs.

"No. Don't," she said.

Gunner sat back and waited.

Eventually, she wiped her eyes with a handkerchief he'd given her, staring straight out the windshield to avoid his gaze, and said, "I'm sorry. I didn't intend for you to see that."

"It's okay," Gunner said.

"No. It's not. I should have developed a much thicker skin by now. It's ridiculous, a person in my line of work not being able to handle this sort of thing better."

"It's not ridiculous."

She finally turned to face him, blue eyes blazing, and said, "You didn't have anything to do with it, did you? When you

went out to see her yesterday, I mean? Because if you
*did*—''

"Me? What could *I* have done to cause this?"

"I don't know. I only know Otha was a very jealous man,
and something must have triggered his attack. I just thought,
if you had words with him yesterday, if you gave him any
reason at all to believe you and Agnes were seeing each
other . . .''

Gunner shook his head, said, "I never said a word to the
man. In fact, I never even met him. I saw somebody outside
their apartment building who I *thought* might be him, yeah,
but that was about it.''

She studied his face for a moment, then nodded, believing
him. "Of course. I don't know what I was thinking.''

"Forget it,'' Gunner said, smiling so she'd know he was
being sincere.

He hadn't thought the gesture would earn him a smile in
return, but it did—and he knew right then it was time to
reevaluate his opinion of her.

She wanted to go back to Sisterhood House immediately,
but he talked her into sharing a late breakfast with him instead. She looked different to him somehow, now that he'd
caught a glimpse of the woman behind the mother figure,
and he was curious to find out what it would be like to spend
some time with her outside of her work environment.

They went downtown to the Pantry Cafe and sat at a booth
in the back. The early-morning rush was over, but the famous
establishment was still busy, filled with wonderful sounds
and aromas, the air thick with a hundred conversations going
on at once. They both had coffee, Gunner with patty sau-
sages, eggs, and pancakes, Singer with oatmeal and raisin
toast, no butter.

"I need to ask you a question,'' Singer said at one point.
Gunner said, "Sure.''

"Not that I think you're an expert, or anything, but . . .
you might have some insight on the matter.''

Gunner watched her stir sugar into her coffee and waited.

"Why do black men do it? Hate their women, I mean.
What's the reason for it, exactly?''

"I didn't realize we all had that problem," Gunner said.

"I'm sorry. I phrased that badly, didn't I?"

"No, no. You just made a sweeping generalization. Maybe you should try it again. Ask me something like, why do *so many* black men *seem* to hate their women?"

"All right. Why do they?"

"I don't know. You said yourself, I'm no expert on the subject. You, on the other hand, have experience in the field. *You* should be telling *me* how it works."

"I know. I should. But I'm curious to hear your perspective on it. Being a black man yourself—"

"We don't all think alike, Ms. Singer. No more than we all look alike. Men like Otha are as foreign to me as they are to you—*I* don't know what makes them tick."

"But you can guess."

"My guess would be that brothers like Otha have a self-esteem problem, number one. And number two, they can't handle the pressure they feel black women put on them to be perfect. Perfect lovers, fathers, providers—the works."

"Would you care to elaborate on that a little?"

"Elaborate? No. What's to elaborate?"

"Well, when you say these men have a self-esteem problem—"

"I mean that they feel worthless. Like they're society's most expendable objects. They consider themselves powerless, incapable of controlling the direction of their own lives, so—"

"So they seek control elsewhere."

"Yes."

"And the pressure to be perfect? What did you mean by that?"

"I meant that the standard some black women hold a man up to is unreasonably high. And that failing to meet that standard can sometimes do as much to cut a man down at the knees as anything another man could ever do to him. Possibly even more."

"You're saying the black woman's expectations are too great."

"I'm saying generations of abuse have made skeptics out

of a great number of black women today, and skeptics are the hardest people in the world to satisfy. Never mind love and respect.''

"And this is why black men feel entitled to hate them. To call them bitches, and hos, and all that.''

Gunner glared at her. "You asked me where the hostility comes from, and I told you what I think. I wasn't attempting to justify anything.''

"Do you think you could?''

"I wouldn't try. Look, I told you Tuesday, I don't beat women, and I don't care for the jerks who do. You don't want to take my word for that, fine, but please stop asking me to defend myself every fifteen minutes. All right?''

Singer started to say something, but chose to remain silent instead.

"What is it? Do I remind you of somebody, or something? Some guy you used to know who treated women badly? Is that it?''

"No,'' Singer said. "It isn't you. It's me. Generations of abuse have made skeptics out of *all* of us, Mr. Gunner. Black women, white women—all of us. Only some of us are better at working around it than others.''

She'd said it like it was a deep, dark secret, her eyes darting here and there, head turned away from him, the fingers of both hands drumming silently on the sides of her coffee cup. And suddenly Gunner saw something in her he had never seen before: a victim. A woman who knew how to survive abuse, because she had survived it herself.

"Who was it?'' Gunner asked her.

Singer opened her mouth to say something, stopped, and then said, "Let the cat out of the bag, did I?'' Trying to smile.

"You don't want to talk about it, we don't have to,'' Gunner said. "It's none of my business, really.''

"He was my second husband. Tony,'' Singer said, jumping right into the story before she could lose the nerve to tell it. "I was twenty-six, he was thirty-one. We met at a going-away party for a mutual friend. He was a print ad salesman, very successful, very handsome. Tall, dark, and all that. I fell in love with him immediately. He never said a cross word to me until the third day of our honeymoon. He'd brought some work along with him to do while we were at the hotel, and I was trying to get him to put it away . . . so he slapped me. Just once, with the back of his hand. He knocked me to the floor, and never said a word.

"Two years later, he was still doing it. Two, sometimes three times a week. Anytime he was upset, he felt like he needed to let off a little steam, he'd slap me around some. Always with the back of one hand, always to the face. That was his routine. He'd have been a puncher, somebody who likes to use his fists on the body as well as the face, he would've killed me eventually, I'm sure of it. But he wasn't. I was lucky. I didn't feel lucky at the time, but I was."

"How long ago was this?" Gunner asked.

"A little over eight years ago."

"And where is Tony now?"

Singer shook her head. "I don't know. Last I heard, he was up in Sacramento. I haven't spoken to him in years."

"You're divorced, I assume?"

"Yes."

"He didn't have a problem with that?"

"You mean, did he fight it?"

"Yes."

"Well, he wasn't happy about it, but he didn't contest it. I guess that was another way in which I was lucky. Aside from a bitter argument or two, he let me leave rather quietly. Most abusers won't do that. They hang on for dear life, no matter what you do to get free of them.

"So yes, my work at Sisterhood was born of personal experience. But surely, you always suspected that."

"Actually, I never gave it much thought. I suppose if I had, though, I'd have presumed you were an abuse victim yourself, yeah. Thing is . . . you really don't look the type to me, you want to know the truth about it."

"I don't?"

"No. Not at all. You always struck me as someone too self-assured and confident to ever tolerate that sort of thing. From anyone."

Singer smiled. "You'd be surprised. By all the different 'types' there are, I mean. Because anyone who's ever needed to be loved by another human being is vulnerable to abuse, Mr. Gunner. Anyone. I don't care how 'confident' and 'self-assured' they seem to be."

Their waiter came by to refill their coffee cups, then disappeared again, but they held on to the silence he'd brought to their table for several minutes longer, neither one of them sure what direction they wanted the conversation to take from here.

Finally, Gunner said, "I talked to Trini Serrano yesterday." Deciding it was time to start treating this meeting more like an interrogation and less like a first date.

"And?"

"And she told me the real reason she's no longer welcome at Sisterhood House is because you suspected her of luring Nina into a lesbian affair."

Singer thought that over a minute, looking to be building up to something explosive, but finally all she said was, "So now you know."

"In other words, it's true."

"More or less. Yes."

"So why didn't you tell me that Tuesday? Why give me all that crap about her no longer being available to come by?"

"I was trying to spare her some embarrassment. Obviously."

"She insists it isn't true. That she and Nina were only good friends."

"They were. Only she wanted them to be more than that."

"And if she did? Why was that a problem?"

"Because women come to Sisterhood House to get well again, Mr. Gunner. Not to get laid. They're hurt, and they're damaged, and they're extremely susceptible to all manner of suggestion. So for that reason alone, I have always been very outspoken in my opposition to people becoming romantically involved during their stay with us. *All* people. Nina was in no condition to be courted by anyone, and Trini knew that.

But she was trying to get Nina into bed anyway, and that's what eventually led Nina to leave us. Weeks before she was ready, I might add.''

"Did Nina tell you that?"

"Yes."

"She said *Trini* was pressuring her into a lesbian relationship?"

"In so many words, yes. She did."

"You ever see any evidence to that effect? Anything tangible, I mean?"

"Anything tangible?"

"Like a bracelet, for instance. Inscribed. Something Trini might have given Nina to demonstrate her affection for her. That sort of thing."

Singer shook her head. "I never saw anything like that, no. Who—"

"Trini says she gave Nina a bracelet like that just before Nina left the house. She said it was inscribed with some words of friendship that Nina mistook for something else. Something more intimate. You're sure you never saw it?"

"I'm sure."

"In that case, I'm confused. If Nina was trying to get you to believe that Trini was interested in her sexually . . ." Gunner fell silent, thinking.

"What?"

The investigator shook his head, said, "Never mind. Scratch that."

"Scratch what? What were you going to say?"

"Well . . . I was going to say she should have shown you the bracelet. What better way to prove to you that what she was saying about Trini was true? But then I remembered that Trini said Nina had lost it. Lost it or chucked it, one or the other, she didn't know which. Either way, Nina didn't have it anymore. And that would explain why she didn't show it to you, of course. If she no longer *had* it . . ." He shrugged.

"What else did Trini tell you?" Singer asked.

"About what?"

"About anything. I'm curious to know."

"You think she might have fed me a pack of lies, is that it?"

"I'm concerned that she might have misled you about some things, yes."

Gunner didn't answer for some time, waiting until he was sure how much he did and did not want to say. Finally, he said, "She told me she wasn't the only woman at Sisterhood pursuing Nina sexually, for one thing."

"Referring to Shirley Causwell, of course."

Gunner's face registered his surprise.

"I told you, Mr. Gunner. It's my job to know what happens in my house. Shirley had eyes for Nina too, I saw that right away."

"Then why—"

"Why did I ask Trini to leave and not Shirley? Because Shirley I had some control over. Trini, I didn't. Shirley is a resident, Trini wasn't. When I asked Shirley to back off, she listened to me. Trini wouldn't."

"Shirley agreed to leave Nina alone?"

"Reluctantly, yes. I told her she could have any kind of relationship with Nina she wanted to have, once they were both out of the house, but until then, I wanted her to treat Nina as a friend, and nothing more. And that's what she did. If Trini told you it was Shirley who drove Nina from Sisterhood, she was lying. Trini was the one who wouldn't stop badgering Nina, not Shirley."

Again, Gunner fell silent, trying to absorb what she was saying.

"You didn't think I needed to hear any of this before now?" he asked.

"I told you Nina had friends, but no enemies. And that was true. Why should I have wanted to say any more than that?"

"Because unrequited love is an excellent motive for murder, Ms. Singer. That never occurred to you?"

"Frankly, Mr. Gunner, no. It didn't. Look, I've already told you who murdered Nina. If you choose not to believe me, that's your business."

"But if both Trini and Shirley were in love with her—"

Singer shook her head vigorously and said, "It doesn't matter. They didn't do it. They didn't do it any more than Virgie Olivera did."

"Virgie Olivera?"

"Yes. You don't remember Virgie? She was the girl you asked me about Tuesday before you left. The one Angela told you had once pulled a gun on Nina out in the field."

"And you said her boyfriend made her do it. The Mexican Mafia hero."

"Ricky Salcido. Yes."

"So what about her?"

"She's dead. Her and Ricky both. I'd been thinking about calling her ever since you reminded me of her, just to see how she was doing, and yesterday, I did. The number we had for her was at her sister's place. Rosie. You never called her yourself?"

"No."

Looking up Virgie Olivera had been something he was saving as a last resort, judging her to be the least of his possible leads. Sometimes, he was clairvoyant like that.

"Anyway, Rosie told me they were dead," Singer went on. "They were both killed at a party last Christmas. They were standing out on the lawn with a group of other people when an argument broke out and . . . somebody drew a gun." She gave her shoulders a little shrug and left it at that.

"Okay. So them I can scratch off my list," Gunner said, actually thankful to have had even this small part of his job done for him.

"And Trini and Shirley?"

Gunner just shook his head.

Singer told him she was ready to go home.

# f o u r t e e n

SHIRLEY CAUSWELL'S RESPONSE TO GUNNER'S ASSERTION that she had been in love with Nina Pearson was surprisingly succinct: "Yeah, so?"

He wasn't sure what else he had been expecting her to say, but he was taken aback nonetheless.

"Then you admit that it's true," he said.

"You think of any reason why I shouldn't?"

"No. But then, I can't think of any reason for you to take this long to tell me about it either."

"You can't? How about, it's none of your fucking business? That's a good reason, isn't it?"

They were standing out in the front yard, beneath the giant avocado tree where Gunner's red Cobra was still parked. They talked with the car between them, because that was how Causwell wanted it. She kept her back to the house's front door, seemingly ready to retreat at any time, given just the slightest provocation.

She was wearing a pale blue summer dress, and sandals. Like a college girl dressed for a spring-morning walk on campus. Gunner tried to focus on her anger, and not her beauty, but it was hard; he liked what he saw, despite himself.

"You didn't think I'd find out anyway?" he asked her.

"I figured somebody would tell you, sure. But so what? What do I care what you know? Who the hell are *you*?"

"I'm the man who's trying to find Nina's murderer. I told you and Angela that two days ago."

"And we told you, the cops already *have* Nina's murderer. Only you're too thick-headed to understand that."

"Meaning Michael again."

"She loved him. She *loved* that sonofabitch!" She was trembling, tears suddenly rolling down both cheeks. "He was a filthy, dirty, mindless piece of shit who didn't deserve to breathe the same air as she did! He made her feel small! He made her feel ugly!" She pounded her chest with one fist, said, "But *I* loved her. *I loved her!* And I could have made her happy, if . . . if . . ."

"If she had let you," Gunner said.

"No! Not if *she* had let me! If *they* had let me! If all her so-called 'friends' had just left us alone and let her make up her own mind about what she wanted to do, and who she wanted to be with. If they had just left us *alone*—"

"Nina wouldn't be dead right now."

"No! She wouldn't! She'd be okay. She and I . . ."

Her voice trailed off.

"What? What would you be?" Gunner asked.

But Causwell was shaking her head at him, a tiny smile playing over her tear-streaked face. "Oh, no. Oh, no, no, no, no, no," she said, laughing now. "Nice try, Mr. Gunner, but no."

"Excuse me?"

"*I* didn't kill her! All right? So you can get that thought out of your tiny little mind right now. I loved her, yes, and I was hurt that she didn't want me, yes—but I didn't kill her. I'm sorry."

She had caught him trying to maneuver her toward a hasty confession, and now he didn't know quite what to say.

She had all the anger and rage a man could ever want to find in a potential murder suspect, but it was all misdirected. If the victim had been anyone else—Singer, Serrano, Angela Glass, or Agnes Felker, even—she'd be perfectly suited for the crime. But Nina? As much as he hated to admit it, Gunner could no longer see it.

"Tell me about Trini and Nina," he said, trying not to

sound as unnerved as he was. "Was Trini trying to seduce her, or not? That's the question."

Causwell smiled again. "What do *you* think?"

"I think I'm asking for *your* opinion, not mine. Am I going to get to hear it, or not?"

"No."

"No?"

"No. She wasn't. Nina thought she was, but she wasn't. It wasn't like that with Trini."

Gunner would have bet money she was going to say just the opposite.

"Are you sure?" he asked.

"Am I sure? No. You asked for my opinion, so I gave it to you. All Trini wanted to be with Nina was friends. Nina only thought she wanted to be more because Wendy had her spooked into thinking that way."

"What about the bracelet Trini gave her? The one with the amorous inscription on it?"

"Bracelet?" Causwell shook her head. "I don't know anything about any bracelet."

"You never saw Nina wear one?"

"A bracelet? No. Only jewelry I ever saw Nina wear were rings. Trini told you she gave her a bracelet?"

"Yeah. But I'm beginning to think she was putting me on."

"You mean she lied to you."

"Somebody's been lying to me," Gunner said.

There'd been an accusation hidden in the comment, of course—but Causwell acted like she hadn't heard it.

Speaking to Angela Glass again wasn't on his agenda, but he asked for her anyway, figuring as long as he was here he could ask her about Nina's bracelet. Give her the same chance he'd given Singer and Causwell to say she'd never even heard of such a thing, let alone seen one. Singer told him she was out.

He called both Ziggy and Mickey from Sisterhood before he left, and each man told him the same thing: No one from the LAPD or the DA's office had called this morning looking for him. Yet.

Because it was no longer fair to Mickey to do otherwise, he finally brought his landlord up to speed on Russell Dartmouth, making him promise to call the cops at the first sign of anybody who even resembled the crazed maniac. Mickey made noises like he was stupid enough to try and take Dartmouth on by himself, he showed his face around the shop, but they both knew he was only talking.

What Gunner planned to do now was turn his attention to Gary Stanhouse, dig up a home address for the attorney and prepare to shadow him all weekend long, if necessary. But three blocks from Sisterhood House, on his way in to Mickey's, he was sitting in the Cobra at a crosswalk, waiting for a trio of women to cross from the south side of Adams Boulevard to the north side, when a flurry of activity to his right caught his eye. He turned to see two black people going at it, a man and a woman, the man trying to force the woman into the passenger seat of a parked car, the woman trying to pull out of his grasp. It was a heated, noisy altercation, but it didn't turn really ugly until the man got tired of pushing and pulling and slapped his larger partner twice, hard. Gunner could actually hear the blows land from where he was sitting in the car. He also recognized the woman who had absorbed them.

Angela Glass.

He yanked the Cobra's wheel, turning right off of Adams onto Cimarron, and parked across the street. Neither Glass nor her friend noticed as he sprinted toward them, the man too busy cramming Glass's sobbing form down into his car, Glass herself too busy trying to keep him from closing the door on her. Coming up behind him, Gunner clapped one hand on the man's right shoulder and said, "Hey."

The smaller man turned around and Gunner slapped him with an open right hand across his face, trying to leave an imprint of his palm on the man's left cheek he would have to live with for the rest of his life. With a sound equal to a small thunderclap, the blow lifted the man off his feet and onto his ass, his eyes filling with tears and his face already starting to swell. He tried to scramble to his feet, but Gunner closed on him quickly to stand directly over him, looking like someone who wanted very badly to put him in his grave.

"That's called being bitch-slapped," the investigator said, his voice even, his expression neutral. "Hurts like hell, doesn't it?"

Again, the smaller, lighter-skinned man tried to rise, his humiliation driving him, and Gunner said, "Get up so I can give you some more. Come on. You've got some teeth on the east side of your head need to be over on the west side, let's go."

"Mr. Gunner, no!" Glass cried behind him.

"Who the fuck are you?" her friend demanded, trying to clear the tears from his eyes with the back of one forearm. He looked to Gunner to be in his early twenties, well under six feet in height but heavy, a combination that gave him the overall build of a slimmed-down Buddha. His head was clean-shaven, but his upper lip was not; he had labored to grow a mustache there that you could almost miss if you weren't looking for it.

"I'm a friend of the lady's," Gunner told him.

"A friend?"

"That's right. You have a problem with that?"

"Mr. Gunner, please! Leave him alone!" Glass pleaded, coming up on Gunner's right to take his arm. "You don't understand!"

Gunner finally took his eyes off the man sprawled out beneath him to look at her. "I understand he was kicking your ass for everybody on Adams Boulevard to see. I understand that," he said.

"I know, I know, but—"

"That ain't none of your motherfuckin' bus'ness!" her friend said. "We wuz havin' a private argument!"

"You stupid ass. You were slapping the shit out of a woman on a busy street corner at high noon," Gunner said. "How the fuck do you figure that's a private argument?"

"Don't matter what it was! It didn't have nothin' to do with you, you didn't have no bus'ness jumpin' in it! Tell 'im, Angela!"

"He's right, Mr. Gunner! It was a private argument!" Glass agreed.

Gunner glared at her, incredulous. "Say what?"

"We were just havin' a little disagreement, that's all. Buster wasn't tryin' to hurt me or anything."

"You hear that? You hear what she just said?" Buster said, finally clambering to his feet. He'd been inching away from Gunner steadily, and now he felt far enough out of the investigator's reach to brave standing up. "We wuz havin' a disagreement! I wasn't hurtin' the bitch!"

Gunner looked at Glass, said, "I don't care what he was doing. He's going home, and you're coming with me. Right now."

"No!" Glass said.

"She don't wanna go with you, man!" Buster screamed.

Turning to face him, Gunner said, "I mean it, june bug. You're not in that car and out of my sight in thirty seconds, it's you and me. Till somebody isn't breathing anymore. You think I'm fucking around, keep standing there."

"Mr. Gunner, please!" Glass protested again.

"Angela, goddamnit—" Buster started to say.

"Angela's got no say in this," Gunner told him. "I'm talking to *you*. You've got twenty seconds."

"But Mr. Gunner—" Glass said.

"Shut up and go get in my car. The red one, across the street. Right now." When Glass opened her mouth to complain, he said, "Or would you rather I went back to Sisterhood alone and told Wendy Singer about all this? That what you want?"

Glass didn't say anything.

"Go on and get in the car," Gunner told her again.

She looked at Buster imploringly.

"You get in that car, bitch, it's your ass," he said.

It had been the wrong thing to say. She heard the word "bitch" and her face changed, indecision turning to angry resolve, right before his eyes.

She went and got in Gunner's car.

Both men watched her go, then faced each other once more.

"You're down to five seconds, sweet pea," Gunner said. He was rubbing his right palm with his left hand like he thought he might soon have to use it again.

Buster just stood there, sizing him up, trying to assess his chances against this larger, wiser, seemingly all too earnest opponent, and eventually reached the conclusion any smart man would have: He was way out of his league.

"This ain't over, motherfucker," he said, pointing a finger at Gunner's face even as he walked in a wide circle to get around him. "Don't think it is. You shoulda minded your *own* goddamn bus'ness!"

Gunner watched in silence as he made his way over to the driver's side of the primer-spotted, big-tired Toyota Corolla sitting at the curb.

"Next time you see me, I'm gonna have somethin' for you," Buster said.

"Shit. The next time you see me, you'd *better* have something for me," Gunner said, smiling. No one was ever as bad as they were *going* to be, the next time Gunner saw them.

Glass's friend jumped in the car, then glared out the open side window at the woman sitting in Gunner's red Cobra over on the opposite side of the street. "I'll talk to you later!" he promised Glass, before starting the Toyota's engine and roaring away, laying down a long trail of rubber on the pavement behind him.

After a while, Gunner joined Glass in the Cobra and said, "What the hell are you doing?" Careful to sound more disappointed than angry, because he wanted her to feel stupid, not defensive.

"I didn't need your help," she said.

"You need *somebody's* goddamn help. Running around with a gutless punk like that."

"He's not like that, Mr. Gunner. You don't know him."

"I know he thinks your name is 'bitch.' And that when he wants you to do something you don't want to do, his answer to the problem is to put his foot in your ass. I know that."

Glass shook her head, said, "You don't know what you're

talkin' about! You don't know him! He ain't like that!''

''You won't get in the car, so he's going to *put* you in the car. Right? Even if he has to break every fucking bone in your body to do it!''

''That's not how it was! I . . . He wasn't ready for me to go yet. That's all. He *loves* me. He loves me, an' it's hard for him to say good-bye, we only been together a few minutes. It's *hard* for him.''

''But it's not hard on you, huh? When he feels like putting a fist down your throat because you've done something to piss him off. That's not hard on *you*.''

''He's gettin' help! All right? He's tryin' to change! You think I'd be with 'im if he wasn't tryin' to change?''

Gunner shook his head, hoping to end this conversation before it could go any further, and said, ''Save it, Angela. He was right, this was none of my business. He likes treating you like a speed bag, and you like being treated like one, so forget about it. It's a marriage made in heaven—forgive me for butting in.''

''Mr. Gunner . . .''

He started the car.

Glass grabbed him by the arm and, screaming to be heard over the Ford V-8's throaty rumble, said, ''You can't tell Wendy about any of this! Please! She'll throw me out if she finds out!''

Gunner studied her face, looking for whatever real emotion lay behind it. She was faking it, he could put her out of the car and leave without a backward glance, but if she wasn't . . .

He killed the Cobra's engine again, knowing naked desperation when he saw it.

''How long has this been going on?'' he asked.

''What?''

''All right, get out of the car. You want to play dumb and dumber, go find another partner.''

''No! We . . . Three weeks. It's been goin' on for three weeks.''

''You've been sneaking off to see that idiot for three weeks?''

"Yes. But he's not an idiot."

Gunner grew quiet for a moment. "That's where you were last Tuesday night. With him."

"Yes."

"So that whole story about being at the library—"

"Was a lie. Yes. I'm sorry."

Gunner turned his head away in disgust. "Jesus Christ." He didn't speak again for a long time.

He took her back to Sisterhood House and just dropped her off, never getting out of the car. She was terrified he'd tell Singer everything, but he couldn't see the point. If she wanted to make a joke out of Singer's hospitality and naiveté, that was her choice to make. She couldn't see where she was doing anything wrong in any event, since Buster was ostensibly seeing a counselor about his "aggression problem" twice a week, not because he'd been ordered by the court to do so, but because he loved her and wanted to stop mistreating her. Gunner just shook his head.

He knew that anything he had to say to her, Singer had already said, no doubt a thousand times, but he gave her a brief lecture on the way to the House anyway, if only to give himself the satisfaction of telling her how pathetic she'd just become in his eyes. She wanted to go on being Buster's fool, he couldn't stop her—but he'd be damned if he wasn't going to make her feel bad about it. *He* felt bad about it, why shouldn't *she*?

He drove to Mickey's deep in thought, wondering how many more people he'd once suspected of committing Nina's murder he'd have to write off before the day was done. He was essentially down to two viable candidates, Stanhouse and Serrano, both Causwell and now Glass having given him cause to all but eliminate them from the running. Neither had proven their innocence, exactly, but he could no longer generate any real suspicion about either of them. Causwell, because she'd apparently loved Nina too much to kill her, and Glass, because she'd allegedly been too busy loving someone else, some*where* else, at the time of Nina's death.

Serrano, meanwhile, was looking more and more like a liar—if not a murderer—every minute. Because Glass couldn't remember ever seeing this bracelet the photographer had told him about either. That made three people he had asked about it, and three people who'd claimed ignorance of it. Singer, Causwell, and Glass, a perfect three out of three. Either Nina had been so embarrassed by the gift that she'd never shown it to a living soul, or it was a figment of Serrano's imagination. Something she'd just invented as an excuse for going through Nina's things at the House.

Making his second attempt to drive out to Mickey's in less than two hours, Gunner would have spent the entire trip trying to guess what else, other than the bracelet, Serrano could have been looking for among Nina's possessions, had he not been busy trying to shake the recurring feeling that he was missing something. A word or an object, something seen or heard over the last two days that his conscious mind should have latched on to, but didn't. He thought if he retraced his steps, did a mental review of where he'd been and who he'd talked to since early Tuesday, he might come up with something, but nothing ever clicked. It was maddening. More so now than it had been the night before, when the feeling had last come over him, because now he had to believe it was genuine, that it wasn't just a trick his mind was trying to play on him.

Still, he pulled the Cobra up in front of his landlord's barbershop as confused by the feeling as ever.

He came through the door to find Mickey having a red-letter day. Four customers waiting, one being served. A red-haired brother Gunner knew only as Appleton was sitting in Mickey's chair, head bowed down as the boss man himself put the clippers to the back of his neck; everyone else in the shop was a stranger to Gunner.

Mickey said, "You've got company." Tilting his head sideways toward the rear of the shop.

Gunner stopped walking, wondering if it was already too late to turn around. "Five-oh?" he asked, using the common vernacular for the police.

Mickey shook his head. "A civilian. Said his name is

Stanhouse. Gary Stanhouse. I told him you weren't here and I didn't know when you'd be in, but . . ." He shrugged. "Man said he wanted to wait. Only been back there about five minutes."

Gunner looked at his watch: It was nine minutes after twelve. Right around lunchtime at Bowers, Bain and Lyle.

Stanhouse was sitting on the couch when Gunner came in, fingering the pages of a magazine he'd brought in from the waiting area out front. Gunner didn't notice what it was. Wearing a form-fitting, lightly pin-striped double-breasted suit in a tasteful, earth-tone brown, the attorney stood up upon Gunner's arrival and said, "I hope you don't mind that I waited in here. The barber outside said—"

"It's okay," Gunner told him, before taking a seat behind his desk. "What's going on?"

Stanhouse walked over to the other chair in the room but didn't sit down in it, said, "I thought I'd save us both some trouble by coming to see you, before you could come looking for me again."

"How did you find me?"

"I'm an attorney. It was easy." He wasn't bragging, just stating a fact. Gunner thought he looked nervous, but not upset. Like he'd come here more to negotiate than to dictate terms.

"I hadn't seen the last of you yesterday. Had I?" he asked.

Gunner shrugged and smiled. "That's hard to say."

"No, it isn't. You made it very clear that I was somebody you intended to keep an eye on in your ridiculous search for Nina's murderer. And I can't have that, Mr. Gunner. I cannot function with that kind of thing hanging over my head. Do you understand?"

Gunner didn't say anything.

"So I came here today to try to reason with you. I want you to believe me when I tell you I had nothing to do with Nina's murder. I want to be able to leave here today knowing our paths will never cross again."

"I can't promise you that, Mr. Stanhouse."

"I'm not asking you to promise me anything. I'm just

asking you to hear me out. You can do that much, can't you?''

Gunner fell silent again, thinking it over. "All right. You want to talk to me? Talk to me," he said finally. "But start with where you were two Tuesday nights ago. From six in the evening to about two A.M., specifically.''

"The night Nina died.''

"That's right.''

"I was at home. Working on a brief.''

"Alone?''

"Yes.''

"You didn't leave your home at all that night?''

"No. I didn't.''

"Anybody see you there? Like a pizza deliveryman maybe, or somebody trying to collect for the paper? Anybody like that?''

"No.'' Stanhouse shook his head.

"That's too bad,'' Gunner said.

"You mean because I don't have an alibi.''

"One would have come in handy, don't you think? You wanted to convince me of your innocence?''

"I should have lied to you. Is that what you're saying?''

"I'm saying I haven't heard a damn thing yet that would lead me to believe you're being honest with me, Mr. Stanhouse. And you've been talking for fifteen minutes.''

"What do you want me to say? That Nina got a raw deal at the firm? Okay. She did. You're right, all the charges we made against her were false. I made them up in retaliation for the charges she made against me.''

"Even though they were true.''

"No!''

"You weren't harassing her at work?''

"I wasn't harassing her, no. I was . . . strongly attracted to her, yes. I admit that. And I made the mistake of admitting it to her, on several occasions. But did I ever harass her? No. Never. I was never rude or impolite to Nina in any way.''

"And yet she went to your superiors to try to get you fired.''

"Yes.''

"How do you explain that? If she wasn't being harassed—"

"She overreacted. That's all. We could have worked out our differences alone, given time, but she wouldn't wait. She was too impatient to get away."

"To get away from you."

"Yes." When Gunner just stared at him, Stanhouse said, "She wouldn't give me a chance to prove myself. To show her that I meant her no harm. She thought I *wanted* her. That I was looking to get her in bed, and nothing more."

"But of course you weren't."

"No. It was never like that with Nina. My feelings for her went much deeper than that."

"You were in love with her."

"From the day I first laid eyes on her. Only I could never get her to believe it."

"It isn't possible she believed it fine, she just wasn't interested?" Gunner asked.

"No. That's *not* possible."

"Why not? You think every time a man falls for a woman, the feeling has to be mutual?"

"We're not talking about what happens every time. We're talking about what happened with *us*. Nina and me."

"There *was* no Nina and you, Stanhouse. There was only you. And I think that's the problem you found yourself with right there."

"I don't have a problem."

"You don't think so? You harass a woman by day, and stalk her by night, my brother, you've got a problem. Ask any shrink in the business."

"I never 'stalked' anybody," Stanhouse said angrily.

"Call it what you will. You were following Nina home when you weren't calling her there on the phone, that's stalking. In anybody's book. Whether you did it for love, or not."

"I told you. It wasn't like that."

"You never followed her home at night?"

"Yes, but—"

"But what?"

"But I wasn't *stalking* her. I was *protecting* her. Making sure she was okay. She was going home to a psychopath, Gunner. Her life was in danger every minute she spent with that sonofabitch. So . . . I checked in on her a couple of times, yes. And I called her, yes. But only because I was afraid for her, and I wanted to be there if that coward she was married to started in on her again.''

"It all sounds very noble, Stanhouse, but—"

"But what? It's the *truth*. I swear it!''

"Look, I'd like to believe you, man, but why would I do that? Because you've got a sincere face?''

"You want proof? Read her diary. No matter what she told everyone else, she wouldn't write lies in her diary. No woman ever does.''

Gunner sat up in his chair. "Her diary?''

"Yes. She kept a diary. You didn't know that?''

Gunner didn't answer the question, because he never heard it. His mind was suddenly spinning, formulating thought faster than he could assimilate it.

"Who told you she kept a diary? Nina?''

"She didn't have to tell me. I saw it. She used to write in it during her breaks sometimes.''

"What did it look like? Describe it for me.''

Stanhouse told him it was a small, paperback-sized book bound in red cloth. Something one could buy in any drugstore or stationery shop.

Gunner asked him if he'd ever had an opportunity to read any part of it.

"No. Of course not,'' Stanhouse said. As if it should have been obvious to Gunner that he was above committing such a grievous breach of etiquette.

"Then how do you know what was in it? You never read it, what makes you think it would prove your version of things, and not hers?''

"I told you. Because nobody writes lies in their diary. What the hell's the point of keeping one otherwise?''

It was an arguable point, but just barely. Some people mixed fact with fiction in their personal diaries, but not many. A diary was generally reserved for the truth, existing as it did as the one place its author could feel comfortable relating it.

If Nina had been keeping one, Gunner had to find it. And not just because it might tell him whether or not Stanhouse was being straight with him now.

He knew exactly where to start looking.

# f i f t e e n

HE FOUND A NOTE ON THE COBRA'S WINDSHIELD WHEN HE went to leave. He had an idea what it would say even before he took a look at it:

*I can see you, motherfucka!*

He scanned the street, but saw nothing out of the ordinary. If Dartmouth was still around, he was hiding; it wouldn't be hard. Gunner stood there in the street for a long minute, to see if the man cared to finish their business right here, right now, but Dartmouth never made a move. He was probably gone.

Gunner tossed the balled-up note to the curb and got in the car.

"I don't know what you're talking about," Mimi Hillman said. But her eyes had already told him that she did.

"Momma, I need to see it. If you have it, you've got to give it to me."

"I don't have it. I'm sorry."

She was moving back and forth across her kitchen floor, cooking, but being evasive didn't help her any; she was lying to him, and Gunner knew it. She simply didn't lie often enough to be any good at it.

"I don't believe you," the investigator said.

Mimi ignored him, acting as if the tomato she was slicing on a breadboard had her complete attention.

"You knew about Nina and Shirley Causwell. That's why you told me not to believe everything I heard about her. You were adamant about that."

"Aaron, I don't have time for this."

"I didn't know what you were talking about at the time, but then I found out about Gary Stanhouse, and what it was that really cost Nina her job at Bowers, Bain and Lyle. I figured you were warning me about him, in case he tried to tell me what he'd been telling everyone else, that *she* had been in love with *him,* and not the other way around. But you weren't, were you? It wasn't Stanhouse you were warning me about at all."

"I'm not listening to this. I'm not!"

"Nina would have never told you about it herself. She would have known how you'd react, what you'd think it meant. So you had to have found out about it some other way. Either by hearing it from someone else—or reading about it somewhere. In her diary, Momma Hillman. You read it in her diary."

"No!" She threw the knife in her hand into the sink and turned to face him, furious.

"If the police have it, you can't help me. Or if it's in her house with the rest of her things, same thing. I'll never see it in time to do anything with it. But if *you* have it—"

"What do you want to see it for? Because you think it's *true*? Is that what you think?"

"Momma . . ."

"She was making it up! The things she wrote about in that book—not a word of it really happened. Not one word! My baby wouldn't do anything like that. She *wouldn't*!"

She was shaking, standing there in front of him with both fists clenched like the secret she was trying to defend was the difference between life and death. He could debate the veracity of the diary's contents with her for the next twenty-four hours, he wanted to do that, and it wasn't going to change her mind. He recognized that immediately.

So he let it go. She could believe what she wanted to believe, as long as he got to see the book.

Ten minutes later, he did.

He read it while sitting in the Cobra, in the empty, shadeless parking lot of Athens Park, on Broadway and El Segundo.

Mimi had removed it from Nina's home the day they found her body, before the police could seal the place up and maybe come across it themselves. She'd discovered its existence a month or so earlier, the night Nina had come to visit and carelessly left her purse open on her mother's kitchen table. Mimi hadn't meant to be nosy, but the book had piqued her curiosity; she'd never known her daughter to keep a diary before. So she'd opened it and started reading, intending to put it down after a page or two. She ended up reading fifteen or twenty, she wasn't sure anymore how many, then closed the book forever.

Horrified.

It had been her misfortune to stumble upon the pages that related to Nina's one-night stand with Shirley Causwell, an episode that could only have had the disastrous effect it did upon a devout Catholic of Mimi's stature. Her initial reaction had been shock, but regret had soon followed. She knew something now that could only make her miserable, something she could never ask Nina to clarify or explain away. All she could do was feign ignorance, and hope she could put the memory out of her mind before her daughter could see the effort it took to hold her silence.

Had Mimi read the diary in its entirety, as Gunner did, she would have learned that she had seen its most provocative passages. The rest of it was fairly mundane, just short, uninspired reflections of Nina's life as an abused woman. Heartbreaking stuff, all of it, but nothing particularly memorable or noteworthy—with one possible exception.

The entry in question would have meant little to Mimi had she come upon it, but Gunner was not so shortsighted. He recognized the import of the entry immediately. It may not have been the reason someone feared Nina enough to murder her, but it had that potential.

And it answered one question, at least, that Gunner had been getting nowhere trying to answer on his own.

"Tell me about Alvin Bascomb," Gunner said.

He hadn't given Trini Serrano any time to gear up for his visit, hadn't called ahead to say he was coming, or bothered to say hello when he came through the door; he'd just shown up at her Hollywood studio for the second day in a row and dropped Bascomb's name like a greeting, watching her face for fireworks. He didn't get fireworks, but he did get recognition, and the minute she realized she'd shown him that much, she knew the jig was up. Telling her he'd read Nina's diary had almost been unnecessary.

Still, she didn't say a word about Bascomb until she'd asked some questions of her own. More to satisfy her own curiosity than to stall for time.

"Where did you find it?" she asked.

"At her mother's," Gunner said. He could have told her it didn't matter where he found it, just to keep Mimi Hillman out of the picture, but he thought it might help her to be straight with him if he demonstrated a willingness to be straight with her first.

"Do you have it now?"

"No," he lied. Being straight with her was not synonymous with telling her everything.

"Then—"

"Don't worry about where it is. It's somewhere safe, that's all you need to know."

Serrano nodded her head, conceding the point.

"Tell me about Bascomb," Gunner said again.

"Tell me first what Nina wrote about him."

"I think you already know that."

"I know what I told her about him. I know that. But how much of what I said she actually wrote in her diary . . ." She shrugged. "I can only guess about that."

"I'll put it to you like this: The salient points are in there," Gunner said. "What's missing are the details."

"And the salient points are?"

"A dead man, a wife who confessed to killing him, and

a shutterbug friend of the wife who actually *did*. Do I need to go on?''

Serrano's face fell, all hope that Gunner had been bluffing suddenly gone.

''I didn't think so,'' Gunner said.

''All right. So the skeleton in my closet has finally seen the light of day. What happens now, Mr. Gunner?''

''I just told you. Now I want the details.''

''The details? What for? So you can have even more dirt to blackmail me with?''

''Who said I wanted to blackmail you?''

''You didn't have to tell me. Not being as stupid as I look, I figured that out all by myself.''

''Well, you figured wrong. I'm no blackmailer. But I *am* the man holding Nina's diary, and I'll be more than happy to turn it over to the police if you don't stop hemming and hawing and start talking to me. Right now.''

''But I still don't understand—''

''I'll give you two minutes, Ms. Serrano. Take it or leave it.''

She took it, but not before all of the allotted 120 seconds had come and gone.

''Alvin Bascomb was a terrible man,'' she said. ''One of the most sadistic people I've ever known. He was big, and he was ugly—about six seven or six eight, at least three hundred pounds. He was a bear. And he towered over Doreen, his wife, like a skyscraper over a toolshed—she was just as tiny as he was huge.

''Anyway, I met Doreen one night I was doing a ridealong with the police out in Culver City, taking pictures and talking to the victims whenever a domestic disturbance call came in. Bascomb had beat her up pretty bad and she'd called the police on him. I'll never forget her face that night. She had this giant gash over her left eye that wouldn't stop bleeding, and when they asked her how she'd gotten it, she told them her husband had hit her over the head with a stereo speaker. Can you believe that? They found it sitting on the living room couch, the wires still hooked up to it, and everything.''

"Where was Bascomb?" Gunner asked.

"In the bedroom. Asleep," Serrano said. "That was apparently his pattern. Drink heavily, beat Doreen silly, then pass out."

"They take him in?"

"Yes. Of course. It was either that or kill him. Those cops were almost as furious as I was, and that was before they woke him up and he started acting like he hadn't done anything wrong. Like it was the most natural thing in the world for a man to beat his wife with a stereo speaker before retiring for the evening."

"He do any time?"

"Three months. He was sentenced to twelve, but nine were suspended." Serrano hesitated, having reached the part of the story she was most reluctant to tell. "We became friends, Doreen and I. I liked her. She wasn't very smart, but she was sweet. Very kind, very generous. I devoted a whole section of one of my books to her. But then Alvin got out of jail."

"And she took him back."

"Yes. It was crazy. Insane. I tried everything I could to talk her out of it, to persuade her to leave him before he was released, but she wouldn't do it. They had three underage children in private school, and she was only working part-time. She needed his financial support.

"When he came back, I tried to spend as much time with Doreen as I could, thinking he wouldn't touch her as long as my camera and I were around. And for a while, I was right. He didn't like my being there, but there wasn't much he could do about it. He knew if he ever messed with me, I'd have the pictures to prove it. Then one night—he'd been home about three weeks, I think—he lost it. Big-time. Something at the garage he owned in West L.A. had set him off and he came home already drunk and in a rage. He walked through the door and went straight for Doreen, too angry and shitfaced to even notice I was there. He had her down on the kitchen floor before I could blink, choking her with one hand and punching her with the other. When I tried to pull him off, he turned on me. He threw me backward and I fell. He came after me and I reached out for something to hit him with . . .''

''And found a knife instead.''

Serrano nodded. ''Yes. I'd knocked down an open drawer when I fell and spilled utensils all over the floor. I grabbed a knife and I stabbed him, once, in the chest. I didn't think about it, I just did it. It was instinctive, not premeditated. We called the paramedics for him, but he died before they could get there.''

''Where were the kids?''

''The kids weren't there. They were over at a neighbor's that night.''

''So they didn't see anything.''

''No.''

''Whose idea was it to let Doreen take the blame for Bascomb's death?''

''It was hers. I know you won't believe that, but it's true. She's a very beautiful person, like I told you. She knew I might have trouble getting the police to believe I'd killed him in self-defense, so she offered to tell them she'd done it. She had the bruises to prove he'd attacked her. I didn't.

''At first, I was against the idea. I didn't like the thought of lying to the police about a homicide. I wasn't afraid anything would happen to her—one look at her and I knew they'd accept her story without much of an argument, especially considering Alvin's long history of abusing her— but I was worried there could be complications later, our lie was ever discovered. So I told her no, let's just tell the truth. Say what really happened, and take our chances.''

''But that's not what you did.''

''No.''

''You changed your mind.''

''Yes. I changed my mind.''

''Why?''

''Because at the last minute, I thought about my career. I considered what might happen to it, word got out I'd killed the abusive partner of one of my photo subjects. Self-defense or no self-defense.''

''You mean that you'd be ruined.''

"I don't know about ruined. But getting the same access to people I'd been accustomed to getting would have certainly become more difficult for me, if not outright impossible. I get invited into the homes of abused women because they trust me to *record* their lives, Mr. Gunner, not interfere in them. If I'd admitted to killing Alvin, I might never have been trusted by anyone that way again. So I decided to go along with Doreen's suggestion. We told the police she'd killed Alvin, not me, and they believed it. They had no reason not to."

"Any regrets?" Gunner asked.

"To tell you the truth? No. Not until this very moment." She shook her head and smiled.

"How did you end up telling Nina all this? What made you decide to confess to her?"

"I don't know, really. It just happened. We were close, like I told you earlier. I trusted her. One day we were going over one of my books together, and she was asking me to talk about each segment. You know, give her some background on the people involved—who was who in this shot or that, what was going on at the time it was taken, et cetera, et cetera. Anecdotal stuff, in other words."

"And when you got to the segment on Doreen Bascomb . . ."

"I told her how Alvin had really died. Yes." She shook her head, recalling her folly. "It was a stupid thing to do, of course. But I wasn't really sorry I did it. Not until—"

"Until you found out she was keeping a diary," Gunner said.

"Yes. I never knew. She never had it out around me. I didn't know she had one until one night out at the house, I caught her writing in it. I'd gone up to her room to say good night and surprised her. She rushed to put it away, but it was too late; I'd already recognized it for what it was.

"I didn't think anything of it at first, but then I remembered what I'd told her. About Alvin Bascomb. And I began to worry. I knew she'd never tell anybody about it, but if she'd written about it in her diary, and somebody at the house happened to get their hands on it . . . The thought of that started to frighten me.''

"Did Nina admit she'd written about Bascomb's death in the diary?"

"No. She wouldn't admit anything. She wouldn't even admit she *had* a diary, even though I told her I'd seen it. All I wanted her to do was promise me she'd destroy any entries she might have made mentioning the Bascomb affair, but she wouldn't do it. She denied everything."

"Leaving you no choice but to find the diary and delete the offensive entries, if they even existed, yourself."

"Yes."

"And that's what you were looking for in her room when she caught you. Not the bracelet you told me about, but the diary."

"Yes."

"The bracelet never actually existed. Did it?"

"No. I'm afraid it didn't."

Gunner didn't say anything for a minute. "You want to tell me the rest of the story now?"

Serrano looked at him, her eyes blank. "The rest of the story? I don't—"

"When you couldn't find her diary, and Nina wouldn't agree to edit it, that left you in kind of a tough spot. Didn't it? I mean, what you said earlier is true: Word gets out you took an active role in the affairs of a photo subject like Doreen Bascomb, nobody's going to trust you to be nothing but a sideline player ever again. And if they can't trust you to stay on the sidelines . . . you probably don't get in the front door. And if you don't get in the front door—"

"What are you trying to say, Mr. Gunner? Spit it out, please."

Gunner waved a hand around the room, said, "Well, this is your livelihood we're talking about, isn't it? All of this isn't a *hobby* of yours. So you lose your ability to do this kind of work, you're not just losing a little. You're losing a lot. You're losing damn near everything, I'd imagine."

"And that leads you to conclude what? That I murdered Nina to keep her silent?"

"You make it sound like an impossibility."

"It *is* impossible."

"Not from where I sit."

"Then you're sitting on your *brains*. I couldn't have killed Nina even if I'd wanted to."

"And why is that, Ms. Serrano?"

"Because I was in Eugene at the time, Mr. Gunner. Almost a thousand miles away."

"Eugene?"

"That's right. Eugene. It's in Oregon. Ever hear of it?"

"But you told me it wasn't true. That what Wendy Singer and the others at Sisterhood said about your being out of town at the time of Nina's death—"

"I told you that that wasn't the reason I was no longer spending time there, Mr. Gunner. That's what I told you. I also said I hadn't been anywhere on the East Coast, which I hadn't. That was the specific question you asked me, had I been anywhere on the East Coast when Nina died? Had you asked me simply whether or not I'd been out of town at the time, I would have told you yes, I was. I was in Eugene, Oregon, for six days, starting the Friday before Nina was killed, to the Wednesday afterward, and I have the photographs to prove it. But that's not the question you asked. You check your notes again, I believe you'll see that."

Gunner did.

And she was right.

His notes weren't detailed enough to reflect that, but the more he thought about it, the more he seemed to recall that it had happened just the way she described it. He'd asked the wrong questions, and she'd answered them. Nothing more, and nothing less.

"Guess I owe you an apology," he said.

Serrano folded her arms across her chest and waited for him to get started.

# sixteen

LOOSE ENDS. THAT WAS ALL GUNNER HAD LEFT TO WORK with now.

Back in his office at Mickey's, sitting behind his desk like the despondent CEO of a bankrupt savings and loan, he sorted through the pieces of his investigation, looking for some clue as to what direction he should move in next, and found not a one. Discovering Nina's diary had given him the idea he had found the mother lode, the key, central piece of evidence around which every murder investigation revolved. Who better to tell him who might have wanted Nina dead than Nina herself?

But the diary had been a false lead.

Reading it from cover to cover two more times had convinced him of that. With the exception of Nina's account of the Alvin Bascomb killing, the book neither enhanced his knowledge of the people in her life he was already acquainted with, nor introduced him to any he had not previously been aware of. The diary confirmed and explained a number of things he'd had lingering questions about, yes— such as the nature of her relationship with Trini Serrano, which had, apparently, been sexual only in Nina's rather paranoid imagination—but other than that, it was useless to him. Just a sad reminder of what a hodgepodge of confusion and disappointment Nina's life had been toward its final days.

So he tossed it, reviewed what remained of his hand, and saw nothing. Nothing but discards and jokers. Serrano was out of the picture, having motive but no opportunity; Causwell and Singer had opportunity, but no clear-cut motive; Stanhouse had motive and opportunity, but hadn't yet shown Gunner the backbone of a murderer; Felker had a weapon, but only a water-thin motive at best; and Glass had neither motive nor opportunity. Put them all in a lineup, and what did you have? A rogue's gallery of unlikely suspects, with the emphasis on "unlikely."

Gunner called Matthew Poole, unable to think of anything better to do.

"Well. The mountain comes to Mohammed," the police detective said, surprising Gunner by actually answering the phone himself.

"That doesn't mean what I think it means, I hope," Gunner said.

"Please. You'd be eating dinner on the county right about now, that was true. I was just making a joke."

"A joke by definition is funny, Poole. Better not tell any more until you can remember that."

"State your business, Gunner. I'm busy."

"I'll do that in a minute. But while I've got you on the phone, you might as well tell me what your intentions are. Just so I'll know."

"My intentions? You mean for you?"

"I figure it's been half a day now, you wanted to hold me accountable for Pearson, you would've picked me up by now. Maybe I'm wrong."

"You want me to tell you you're in the clear? That what you want?"

"Only if it's true, Poole. If it's not—"

"I'll put it to you like this, Gunner: You wanna make plans for dinner tonight, go ahead. Same for lunch tomorrow, 'less I miss my guess. Beyond that, I can't tell you. The DA's office has been talkin' like they might be interested in prosecuting, but it's probably just talk. I won't know for sure until sometime tomorrow."

He waited for Gunner to comment, but all he heard coming back over the line was silence.

"Hey. You still there?"

"Yeah, I'm here. Thanks, Poole."

"You're welcome. That all you wanted to know?"

"Actually, no. You never called me back about the gun. When I called you yesterday. You didn't get my message?"

"I got it. But here's the problem: This ain't a goddamn research library. It's a police department. So it's not my job to hop to every time you call looking for information. Especially if it relates to an ongoing homicide investigation."

"I had a reason for asking the question, Lieutenant."

"I'm sure you did. But so what?"

"Listen. Enough with the snappy dialogue. I found out yesterday one of Nina's old girlfriends out at the shelter happens to own a shotgun. I know, because I saw it. Up close and personal. It looked like a Browning, single-barrel pump action, but I'm not sure. I thought if Nina was killed with something similar, you might want to check it out."

"Who's this girlfriend we're talking about? Give me a name."

"Her name's Felker. Agnes Felker." Gunner spelled it. "And guess what, you lucky bastard?"

"What?"

"She used the gun in question to kill a man last night. Her boyfriend Otha. He put her in the hospital, and she put him in the morgue. Seems she shot him after he beat her half to death, she's out at County-USC as we speak."

"Then there ought to be an open ticket on her somewhere."

"Yeah. And with the gun being held in evidence—"

"I get it, I get it. I get with ballistics, see if we can make a match between this weapon and ours."

"Right."

Poole said he'd see what he could do. Coming from him, that was like a guarantee in writing.

"So what else you got going, cowboy?" he asked.

"Plenty. I'll be filling you in later, don't worry."

Poole laughed, said, "You're full of shit. You've got nothin' going, Gunner, and you never will. Because the man who killed Nina Pearson is dead. All this runnin' around you're doin' trying to find another perp is a big waste of time. Yours *and* mine.''

"I don't think so, Lieutenant. But I want to thank you for sharing that opinion with me,'' Gunner said.

"Don't mention it. Have a nice day.''

And with that, Poole was gone.

It took some doing, but he found a number for one of the detectives working the Roman Goody murder case, the brother named Bunche, and called him, just to let him know Russell Dartmouth had been in the neighborhood earlier. Bunche said thanks for the info, he and his partner Bertelsen would get right on it.

After that, Gunner drove over to the Acey Deuce for a drink. It was only four o'clock in the afternoon, but that was too bad; he was down and he was tired, and he needed something to take the edge off his self-deprecation.

"You start any shit in here today, boy, you're gone for good,'' Lilly said, soon as his ass hit a stool at the bar.

Gunner looked around for the barkeeper's benefit, first over one shoulder, then the next. His entrance had brought the number of patrons at the bar to a whopping five.

"You see anybody in here to start any shit *with*?'' he asked.

"I don't care if there ain't but you an' me in here. I catch you sayin' an unkind word to your shadow on the wall, you gonna be lookin' for someplace else to do your drinkin'. Try me an' see.''

She poured Gunner his usual and went away, confident nothing further needed to be said.

For the next fifteen minutes or so, Gunner sat there alone, ruminating. Thinking about Stanhouse, mostly. Trying to decide how much sense it would make now to put a tail on him over the weekend. It was still the only thing left he could think to do, but he couldn't see how it would accomplish anything. Even if Stanhouse didn't know it was coming, the chances that he would do anything to incriminate himself—like lead Gunner to the weapon he'd used on Nina—were almost nonexistent. With the lawyer *expecting* to be put under surveillance—as he'd practically come right out and said he was when the two men had spoken earlier in the day— the odds became greater still that Gunner would learn nothing whatsoever from watching him. Not today, not tomorrow, not ever.

When Lilly inevitably came back around to check on him, Gunner asked her to hang for a while, he had a question he wanted to ask her.

"What kinda question?" the ruby-lipped giant wanted to know.

"I was just wondering whether or not you've ever been with somebody who liked to slap you around," Gunner said.

"Slap me around? What, you mean a man?"

"A man, yes. What the hell else would I be talking about?"

Lilly laughed. Not at his sorry wisecrack, but at the question he was asking. Like she hadn't heard anything so stupid all day. "Lemme ask you somethin', Gunner," she said. "You was my man, would *you* wanna try slappin' me around?" She threw her head back and laughed again, genuinely amused.

And hell if she didn't have a point. Lilly was bigger than half the men Gunner had ever seen in his life, and meaner than all but maybe a dozen. Any man who put his hands on her, she didn't *want* his hands on her, was playing with his life.

"No offense, Lilly, but size isn't everything," Gunner said. "You might not take any shit in here, but that doesn't mean you won't take any in the bedroom. Does it?"

"I don't take any shit from anybody *anywhere*," Lilly said.

"You still haven't answered my question."

The big woman stood on the other side of the bar and looked at him, the broad grin she'd been wearing slowly leaving her face. It took some time to disappear completely, but when it did, she said, "You ain't gonna believe this, but I only had one man in my life ignorant enough to put his hands on me, an' that was J.T., back when we first got married."

She was right; Gunner didn't believe it. Her late husband had been almost as big as Lilly, but most of the man was heart; J.T. could raise hell if he had to, but friends didn't come any better.

"J.T.?"

"He only did it once. We'd been married three weeks, just found a place and moved in together, over on Wadsworth Avenue near Ninety-first Street. This was almost thirty years ago, September 1968—I was nineteen, an' he was twenty-one. He come home late one night, smellin' like liquor an' some other woman, an' I let 'im hear about it. So he slapped me. One time, hard, on the left side of my face right here." She pointed to her left cheek like the blow had left a mark that could still be seen.

"What did you do?" Gunner asked.

"I'll tell you what I did. I called the cops on his ass. Cried into that phone like he'd tried to kill me, told every damn lie I could think of to get him put in jail. J.T. about wet his pants."

"I take it he ran."

Lilly shook her head. "He never did run. He was too afraid to. I think he thought it would be better for him, he stuck around to tell the police *his* side of the story, 'fore I could tell 'em mine. But they never let that poor man open his mouth. Those two cops come in that apartment an' had the cuffs on him soon as I pointed him out. I should've known what was gonna happen to him right then, but I was still too mad to care. I just let 'em take him away."

"Down to the station."

"Yeah. Down to the station. I didn't see or hear from him again for two days."

"Two days?"

Lilly nodded, said, "They took that man to jail an' whipped his ass for two whole days. He'd called his momma that first night to bail him out, but she didn't have the bail money, so she called me. Beggin' me to drop the charges against him an' get him released, 'fore they could kill him in there. By that time, I wasn't angry no more, so I did what she said, I went down to the police station to get him out.

This was the next day. Only they said they couldn't find him. They said he'd been transferred to another jail overnight, and they didn't know which one, 'cause his paperwork was lost. Some bullshit like that. Back then, they could do that kinda shit to black folk, it happened all the time.''

"So when did they finally 'find' him?"

"'Bout six in the morning the next day. They didn't call me or nothin', they just let him go. I didn't know he was out till he walked in the door. An' if you could've seen what those policemen had done to him . . .'' She shook her head, almost thirty years later still haunted by the memory. "Lord, it broke my heart. 'Cause I was the one turned him over to those animals, right? I hadn't told all those lies on him—''

"Bullshit. You did the right thing," Gunner said.

"Brother, I was lucky. I might've done the right thing, but I was lucky."

"But he never put his hands on you again. Did he?"

Lilly shook her head again, said, "Never. He never *raised* his hand to me again after that. And we were married twenty-one years."

"What would you have done if he *had* tried it again? You ever ask yourself that?"

"I know what I woulda done. I'd've left him. Quick as a flash. What do I need you around for, you can't treat me with some respect?"

"That's a good question. It's a shame more women don't ask it."

"More *women*? You mean more *men*."

"I mean everybody. Men *and* women. Respect is something we all deserve—we received a little more of it, maybe we'd get along a little better."

"Kinda hard to respect a nigga don't wanna work, Gunner. Just wants to drink, and sleep, and chase tail all the time."

"Jesus. Here it comes."

"You know it's true."

"The hell I do. As long as your image of the black man is that fucked up—''

"I never said I was talkin' 'bout all of you. Just most of

you. Ask any sister on the street, she'll tell you. A woman would have better luck findin' diamonds on the sidewalk than she would a decent black man.''

"Maybe the trouble is, most women want both. The diamonds *and* the decent black man.''

"Shit. Now you soundin' like the fool wrote that book. You know the one I mean.''

"What book?''

"The one that sister wrote a few years back. Talkin' 'bout how all the black man's problems are the fault of the black woman, an' shit. I forget what it's called.''

*"What Every Black Man Needs to Know to Understand the Black Woman,"* Aubrey Coleman said, moving over to Gunner and Lilly's end of the bar. The Deuce's resident academic, he'd been sitting a few stools down talking to Eggy Jones, going on about some movie he'd recently seen on TV, when he overheard Lilly's description of the book.

"That's it,'' Lilly said, snapping her fingers. "That's the one. What's the fool's name wrote it?''

Coleman shook his dreadlocked head, said, "I never read it. I just heard what people were sayin' about it, back when it came out. The sister was a Muslim, though, I remember that.''

"The one did all the talk shows? That sister?'' Gunner asked.

"Yeah. Her,'' Coleman said, putting his drink on the bar and sitting down. *"Oprah, Donahue, Sally Jessy Raphael—* she was on all those shows. Had sisters in the audience rushin' the stage, tryin' to get at her ass. Remember?''

Now Gunner did. The book in question, a self-published paperback sold almost exclusively in independent black bookstores, had been a powder keg of controversy, espousing as it did the philosophy that every fault and shortcoming of the Afro-American male could be directly traced to his female counterpart, the Afro-American woman. It was her overdemanding, gold-digging, trash-talking inner nature that drove the black man to do the terrible things he did to her, and only a good stiff uppercut delivered on a regular basis could keep her from destroying him altogether.

It was the worst case of black-on-black crime since the assassination of Malcolm X.

"That bitch was crazy," Lilly said. "Tryin' to blame what you worthless niggas do on *us*."

Gunner and Coleman glanced at each other, catching the irony in the bartender's comment that Lilly herself was unaware of.

To Gunner, Lilly said, "And you're just as crazy for agreein' with her."

"Agreeing with her? I don't—"

"You didn't just say a woman don't want a man 'less he can shower her with diamonds and furs?"

"I said *some* black women are like that, yes. They want a good man, sure, but a good man's not enough. They've got to have the green, too. Man can be as good and decent as he wants, but if he can't deliver the goods—"

"See ya!" Coleman said, finishing Gunner's thought with a farewell salute aimed at Lilly. He and Gunner then put their fists together, top to bottom, bottom to top, congratulating themselves on the clear vision they obviously shared on the intricate workings of the female mind.

"I don't remember askin' you to be a part of this conversation, Aubrey," Lilly said, unmoved by the beautiful show of male bonding she had just witnessed. "Get on back over there with Eggy where you were an' leave me an' Gunner alone."

"But—"

"You heard me. Go on over there an' finish tellin' him 'bout that crazy-ass movie you was talkin' about, that 'alien surgery' shit, or whatever you called it. Alien somethin', it was."

"*Alien Autopsy*," Coleman said. "It was on Channel Eleven last night at ten o'clock. Did you see it?"

"No. I see alien autopsies in here every week, what the hell do I need to see the movie for?" She cracked up, and Coleman did too. Even Eggy Jones at the far end of the bar was laughing.

But not Gunner.

Gunner wasn't laughing because he'd just had a revelation.

That thing that had been clawing around at the back of his skull for almost twenty-four hours, working from the inside trying to get out, was finally free. He could see it now for what it was, and understand why he had always known its role in Nina's murder was significant. It was, in part, a word. And Coleman had just said it.

*Autopsy.*

The Gatewood autopsy.

# s e v e n t e e n

BUNCHE DIDN'T WANT TO TALK TO HIM. TWO CALLS IN THE same day from a private operator he barely knew was more than the cop could stand. It was late in the day, and he was tired. But Gunner had left three messages for him in the span of an hour, and Bunche admired persistence in a man almost more than anything else.

"What business is the Gatewood case to you?" the detective asked when Gunner had stated his reason for calling.

"I don't know that it *is* my business," Gunner said. "Yet."

"So what makes you think it might be?"

"The name. Gatewood. I know a woman by that name."

"Let's hear it."

"Florence Gatewood. Black woman in her mid-forties, about five nine, five ten, one hundred and sixty pounds or thereabouts, dark hair, dark complexion, no discernible marks of distinction. Sound familiar?"

Gunner didn't hear anything, until Bunche threw some mints in his mouth and began chewing loudly into the phone.

"Detective?" Gunner said.

"Sorry, friend, but that's not our deceased."

Which would have been bad news, save for two things: Gunner's relative fondness for Gatewood, and the time Bunche had taken to answer the question.

"But she does sound familiar," Gunner said.

More chewing at the other end of the line. "Maybe."

"Bunche, please. Don't play with me, man. This is a charity call, I need a break."

Bunche thought about it, taking his time. "And when I need a break later? You gonna be there to help *me*, brother?"

"You don't ask for anything unreasonable, I will be, sure."

"Who's to say what's reasonable or unreasonable? Me or you?"

"Me. Same as you're deciding right now whether what I'm asking for is reasonable or unreasonable."

"That ain't my standard deal, partner," Bunche said. "But what the hell. You or the United Way, what's the difference." He treated Gunner to one more long silence, then said, "The victim in our case is one James Gatewood, Junior, or Jimmy to his friends and loved ones. A dirtbag. A low-level errand boy in the drug trade, been a wart on the community's ass for every one of his twenty-eight years. God bless his soul."

"And Florence Gatewood is his mother."

"A Florence Gatewood who fits the description you just gave me claimed to be his moms, yeah. I got her address around here somewhere . . ."

"Lady I'm talking about lives on Ninety-fifth Street. Two-oh-nine East Ninety-fifth, near Watts."

"Ninety-fifth, right. We must be talkin' about the same lady, all right. How is it *you* know her?"

"I don't. I just had a few words with her a couple of days ago, in the course of looking for witnesses to a murder I've been investigating. When was her son killed?"

"Last Thursday. Late. What murder you talkin' about, Gunner?"

The investigator told him about Nina Pearson's murder in brief, avoiding the question of what a private citizen like him was doing sticking his nose into an open homicide investigation altogether.

"Detective in charge of the case is a guy named Matt Poole out of the LAPD's Southwest," Gunner said, "you want all the details."

"You say this Nina Pearson was shot?" Bunche asked.

"That's right. Shotgunned. Same as your boy Jimmy, I'll bet."

"And you think that proves they're connected? Your homicide and ours?"

"It's beginning to look that way to me, yes."

"Just because Gatewood and your girl were neighbors?"

"And the commonality of the weapons used, yeah. You don't—"

"Forget about it. You're reachin'."

"Reaching?"

"That's right. You're reachin'. You're forgettin' one very important fact."

"And that is?"

"Think about it, smart guy. What department do I work for? Compton PD. And if Jimmy Gatewood had been murdered at home—"

"LAPD would be handling the case."

"Exactly."

"So he was killed somewhere in Compton."

"At a girlfriend's house on Whitemarsh Avenue, between Greenleaf and Alondra. Which is what? About ten or twelve miles from where your victim got it?"

"That supposed to mean the same person couldn't have killed them both?"

"No. It's just supposed to mean it ain't likely. Besides which, the suspect in our case had a motive for killing Gatewood. But the lady—"

"You have a suspect? In custody?"

"Not in custody, no. At large. But that should be changin' any minute now."

"This suspect have a name, Detective?"

"He's got a name, sure. What suspect don't?"

"Do I get to hear it?"

"I don't know. You got a reason for askin'?"

"I don't know the man's name, Bunche, I can't give you a call, I happen to see or hear something you might wanna know. Can I?"

"I'm gonna pretend to be ignorant enough to believe that

bullshit, and tell you the man's name is Dobbs. Angelo Dobbs.''

"Never heard of him."

"Well, don't lose any sleep over it. He's one for the psycho ward. Got a jacket so full of felony arrests we can't close the fuckin' thing."

"And he killed Jimmy Gatewood because . . . ?"

"Because that's what he was paid to do. He's an enforcer, Angelo. A drug trade gun-for-hire. Way we understand it, a local Blood set known as the Trey-Kays put a contract out on Gatewood, and Dobbs was the one picked it up. Seems Gatewood was the inside man on a theft at one of the Trey-Kay rock houses, and that put him at the top of their shit list."

"You have the weapon Dobbs used on him?"

"No. But when Dobbs turns up, it will too. Just a matter of time."

"You've got a line on him?"

"Let's just say, he ain't in our custody this weekend, I'll eat my hat."

When Gunner became quiet, Bunche said, "So now you know why Dobbs killed Gatewood, you can tell me why he killed your Nina Pearson. Was she in the rock biz, by any chance?"

"No."

"You sure about that?"

"Positive. That wasn't her scene, believe me," Gunner said.

"Then maybe she had a friend—"

"No. I don't think so," Gunner insisted.

"Then where's your motive, Gunner?" Bunche asked. "Every murderer's got one, right? What's Dobbs's for killing *her*?"

After some deliberation, Gunner said he didn't know.

But he could make a wild guess.

The address marker on Nina's house was missing a 6—the last digit of three—leaving the marker to tell the big lie that this was 10 East Ninety-fifth Street, instead of 106 East Ninety-fifth.

It was well after seven o'clock and it was dark, but with the help of a flashlight, Gunner was able to find the missing brass 6 right where he had suspected he might, beneath the truncated address marker in the dirt, behind some of the shrubbery planted at the foot of the front porch. The investigator picked it up, brushed it off a little, and placed it up on the pillar from whence it had fallen, only upside down and just below its original position, the way he figured it might have been hanging the night Angelo Dobbs came around looking for Jimmy Gatewood's house in the dark.

"I'll be goddamned," Bunche said.

Now the address marker suggested this was 109 East Ninety-fifth Street. Another big lie.

It was Florence Gatewood who lived at 109 East Ninety-fifth Street.

"I remember her saying something Tuesday about Nina getting her mail by mistake," Gunner said. "It didn't mean anything to me at the time, but now . . ."

"I'll be god*damned*," Bunche said again, clearly impressed.

"It could just be a coincidence, sure. But—"

"It ain't no fuckin' coincidence," the detective said. "The dumb shit went to the wrong address. I'd bet my pension on it."

"And killed the first person he found at home."

"Yeah."

"He have a reputation for being that stupid?"

"Stupid and loaded at the same time, hell yes. He's a crackhead. Crackheads do dumb shit like this all the time."

It was true. The haze most rockheads were in half the time, it was a miracle they could work the fly of their pants without fucking something up. Making the mistake they were assuming Angelo Dobbs made the night Nina was killed would have been easy for somebody who'd just been on the pipe.

"You going to talk to Poole?" Gunner asked Bunche.

"Looks like I'd better, now. And while we're talkin'

about our future plans, let me tell you what *yours* are . . ."

"Go home and read a good book. You took the words right out of my mouth, Detective," Gunner said.

Telling a big lie of his own.

Del Curry was not Gunner's only living relative.

His mother, Julliette, had suffered a fatal heart attack in 1966; his father, Coleman, succumbed to lung cancer less than two years after that. And two of his four siblings were also dead: his older brother Joshua and his older sister, Ruth, who had passed on in 1968 and 1991, respectively. Gunner's baby sister, Josephine, and his older brother John, however, were both still alive; Jo lived in Seattle, had for eleven years now, and John, a career Navy man, was stationed in Norfolk, Virginia—or at least he had been back in 1989, when Gunner last had heard from him. Maybe he was dead too, Gunner didn't know. No one ever knew with John.

Gunner also had several living aunts and uncles, first and second cousins—and a plethora of nieces and nephews.

Alred Lewis was one of his nephews.

His late sister Ruth's oldest child, Alred was young, good-looking, and better off financially than his Uncle Aaron could ever hope to be. You saw him on the street, you'd think he was a power forward for the Clippers, but he wasn't. He wasn't in the music business, either. Or the movies, or television. The thousand-dollar suits he wore, and the canary-yellow Porsche Carrera he drove, had not come to him via any such pedestrian pursuits as these. Oh, no.

Ready was a dope dealer. And a damn good one, apparently.

That was the boy's name in the trade, "Ready," but Gunner still called him Alred. It was his way of refusing to acknowledge his nephew's role in the business he was in. He couldn't look at Alred without thinking about Alred's mother, Ruth, and how she would spin like a top in her grave if she could see what her baby had become. Most everyone else in the family had always known this was coming, having seen the signs early on, but not Ruth; she had always thought her boy's selfishness and egomania were faults he would outgrow with time.

She had been wrong.

Without his mother around to restrain him, Alred had blossomed in the criminal world like a garden show carnation, impressing everyone he came in contact with with his gleeful willingness to commit any crime, anytime, anywhere. He had ambition, he had nerve, and he had no conscience whatsoever. He was a big player now, and he was going to be a bigger one later, he didn't get himself killed or busted first.

Gunner wanted nothing to do with him.

Which was why it pained him so to seek his nephew out Thursday night, less than twenty minutes after parting company with Bunche. Not yet twenty-five, Alred was part owner of a dance club out in the Crenshaw district called Ruff 'n Ready's, on Crenshaw Boulevard between Stocker and Forty-third Street, and Gunner looked him up there, knowing if he wasn't around, this was as good a place as any to leave a message for him.

But Alred *was* around; the yellow Porsche with the oversized wheels and tires he drove was parked out back when the investigator arrived, just after eight o'clock. A line of young black people had already formed outside the doors, smartly dressed men and women anxiously awaiting their turn to party inside. The bass line of the music playing within was loud enough to rattle teeth two doors down the block. Gunner went straight to the front of the line and flashed his ID at the doorman, a behemoth in suit and tie who would have had no difficulty at all picking Gunner up and throwing him a good ten yards, that was what he decided to do.

"I'm looking for Alred," Gunner said.

"Ready ain't here," the doorman replied.

"Okay. I believe you. But do me a favor anyway, huh? So it doesn't look to all these people like you just dissed me?"

"What's that?"

"Take one of my business cards here, go inside for a

minute, and just *pretend* you told him his Uncle Aaron's
outside looking for him. All right?"

"His *uncle*?"

"That's right. His mother, Ruth, was my sister. I'll wait
right here."

Gunner smiled good-naturedly and handed him a business
card, then watched the big man disappear inside, leaving his
doorman's duties to another, similarly sized co-worker standing nearby. The couple at the head of the line to Gunner's
left were eyeing him with open contempt, resentful of what
they thought was just a brazen attempt on his part to gain
entrance to the club without having to wait in line like everyone else, and they seemed about ready to say something
about it when the doorman suddenly returned, having been
gone all of sixty seconds.

"Come on in, Uncle Aaron," he said, smiling.

Gunner's nephew had an office at the far rear of the club,
beyond a door marked "Employees Only" on the other side
of the dance floor. The doorman and the investigator had to
pick their way through a bumping, grinding, hip-hopping
morass of humanity to get there, rendered all but deaf by the
music a DJ in a glass booth was bombarding the club with.
Gunner tried to ignore the abundance of exquisite female
flesh the club had to offer tonight, meeting only minimal
success. There was one sister in particular, a coffee-and-
cream-colored brickhouse in a two-piece, skintight red Lycra
number, who had the most symmetrical, perfectly formed—

"In here," the doorman said gruffly, holding the door to
the rear of the club open for Gunner to pass through.

When they reached Alred's office in the back, he was
sitting in a large, high-backed swivel chair behind a black
marble desk, watching the same people Gunner had just seen
out on the dance floor move around on a giant-screen TV.
The TV was hooked up to the club's numerous security cam-
eras, affording Gunner's nephew a view of his kingdom that
changed every thirty seconds or so: the dance floor, the front
entry area, the box office, the bar, and so on.

"Uncle Aaron. Whatta nice surprise," Alred said, beam-
ing. He didn't stand up or extend his hand, he just sat there

in his swivel chair and beamed. Dark-skinned, clean-shaven, and completely bald, he was wearing a black, banded-collar silk shirt with an oversized pearl top button Gunner knew must have cost two bills if it cost a dollar.

"I didn't check 'im," the doorman said. Warning his employer that he hadn't patted Gunner down yet.

"Fuck it. He's cool," Alred said, waving the big man out of the room.

The doorman gave Gunner one more hard look, then left the two men alone.

"Have a seat, Uncle. Make yourself comfortable," Alred said.

"No thanks. I'm not going to be here that long," Gunner said. Sounding as ill at ease as a convict in a warden's office.

"What, you can't hang a while? With your favorite nephew?"

"You're not my favorite anything, Alred. Any more than I'm yours. So please, put the family album back on the shelf and let me ask you what I came here to ask you, all right?"

Alred started laughing. "Damn! You always so hostile! What's up with that, man? I ain't seen you in over a year, an' look how you treatin' me!"

"I'm looking for somebody, Alred. And I thought you might be able to help me find him."

Alred let his laughter die down, then said, "You lookin' for somebody? Who?"

"Boy named Angelo Dobbs. The contract psycho who knocked off Jimmy Gatewood last Thursday. I don't have to tell you who Jimmy Gatewood was, do I?"

"Jimmy Gatewood? Lemme see . . ." Alred raised his gaze to the ceiling, like a man laboring to remember something. "That's the fool tried to jack the Trey-Kays' shit, right?"

"Then you know the story."

Alred shrugged and grinned again. "Word 'bout some things gets around to ever'body, sooner or later."

"So what can you tell me about Dobbs?"

"What can I tell you? I can't tell you *shit*. What the fuck you think I can tell you?"

"It's like that, is it?"

"Goddamn right it's like that. Look at you! Can't even sit down, you hate my ass so bad! Like it hurts just to talk to me, or somethin'!"

He was no longer smiling. He stood up and walked around the desk to stand toe-to-toe with his uncle, breathing right in Gunner's face. "You come in here to see me, motherfucker, you give me my props!" he said, slapping his own chest with an open palm. "I don't care who the fuck you are!"

"Your props," Gunner said, unflinching.

"That's right! My props!"

He was asking for something Gunner couldn't give him: respect. But Gunner couldn't tell him that, of course. He wanted to, but he couldn't; not unless he cared to walk away from the premises with nothing whatsoever to show for either his time or his aggravation.

"What would you like me to do, Alred? Kiss your ring?" he asked.

His nephew's right arm flexed and started to go back, then held up. Alred grinned again, teeth flashing, and said, "You think I owe you, huh? That's why you actin' like this, like you can come in here to my place an' talk shit, say any damn thing you want. Huh? 'Cause you think I *owe* you."

Gunner didn't say anything, leaving the younger man to draw his own conclusions.

Five years earlier, Alred had been there at the hospital to witness his mother's passing only because Gunner had seen to it the boy was free to do so. Ruth's son had been busted for possession just three days before, and Gunner was the only member of the family willing to raise his bail money and get him released in time to properly tell his mother goodbye. Gunner had never made an issue of it himself, but Alred's sister Janette had made a point of letting Alred know what his uncle had done, hoping Alred would be so moved by the gesture that he'd straighten up his act.

Like her mother before her, Janette had been dreaming.

Just as Gunner was probably dreaming now, thinking Alred would view something he'd done five years ago as a debt his nephew had never paid.

"Just 'cause you bailed me out that time so I could see Moms . . ." Alred said.

"You don't want to help me, Alred, just say so, I'll get the fuck out of here," Gunner said.

He wasn't going to beg, and he wasn't going to crawl. He wanted that made clear right now, before Alred got the foolish idea he could string his uncle along for a while, dangling the carrot before his nose, then tell him to go fuck himself. It wasn't going to be like that. Gunner didn't need his help that bad.

"Say what?" Alred asked.

"You heard me. Stop fucking around and give me an answer. Can you help me or not?"

Alred folded his brow up in a scowl, incredulous. A small eternity went by as he thought things over. Finally, another toothy grin spread across his face and he broke up laughing, backpedaling away from Gunner to return to his place behind his desk. "You're crazy! Everybody be thinkin' *I'm* the crazy motherfucker in the family, but *you* the one! You ain't got *no* goddamn sense!"

"Is that a yes, or a no?" Gunner asked.

"It's a maybe, Uncle. That's what it is. You got a card, put it down on the desk. Right here." He pointed. "I hear somethin' 'bout the man you lookin' for, an' I feel like tellin' you about it, maybe I'll call you. Or maybe I won't. Depends on if I got somethin' more important to do at the time."

"You mean like drop a little rock on the street," Gunner said, flipping a business card on his nephew's desk.

Alred smiled, waved his right hand at all his luxurious surroundings, and said, "It pays the bills, don't it?"

He threw himself down in his chair and laughed again, as Gunner turned and fled the room.

# eighteen

GUNNER SAT AT MICKEY'S AND WAITED FOR THE PHONE TO ring. At his desk in the back, he had a fast-food chicken bowl at his left hand and Mickey's portable TV at his right, the latter tuned to a broadcast of Roman Polanski's *Chinatown* that played like it had been edited for television with a butcher knife.

All the lights in the shop were on.

Right around eleven-thirty, more than two hours after the investigator's escape from Ruff 'n Ready's, Alred called.

"I got an address for you, Uncle," he said. "You ready?"

Gunner grabbed a pencil and the bag the chicken bowl had come in, said, "I'm ready."

His nephew quickly recited an address in Fontana, then said, "That's his homey's sister's place, he s'posed to be out there right now, chillin' till the heat comes down."

"Got it."

"You know the boy's crazy, right? That he's fuckin' whacked out?"

"I heard that, yeah."

"You thinkin' 'bout goin' out there after 'im yourself? That what you thinkin'?"

"I don't know what I'm going to do yet, Alred."

"'Cause if you are, you dead, Uncle. All right? You thinkin' 'bout fuckin' with a zombie like Angie, you as good as dead, I'll tell you that right now."

"Thanks for the health tip."

"I ain't gotta tell you this evens us up now, do I? That
we all through now, you an' me?"

"No, Alred. You don't."

"Good. 'Cause you ain't got no respect for me, an' I ain't
got none for you. You come around me again, one of us
gonna get hurt—an' it ain't gonna be me."

Gunner let the threat pass, finding it rather sad, and just
said, "Be good, Alred," before hanging up the phone.

He left a message for Bunche at the Compton police station,
labeling it "urgent," turned out all the lights in the shop,
and started out the front door, braced for the long drive out
to Fontana. He wasn't going out there alone, hell no, but he
*was* going; all Bunche had said was don't be a hero, not that
he couldn't be there when Angelo Dobbs was taken into
custody. Besides, Dobbs could slip away in the time it might
take Bunche to reach him; somebody had to get out to Fontana *now,* to watch the house Dobbs was allegedly holed up
in, just in case he decided to go somewhere.

Gunner was out on the sidewalk, locking the barbershop's
door, when somebody behind him popped some gravel un-
derfoot.

Russell Dartmouth had finally decided to make his move.

In the next instant, the crazed black man threw the same
lead right hand he had eight days ago in Venice, aiming for
the side of the investigator's head, but all he connected with
this time was air. Forewarned, Gunner dropped, ducking under Dartmouth's arm, then reached up and helped the big
man with his follow-through, flipping Dartmouth clumsily
over his shoulder. The giant landed hard on the base of his
spine, turned snarling like a wild dog, and caught the toe of
Gunner's right foot flush under his chin, his head snapping
back as far as it would go. Any other man would have been
finished, but Dartmouth was merely dazed. He rolled one
way, then the other, actually trying to get up, until Gunner
brought the butt of his nine-millimeter Ruger down on the
crown of Dartmouth's head, making only a halfhearted attempt to fracture the big man's skull.

That slowed Dartmouth considerably.

Still, he never lost consciousness. As Gunner watched in amazement, staying well out of his reach, the supine giant remained animated, moaning and grumbling, fighting desperately to rise and go after Gunner again. The investigator looked up and down the street, hoping to see some kind of sign that help was on the way, but he saw nothing of the sort. Just a car or two whizzing past him, and a stray dog sniffing a lamppost.

Dartmouth was his and his alone to deal with.

He looked at the big man again and found him up on one knee now, groggy as hell, but improving rapidly. He couldn't yet put much behind the glare he was showing Gunner, but its message was clear, nonetheless: *Wait right where you are, motherfucker. I'll be there shortly . . .*

Gunner sighed heavily and took a full step forward to let Dartmouth have a closer look at the Ruger he was pointing directly at the big man's chest.

"Well, Russell," he said. "I guess now's our chance to find out how crazy you really are."

The world was round and not flat, that had been proven conclusively a long, long time ago, but had the opposite been true—if the earth really had four edges to tumble over, as Christopher Columbus had been warned many times it did— Fontana would almost certainly have been in close proximity to one. Or so it often seemed to anyone who had to drive there from Los Angeles proper, as Gunner did tonight. The San Bernardino County city was that far out of the way.

All told, the trip covered approximately fifty-five miles over three separate freeways, and it was every bit as unscenic as it was interminable. Shopping malls and car dealerships, and one suburban sprawl after another—that was all there was to see. And in the end, desert. Level earth baked to a dry and dusty crisp, sparsely dotted with the feeble attempts of civilization to reach this far into the badlands. You wanted to buy or build a new home anywhere near Los Angeles, this was where you ended up: out beyond the municipal stratosphere by more miles and minutes behind the wheel than any rational person would care to count.

This was the last frontier.

Gunner had to smile, wondering if Angelo Dobbs hadn't been thinking when he'd come here, even if the cops learned where he was, who the hell was going to drive all the way out to fucking Fontana to pick him up?

That amusing thought, along with Russell Dartmouth, was on Gunner's mind as he spurred the Cobra on through the night. Had he been forced to guess, the investigator would have thought a head-case like Dartmouth was nuts enough to try him, Ruger or no Ruger, but the big man had proven himself to have more sense than that. As far gone as he was, he knew he wasn't Superman, and that he'd have to be nothing less, he took another step in Gunner's direction. Rage was no match for bullets, even under the best of circumstances, and Dartmouth was just barely sane enough to realize it.

Gunner had handcuffed his arms around the nearest utility pole and left him for the police to pick up later, whenever or *if* ever he came to their attention.

Then he'd started out for Fontana.

The investigator had studied a street map of San Bernardino County before leaving Los Angeles, so he pretty much knew where he was going. The address Alred had given him brought him just a mile off Interstate 15, only four exits north of Interstate 10. It was part of a huge tract of split-level homes its developer had aptly named Sunset Ranch, according to the overhead sign that welcomed visitors onto its main access road. The tract was the only fully developed parcel of land for miles in either direction, though another, similar complex was going up across the street, its hacienda-style homes sitting in total darkness, silently awaiting completion.

Entering Sunset Ranch, Gunner quickly found the street he was looking for and slowed the red Cobra to a crawl.

These homes had been inhabited for some time, but the black-and-white address markers on the curbs before them were still fairly new and perfectly legible, enabling Gunner to make a reasonable determination as to where the house Dobbs was supposed to be hiding in was situated on the block, without first having to cruise the noisy Cobra past its front door. He could see less than a half-dozen lighted windows on the entire street, making it unlikely his passing would actually attract anyone's attention, but he didn't want to take the chance. He waited until he was nine, maybe ten houses away, then pulled the Cobra over and parked, at the heart of a dark void between streetlights where he hoped he'd be difficult to spot from a distance. From there, he used a pair of binoculars to make a positive ID of the house he was interested in, and found it to be just as dark and relatively lifeless as its neighbors. That was good.

Now there was nothing to do but get comfortable in the Cobra's driver's seat and wait for Bunche to show.

It was 1:22 A.M.

A little more than an hour later, the Compton police detective appeared out of nowhere beside him, standing in the street, and said, "Just what the fuck are you doin' here?" Managing to keep his voice low, when what he really wanted to do was scream.

Without batting an eye, Gunner said, "Waiting for you. What else?" He turned to nod at Bunche's partner, Bertelsen, as the other cop stepped into view, over on the passenger side of the convertible.

Bunche couldn't figure it, why they hadn't scared the investigator shitless sneaking up on him like they had, but all the cop said was, "I don't remember invitin' you to the party, Gunner." He had no mints in his mouth tonight, no doubt a concession to the stealth this mission would soon require of him.

"Like my message said, I didn't think you'd mind, I came out to watch the house until you got here," Gunner said, "considering it was my tip that brought you out here in the first place."

"Yeah, well, you thought wrong, buddy," Bertelsen said, having almost as much trouble keeping his voice down as his partner.

Explaining, Bunche said, "I had that talk with Matt Poole you suggested I have, an' guess what? I found out what your interest in all this is. Revenge. This Nina Pearson you think Dobbs whacked, she was an ex–old lady of yours."

"Forget about it, Bunche. I'd wanted Dobbs dead, I'd have gone in there and put a clip in his ass an hour ago," Gunner said.

Bunche shook his head, said, "Sorry, brother, but you're goin' home. Right now."

"No, I'm not. I'm not going anywhere."

"Look, asshole—" Bertelsen started to say.

"No, *you* look. I've been playing ball with you guys right down the fucking line so far. Right? So what the hell's wrong with letting me help you? If Dobbs has any company in there—"

"We don't need your help, Gunner."

"I won't lay a hand on the sonofabitch! All I want is to see you take him, you have my word on it."

"Not a chance. Say adios, amigo," Bertelsen said.

Gunner turned to Bunche, knowing he would have the last word.

"You just want to see us take him," the black cop said. "That's all."

"That's all. Or if you need me to back you up—"

"You're gonna stay right here, Gunner. Right here in the fuckin' car. You can't see what you wanna see from here, you're outta luck."

"Whoa, whoa, whoa!" Bertelsen cried, regarding his partner with open disbelief.

"You don't think—" Gunner said, still talking to Bunche alone.

"I think you say another word, I'm gonna rescind the offer I just made you," Bunche said, ignoring Bertelsen just as completely as Gunner had. "Okay? You either stay right here till we tell you to move, or you take your ass home right now. What's it gonna be? Me an' Al, we got work to do here."

"Richie—" Bertelsen said, trying once more to be heard.

"Shut up, Al. He's makin' up his mind," Bunche said. He was looking straight at Gunner.

With the gaze of both cops bearing down on him, Gunner shrugged and said, "I'll stay in the car."

Bunche eyed him warily, well short of being thoroughly

convinced. "You must've seen us go by, huh? In the car, I mean. That's how come you weren't scared, we came up to you like this."

Gunner had to grin, amused to see Bunche couldn't let even as little a mystery as this go unsolved. "Those pack mules you boys drive are kind of hard to miss."

Bunche made a little face and started backing away from the car, toward the house he and Bertelsen were about to drop in on. "Don't move," he told Gunner simply. "You move, I'm gonna shoot you. I swear to God."

"You and me both," Bertelsen said, drawing the slide back on his service automatic for Gunner's benefit before moving to follow his partner.

Gunner watched them close quickly upon the house, squirming around in his seat like a house pet that needed to be let outside.

Bunche took the front door, while Bertelsen eased around to the back, disappearing from the investigator's view down the driveway. Gunner grabbed his binoculars again. He saw Bunche step up on the dark porch and press himself to the wall beside the doorjamb, gathering the nerve to knock on the door and let the show begin.

But he never got the chance.

Gunfire erupted from the back of the house, first the lone report of a handgun, then two loud, extended shotgun blasts after that. Bunche stiffened, energized by fear, and came down off the porch to follow the sound to the back, taking the same route Bertelsen had along the left side of the house, albeit slower and with greater care. He never even looked Gunner's way.

The investigator threw his binoculars down and jumped out of the car, hitting the ground running. The Ruger was in his hand before he covered three feet.

Bunche reached the back of the house, slipping from Gunner's sight just as Bertelsen had earlier, and two more shots rang out: a handgun and a shotgun again, this time firing almost simultaneously. Gunner was four doors away now, going on three. A black man sprinted into view, emerging from the same yard Bunche had just entered, and saw Gunner coming. He looked like the wild man in the circus, eyes glowing like drops of molten metal, hair all over his ebony face and head. He was holding a pump-action shotgun in both of his hands.

"Dobbs!" Gunner called after him, stopping in the middle of someone's damp lawn to aim the Ruger at the wild man's chest.

Dobbs took off running.

Gunner fired at him twice, but the man was both fast and lucky; even weighed down with the shotgun, he was able to get away unharmed. Gunner started to go after him, then remembered Bunche and Bertelsen. Both men were probably down and in need of his help, if they were still alive. If he left them to pursue Dobbs now, he could be leaving them to die.

Deciding what to do was a no-brainer.

He found Bunche first, laid out on the driveway where Dobbs had left him, bleeding all over the concrete. His right shoulder looked like something a lion had been chewing on, but he was alive and conscious. Bertelsen was neither. He was joined in death by a young black man who was stretched out on the brick patio beside him, several feet away from a sliding glass door that stood wide open, flooding a lighted kitchen with cold night air. Several giant glass bottles of Magnum malt liquor stood on a patio table nearby, all but one of them empty.

It was an odd scene, but Gunner thought he understood it.

"I thought I told you to keep your ass in the car," Bunche said as the investigator tended to him—in obvious pain but seemingly intent on surviving.

"Save it," Gunner said.

"Is Al . . ."

"Yeah. I'm sorry."

Bunche tried to nod. "Motherfucker must've been waitin' for us, or somethin'. He was tipped off."

Gunner shook his head. "I don't think so. There's another dead man back there besides Al."

"So? What's that supposed to prove?"

"It doesn't prove anything. But the way it looks to me, this guy was out on the patio when Al showed up, and Dobbs was in the house, getting another brew out of the 'box, or something, I don't know. Al popped the other guy, I assume because he made a move, and then Dobbs came out of the house and popped him."

"And me," Bunche said, grimacing like he was about to pass out.

"Yeah."

"Did you get 'im? Tell me you got the sonofabitch."

"No. But he won't get far. How many friends can he have in Fontana?"

"Go get the fucker! He's hurt!"

"You hit him?"

"I think so, yeah." Bunche grimaced again and said, "Hurry up, goddamnit! Before the asshole gets away!"

Hearing voices behind him, Gunner looked over his shoulder to see that neighbors were starting to gather around out on the sidewalk nearby, watching him and Bunche converse.

"You going to be all right?" he asked the detective.

Bunche nodded and tried to elaborate, but he couldn't get the words out through his pain.

"I'll have somebody put a call in, they haven't already, then ask a sister or two to come hold your hand till the troops arrive. Okay?" Gunner stood up.

"Watch your ass, man," Bunche found the strength to tell him.

Gunner nodded at him and said thanks, then was gone.

He hadn't looked like it when he'd fled the scene, but Dobbs was indeed doing a good job of bleeding, himself.

The spotty crimson trail he left behind wasn't as easy to follow along the streets and sidewalks of Sunset Ranch as a painted yellow stripe might have been, but it led Gunner to him, all the same, only eleven minutes after the investigator had started tracking him.

He was hiding in the ghost town–like tract of unfinished homes Gunner had seen earlier, over on the opposite side of the street from Sunset Ranch.

He had taken a long, circuitous route to get here, but get here the killer had. Gunner was certain of it. The blood spilling out of him in greater and greater quantities seemed to leave little doubt. Using a strong penlight, Gunner had traced it across the street, before and beyond the chain-link fence surrounding the property, and down a still-unpaved street to a two-story house that was little more than a wood-frame shell. Its exterior walls were all in place, but the interior they surrounded was in its infancy, consisting of nothing but naked wood and fiberboard, exposed copper plumbing and sawdust. Gunner followed Dobbs's bloody trail right up to the open front door and stopped, considering his options.

As he had only one, he moved forward and slid inside, his pulse racing like a Japanese bullet train.

The house was as silent as a crypt, and every bit as dark. The only sounds he could hear, he was making himself, the floorboards beneath his feet mildly protesting his every step. His penlight was off now, a target beacon he preferred Dobbs didn't see, so the signs that had brought him this far were much more difficult to read; he could try to read them regardless, but he didn't want to. He kept his eyes on the floor looking for blood, instead of on his surroundings, Dobbs was likely to blow his head off. The only way to find Bertelsen's killer now, if he didn't want to risk getting ambushed, was the old-fashioned way: make a slow, methodical search of the premises until Dobbs turned up.

*Shit!* Gunner thought to himself.

He did three rooms on the first floor—the living room, the dining room, and what looked like some kind of den. He found nothing. He was still making the only sounds he could hear in the house, and it seemed to him they were getting louder every minute. If Dobbs didn't know he was here by now, the man was deaf, wherever the hell he and his shotgun were hiding. Around the next corner, maybe?

Gunner started for the nearest open doorway and swallowed hard, his mouth completely dry.

It was a bathroom, with a tub and a separate shower stall. The tall glass door on the stall was still covered by its protective brown paper mask, so that Gunner couldn't see what lay beyond it in the stall itself, if in fact anything—or any-*one*—did. He edged closer for a better look, but it didn't help; he still couldn't see anything. Moving to the far side of the shower, he held the Ruger in his right hand, reached for the door handle with his left, and started to jerk it open—

—when he finally heard someone else make a floorboard creak, off in another part of the house.

He wasn't sure, but he thought it had come from some-where above his head, up on the second floor. He cautiously made his way back out to the front of the house and stood alongside the ascending staircase, listening up. He didn't hear a thing. The old familiar silence of the place was back again, in full force. He began to wonder if he hadn't imagined the creaking floorboard, or if what he'd heard had just been the building settling, the way even completed homes liked to do from time to time.

And then he saw the blood.

It was up about ten or eleven steps from the bottom, a blotchy wet pool soaking into the wood. Gunner hadn't seen it when he'd first come in, his eyes hadn't made friends with the dark yet, and he'd never been this close to the stairs. But standing where he was now, just to the side and at eye level with the step it was staining, he was in perfect position to see the blood, though it still would have been easy to miss, he'd been unlucky enough to do that.

He craned his neck to see what he could of the landing at the top of the stairs, but saw nothing but an ominous mass of shadows up there. The ideal place for Dobbs to await his imminent arrival.

Again, Gunner paused to consider his options, and for the second time in twenty minutes, realized he had only one. He wanted to bring Dobbs in, he was going to have to go up and get him.

Gunner started up the stairs, slowly.

Then he stopped, only two steps off the first-floor landing. He had an idea.

There was a small bucket of spackle sitting on the floor nearby, and he retrieved it. It was about the size and weight of a gallon of ice cream. Standing off to the side of the staircase again, keeping his eyes open for any movement above him, he gingerly placed the bucket on its side about eight or nine steps up, then gently nudged it forward and stepped back. The bucket rolled noisily down the stairs, striking first one step, then a second, then a third . . .

Dobbs made his play when it hit the fourth.

He leapt into view up at the top of the stairs and his shotgun spit fire, twice spraying buckshot down the empty staircase. As Dobbs's face filled with surprise, Gunner reached around the staircase railing and squeezed the Ruger's trigger three times, bringing Dobbs down toward him like a boulder in an avalanche. Dobbs tumbled down the staircase and stopped halfway, his body folded up in the shape of a dead man. Gunner put a hand to his throat, checking for a pulse, and held his breath, hoping the sonofabitch was somehow still alive.

Then he went to tell Bunche the good news.

# nineteen

WHATEVER IT TOOK TO PUT AN ANIMAL LIKE ANGELO Dobbs in his grave, both Bunche and Gunner had failed to do it that Friday morning.

Bunche had hit him once in the right thigh, and two of Gunner's three rounds had put holes in his left arm and upper chest, respectively. But Dobbs would not die. He defied their collective efforts to end his life, and he did so with robust glee, treating his wounds in the days that followed like bee stings he barely felt the need to scratch. Some people were just like that, Gunner knew. So full of evil, so reinforced by it, you couldn't dent them; they were all but immortal.

And they loved to boast about it.

Killers like Russell Dartmouth took no pride in what they did; they saw their acts of violence not as works of art, but as unfortunate measures the world had forced them to take. From the moment he had been picked up off the street in front of Mickey's, early Friday morning after the barber had called 911 to say he was out there handcuffed to a lamppost, Dartmouth had done nothing but rage. He couldn't articulate his motives for murdering Roman Goody, and he had no desire to try. Receiving credit for homicide was of no interest to him whatsoever.

Monsters like Dobbs were different.

The men and women cut from his mold were ashamed of nothing; they treated their every accomplishment like a badge of honor, something to show the world with pride and self-satisfaction. No crime was too vile or too senseless to confess to; no theft, no rape, no disfigurement of the innocent. And certainly no murder. Murder was the greatest trophy of all.

Murder was the private domain of the chosen few, and Dobbs would never commit one he didn't want to accept responsibility for.

"Yeah, I killed the bitch," he said when they asked him about Nina Pearson. Straight out, no hesitation, no worry over how he would say it. He told them he didn't need a lawyer, whatever they wanted to ask him, they could ask him. He was going back to the joint for the rest of his life with or without a lawyer, who the hell were they trying to kid?

Yeah, he'd been looking for Jimmy Gatewood that night.

Yeah, he'd gone to the wrong house.

Yeah, he'd been high when he got there.

And man, they should have seen what it had looked like, that bitch's head flying apart all over her perfectly spotless kitchen, ha-ha.

Gunner heard it all secondhand, of course. Poole gave him a full report. The investigator listened to the disturbing details in silence, not knowing whether to laugh or to cry. He hadn't thought it would make much difference to him, Dobbs surviving the holes he'd put in his ass rather than dying as a result of them, but now he knew he'd been mistaken. It would always make a difference. Not killing Dobbs when he'd had the chance would stand as one of his life's greatest regrets, whether the act would have brought Nina back to him or not.

Naturally, the story broke fast and made the news everywhere, but as early Friday as he could manage it, Gunner delivered it to Mimi Hillman and Wendy Singer personally. Singer took it hard, but Gunner's Momma Hillman took it much worse than that. Having to live with the idea that her daughter had died at the hands of an abusive husband had been difficult enough for her, but to hear now that Nina's death had been the result of mere chance, of something so tragic and meaningless as a loaded crackhead's stupid mistake . . . It was almost too much for her to bear.

And yet, bear it she did. Accepting it, after a time, as one more cross her Father in heaven had decided she should carry, for reasons known only to Him. Gunner didn't understand it, this woman's refusal to shuck her faith under the weight of all her losses, but he envied it too. Because he was going to have as much trouble dealing with the senseless circumstances of Nina's death as anyone, and he had no such crutch to lean on. He and God were not that close.

All Gunner had with which to fuel his recovery from Nina's passing was hope. The vague and smokelike wish that tomorrow would be better than yesterday, and that all of his best days—and prospects for love—weren't behind him.

It was a hope he held for the entire world.

Saturday night at the Great Western Forum, Gunner and Gaylon Brown watched the Lakers run over and around the San Antonio Spurs for just over three quarters. Two minutes into the final period, Cedric Ceballos already had 31 points, and Nick Van Exel had 25; together with the team's new sixth man off the bench, a new/old power forward named Earvin "Magic" Johnson, the pair had forged an 86–71 Lakers lead, and all was well with Showtime.

Then, during a time-out, Gaylon said, "I like the bitch on the end." Pointing to one of the Laker Girls.

Gunner told him to grab his jacket and come on, it was time to go.

The boy must have asked Gunner fifty times what he had done to make the man so angry, before he received an answer. They were in the car, moving east on Manchester Boulevard, headed for home. Gunner's eyes were on the road, but his mind was clearly elsewhere.

"I don't like the word 'bitch,' " he said. "And I don't like 'ho,' either."

Gaylon just looked at him.

"That was a woman you were talking about back there. Not a bitch, or a ho. A woman. Someone who deserves respect, same as you and me. Do you understand?"

The seven-year-old shook his head, confused.

Gunner took a deep breath, said, "All right. Listen to me.

Listen to me *carefully*. Most of the hate in this world starts with one thing, Gaylon. Do you know what that is?''

Gaylon shook his head again.

"Names. The names we give ourselves, and the names we give to others. I'm talking about *ugly* names. Names like nigger and kike, and faggot and gook—and bitch and ho. Names like that. Names that do nothing but hurt people, and degrade people. Do you know what 'degrade' means?''

"No . . .''

"It means to shame. To tear someone down and make them feel bad about themselves.''

"Oh.''

"A real man doesn't treat people that way. A real man doesn't use degrading names for women. He doesn't use degrading names for anyone.''

"So how come everybody says it? That's what everybody says, 'bitch.' ''

"You ever hear me say it?''

"No. But—''

"But nothing. You want to do what everybody else does, get your ass out of my car right now. You don't want to be any better or smarter than those knotheads you run around with, later for you, I'll find somebody else to hang with.''

He jerked the car over two lanes of traffic to the curb and reached across the boy's lap to open his door.

Gaylon looked at him wild-eyed, afraid to move.

"It's like this, Gaylon. I picked you to be my 'boy because I think you're smarter than everybody else. I think you've got a good brain, and a good heart, and I don't want to see either go to waste. But if you don't want to listen to me when I tell you something, I've got no time for you. Because I've got enough disappointments in my life without you disappointing me too. You hear what I'm saying? You can't follow me, and your homies, too. You've got to choose between us. And you've got to choose right now, before I spend another minute messing around with you.''

He killed the Cobra's ignition and waited, locking his gaze onto Gaylon's own.

The boy remained silent.

"A woman is not a bitch," Gunner said. "Say it."

"A woman is not a bitch," Gaylon repeated, not doing much more than exhaling the words.

"Say it again."

Gaylon did, louder this time.

"A woman is a beautiful creature, and if you treat her like one, she'll love you," Gunner said. "Don't you want to be loved?"

The boy nodded his head.

"Hell yes, you do. We all do. That's what makes life worth living, love."

"My momma loves me," Gaylon said.

"I know she does. And she's waiting for us. Close that door so we can go, huh?"

Gaylon did as he was told and Gunner started the car.

They rode in silence the rest of the way home.

Now available in hardcover

# PERSON OR PERSONS UNKNOWN

*A Sir John Fielding Mystery*

## BRUCE ALEXANDER

Putnam